Dan Brewer

JACQUELINE JACKSON
and her husband

Mrs. Jackson, her husband, and their four daughters live in Kent, Ohio, where Mr. Jackson teaches English literature and she teaches children's literature at Kent State University. They spend their summers traveling back and forth to Vermont where they have a cottage on a small lake.

by Jacqueline Jackson

The Paleface Redskins

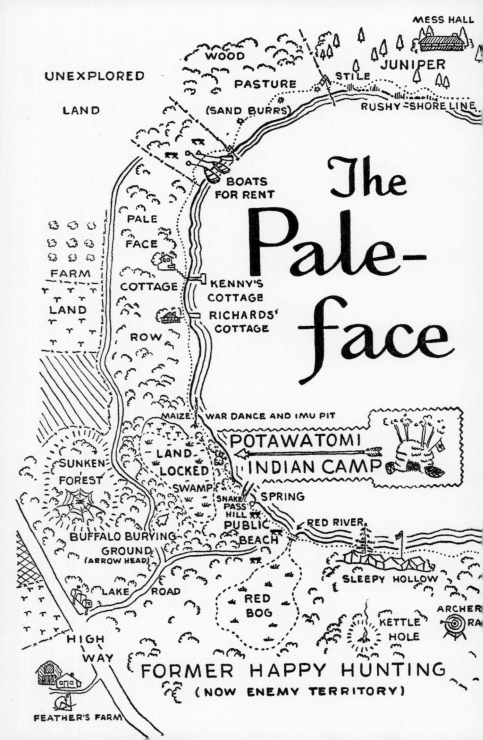

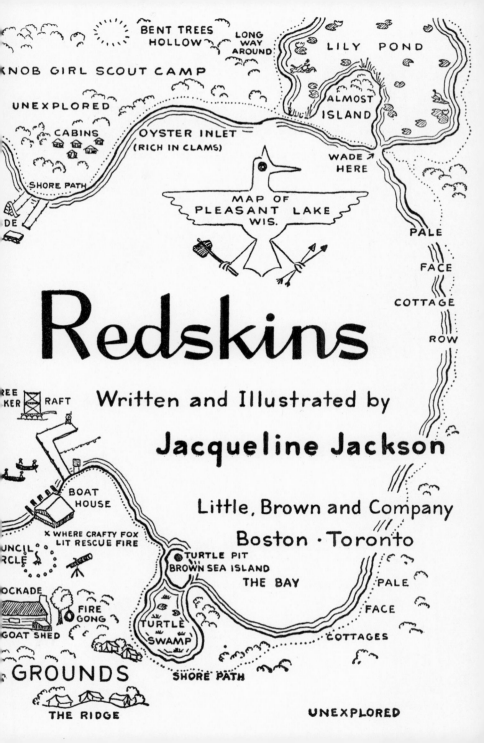

Redskins

Written and Illustrated by

Jacqueline Jackson

Little, Brown and Company

Boston · Toronto

The Paleface Redskins

is dedicated to

V.W.D. ⎫ the parents, who claim they knew more
R.A.D. ⎭   than they let on

Jo ⎫
Bob ⎪
Pat ⎬ the warring Indians
Jack ⎪
Craig ⎭

the long-suffering Boy Scouts of Camp Chippecotton,
Pleasant Lake, Wisconsin, including John Batikis, the
bugler, and his brother Alex, who came to the feast

and to

Roy Cowden, whose help in the telling, and
Franklin Boggs, whose help in the drawing
have made this a better book.

Author's Note

While this story is not autobiographical — although my mother is afraid some might think that it is — many parts really happened.

The Paleface Redskins

Chapter

1

MARCY RICHARDS straddled a heap of blankets in the back of the open truck and watched the road unroll behind. She felt the white feather in the headband above her long pigtails and gave an impatient wiggle.

"Sugarpuss! How can you chew your cud without even a quiver, when we're almost *there?"*

The placid black and white goat tethered beside her crunched on rhythmically.

Marcy peeped around a trunk at her older sister Betsy, who was thirteen. She lay biting her fingernails, and through thick glasses blinked meditatively at cloud puffs in the sky. Her hair was short and tangled, and also bore a feather.

"Owl Eyes!" called Marcy.

Betsy turned her head slightly.

"Has the papoose fallen off yet?"

"Haven't noticed lately."

Marcy scrambled up on the mattress that spread over the luggage. On the end closest the cab her younger brother Thad lay on his stomach. The whistling wind stood his sandy hair on end and made his ragged feather bob and dip like a tailless kite.

"Shh," he said as she crawled beside him. "I'm scouting." He let fly an imaginary arrow at a policeman signboard labeled BOATS, and then bawled toward Betsy's feather fluttering among the trunks below, "Another paleface bit the dust!"

The feather shot up. "Where?" asked Betsy.

"Well, we've passed him now, slowpoke. It was the old policeman sign." He and Marcy slid down beside the trunk.

"Hello, goat," said Thad. "We're almost there."

"She doesn't care," said Marcy.

"She doesn't know what fun it is at the lake." Thad surveyed the receding scenery. "Daddy hasn't passed us yet, has he?"

"No," said Betsy. "He wasn't near finished packing the car when we left, and you know how slow Janice is. She probably forgot something."

Thad looked anxious. "I hope they found Jip."

"He could smell his way to the lake," Marcy comforted. "I bet he was saying good-by to all his rabbit holes."

Betsy jerked off her brother's headband. "Your feather's a mess. Mine's wrecked, too, after it went through the wash that time. I think I'll make a new headband with lots of feathers."

4

"Kenny won't like that," Thad warned. "He says only the chief can wear more than one feather."

"I'll wear all I want. Maybe *I'll* be chief this summer. He can't boss me!"

"If you're chief, can I be a brave like the rest of you?" said Thad eagerly. "I'm almost ten! And I know more about Indians now than any of you, because we just had it all in school. This is the month of the Strawberry Moon, and July is Ripe Berries, and —"

"You can be a brave," Betsy promised. "But, Marcy, you ought to stay a squaw. We need at least one, and with your braids you look the most like an Indian maiden."

Marcy nodded. She sometimes thought of herself as the captive maid in the Indian song:

> From the Land of the Sky Blue Water
> They brought a captive maid;
> And her eyes, they are lit with lightning
> Her heart is not afraid!
>
> But I steal to her lodge at dawning,
> I woo her with my flute;
> She is sick for the Sky Blue Water,
> The captive maid is mute.

That's what she'd been, all winter — sick for the Sky Blue Water!

Betsy kicked off her shoes and wiggled her knobby toes. "I'm not going to wear shoes again till the day we go home!"

"And I'm going to swim across the lake," Thad vowed, "this year, for sure!"

5

"What's the first thing you're going to do when we get there?" Marcy asked.

"I'm going to run out to the end of the pier and jump in with all my clothes on," Betsy declared.

"I'm going to see how the wigwam weathered the winter," Thad said.

"I'm going to —" Marcy began, but was cut short by a bugle splutter, and a loud honking.

"Oh, cabbage!" Betsy exclaimed. "Here comes the car. Now we won't beat!"

"There's Jip poking his nose out the window!" Thad cried.

Mother and Daddy and Janice, their older sister, who was fifteen and would rather ride in comfort, grinned through the windshield. Janice blasted her bugle again as with a taunting blare of the horn the car passed the laden truck. Milton, in the cab, honked back.

The three scrambled up on the mattress.

"Catch up!" Betsy pounded on the cab roof.

"There it is!" Thad pointed frantically through a rift in the trees. "The lake! The lake!"

For an instant a shimmering blue patch was visible against a juniper-dotted knoll.

"I can hardly wait!" Betsy gave herself a frenzied hug.

"There's the row of mailboxes!" cried Thad.

"There's the turn-in to the lake road!" Marcy added, and they rolled on the mattress in a delirium of joy.

The truck drove slowly onto a gravel lane with a stripe of grass down the middle.

"There's the Buffalo Burying Ground!"

6

"There's the Sunken Forest!"

"There's the swamp!" Thad gazed down the hill, fascinated, to where a bright green patch bulged like a fungus on the side of the sparkling lake.

"Here's the Chipmunk Tree! Duck!"

"And the end of the road. We're here! We're here!"

The truck jolted to a stop behind the Richardses' car, and the three children leaped out.

"Maa!" Sugarpuss gave a strangled cry.

"Hold your horses!" Marcy clambered back and undid the taut rope. The goat half twisted through the air, skipped sideways, and dropped her head to crop a dandelion.

A spotted mongrel with short hair and a rubbery nose bounded up the hill.

"Good old Jip!" cried Thad. "Your tail's wagging so fast it's like a propeller pushing you!"

Marcy stood at the top of the hill and took a deep breath. She could smell the cool freshness of the lake and the hot greenness of grass and weeds. The air was filled with the pulse of crickets, the long metallic buzz of a cicada, the squawk of a bluejay. Everything was alive with wispy feelings of past excitements and the thrilling promise of future ones. Her whole body quivered and she let out a long sigh. She was back to the Sky Blue Water! And it was just as she remembered.

"Come on!" yelled Thad.

She raced after him down the hill. Sugar flattened her tail against her back and sprang to follow. Betsy, hobbling like the crooked man on account of her tender feet, brought up the rear.

The familiar porch roof of the brown stucco cottage showed through the trees. Thad threw open the screen door.

"Mommy, we're here! Where are the swimming suits?"

Daddy was teetering on a porch rail, rolling up a green-striped canvas. "How was the truck ride?"

Marcy ran to the front of the wide porch and feasted her eyes on the dazzling blue. Bushy trees hid the shore on both sides, but she could see the length of the lake, the mile-long stretch of water to the tiny cottages on the far end. She took another satisfied breath.

"Dibs on my same bed!" Betsy hobbled onto the porch and sprang onto the bare springs of a cot.

"Dibs on mine!" Thad yelled.

Marcy raced for her old cot. "Dibs on mine! Oh, look —

here's my tooth-on-a-string, still tied to the post! It's been here since I was seven!"

"Don't any of you dare take my bed! My bugle's on it." Janice stuck her head out the window that opened on the porch. "Ha, ha, we beat you!"

"Not by much," said Betsy.

Marcy wandered happily into the musty living room. There was the blackened fireplace with the bent tongs, the rug with the worn spots and frayed edges, the mammoth black piano so terribly out of tune, the leak-stained wallpaper, the antique red-plush rocker that jiggled back and forth on wooden treadles, all the old books — Janice, curled up in a corner, was already reading one.

"Look!" Thad yelled from the kitchen, winding a creaking handle. "Here's the old dumb-waiter, and my tonsils are *still* in it!"

"Who'd want *them,* anyway?" called Janice.

Marcy joined her brother in the kerosene-smelling kitchen and poked in a cupboard. "Here's where we put our bows and arrows, too."

"Children! Help unload!" Mother ordered from the bedroom. "Milton has to get back with the truck."

"Can't we take a quick dip first?" Thad pleaded. "We're so hot!"

"Come on, come on!" Daddy slammed off the porch.

Marcy scampered behind. "Janice is reading."

"Janice!" barked Daddy. "Put down that book and get out here!"

For the next half hour the path was heavily traveled. Faithful Jip panted up and down the hill, but Sugarpuss, after a few mad circuits, wandered into the tall grass and only raised her head to give a murmur of recognition when someone toiled by.

At last everything was heaped on the porch floor. Cartons of groceries, stacks of library books, a ream of Manila paper, crayons, games, red rubber inner tubes, Daddy's wading boots —

"Didn't we leave *anything* at home?" Mother asked, digging hopelessly into the pile. "Where are the paper plates?"

"Now can we go swimming?" Thad danced impatiently.

"Run along," Mother said. "I'll call you for supper."

"I don't think I'll go in today," said Janice. "I want to make up my bed."

The others dived for their suits and stripped in the middle of the porch. Betsy charged down to the dock and plunged off the end. She rose, spouting water.

"It's marvelous! Ish — the weeds have grown."

Thad climbed gingerly onto the pebbly shore. "The lake's gone up. You can tell by that dead stump." He put a toe in the water and then splashed in. "Ooh! It's *cold!*"

Sugar's hoofs clattered as she galloped to the end of the pier. She skidded to a stop, her nostrils dilated at the sight of so much water.

Marcy followed. At her first glimpse of the whole lake she stared, horror-struck.

"What is that?"

"Where?"

"Over there — on our Happy Hunting Grounds! *A huge new dock and boathouse!*"

10

"And there's a building on the top of the hill!" Thad pointed out excitedly.

Betsy thrashed back to the pier and put on her glasses. "And tents in the hollow! Of all the nerve!"

"Doesn't that frost you!" Thad shrilled.

Marcy almost wept. "Somebody's bought that whole side of the lake and we won't have any wild lands to play in any more!"

Betsy scowled. "They'll put up signs saying NO TRESPAS-SING."

"Has anything else changed?" Thad mourned.

They looked anxiously around the shore line, at the tree-veiled cottage row across on the far end, the toothpick docks, and the dazzling fronts of boathouses. They surveyed their own end, where the cottage row was much shorter, and then the wooded sides of the lake, which were pinched in a little at the middle, making the water span there only half a mile wide. On the north bulge were the usual two long docks, one ending in a slide, which belonged to Juniper Knob, the Girl Scout camp. Then their eyes returned to the south shore, which had been their Happy Hunting Grounds, but where now the gleaming pier filled their hearts with dismay.

"Maybe we can still play there," Thad said.

"Fat chance," said Betsy bitterly. "Hullo, there's Kenny. I mean, Chief Thunder Cloud."

A green canoe glided up. In the stern sat a boy clad in khaki pants almost the color of his skin. His hair was bleached white by the sun. He braked the canoe sideways and solemnly held up his arm.

11

"How!"

Three arms returned the salute. "How!"

Kenny jerked his head toward the goat picking her way daintily along the shore. "What's that?"

"Sugarpuss, Marcy's goat," Betsy answered.

"Oh. When'd you get here?"

"Just now."

"Seen that?" He jerked his head toward the new dock.

"What is it?"

"Boy Scout camp."

"Boy Scouts!" Thad sucked in his breath in delight. "I'm going to be one when I'm old enough!"

Kenny gave him a withering look.

"I mean at home I am — maybe. Up here I'll always be an Indian."

Kenny's eyes became narrow slits. "White man take land from Indian."

"Ugh," agreed Thad hastily.

"Clear the land on Happy Hunting Grounds. Burn-um trees. Put-um up paleface dwellings."

All nodded seriously.

"Indian — him mad!"

Betsy's eyes flashed. "Indian — him declare *war!*"

"Ugh!" Kenny agreed emphatically.

"Right away?" Thad was eager.

"No, silly," said Betsy. "We have to have a council of war first; you should know that."

"Betsy! Marcy! Thad! Supper's in ten minutes," Mother called.

"Oh!" Marcy wailed. "And I'm not even wet yet!" She jumped in.

"Churn around some, Thad," ordered Betsy. "Your lips are purple."

"Chief Thunder Cloud call-um powwow tonight," Kenny said, turning the canoe. "All tribe present. Brave Owl Eyes. Squaw White Feather. And papoose. At-um wigwam." He raised his hand in farewell and glided rapidly off, his back straight and his paddle slicing the water with no splash.

The tribe watched him depart, swam around a minute longer, and then climbed to the dock.

Betsy examined a foot. "Here's a juicy bloodsucker. I'm going to save it and drop it by the Boy Scout pier!"

Thad looked doubtful. "The only trouble with declaring war," he said through chattering teeth, "is maybe the Boy Scouts are friendly."

"Never!" glowered Betsy. "The white man was friendly, too, but look what happened to the Indians anyway! We must swear to hate them and not accept their beads or firewater, no matter how friendly they are! Do you want to be penned up on a *reservation* for the rest of the summer?"

"No!" cried Thad and Marcy, horrified.

"Well, that's what they want to do to us," Betsy said firmly. "Let's go eat; I'm starved."

Chapter

2

SLICES OF PINK HAM, potato chips, cottage cheese, garden lettuce, and little green onions had been gobbled up. Songs had been joyously sung, to usher in summer table manners, and then, munching chocolate grahams, the Richardses had hurried to their tasks.

The porch table was cleared, and dishes done in a jiffy. Thad, on a level spot below the cottage, had burned up a miniature village of paper plates and cartons, while grieving gleefully. Betsy and Marcy had made up the cots that ranged head to foot along the long porch rail, and Janice had shepherded herds of dust bunnies into the waiting dustpan.

Mother was still unpacking, but Daddy, who had to return

to work the next day, had bailed out the boat, taken the oars from under the cottage, and gone fishing.

Now the tribe, feathered and bowed-and-arrowed, accompanied by goat and dog, was on its way to the wigwam.

"I could walk this shore path with my eyes closed," said Thad, closing them, but opening them quickly when he stumbled on a root. "Doesn't the dust feel puffy between your toes?"

"Janice asked if we were going to have one of those silly meetings where we sit around and say 'Ugh,' " Marcy remarked.

"She's so grown-up," Thad said.

"I'm never going to grow up," Betsy cried vehemently. "Never, *never!*"

The tribe slid through a lilac hedge and trod single file across the lawn of a boarded-up cottage down to the flat, pebbly shore, where needles of grass pricked up among the stones and water oozed between their toes. They followed the path past another cottage or two, through a squashy place where a water-logged boat was pulled up on shore, and then turned sharply into a willow thicket.

"Here we are!" Marcy cried.

The willows were short and sparsely leafed, but after a few turns of the path they towered overhead and pressed densely in, so that the light filtering through was dim and green.

"Here's the swamp outlet." Thad hopped across the trickle.

Now the ripply lake was on one side of them and the still green swamp on the other, first one, then the other veiled by willows as the path snaked along the narrow isthmus. Then the

15

land widened and there was a grassy spot long enough to lie full length on, beneath the spreading branches of a mulberry tree. Jip was nosing around the trunk.

"He remembers this is where we stop," Thad said. "Cabbage, look at the wigwam!"

"Isn't it brown!" Betsy exclaimed. "And awfully beat up."

The wigwam was built around four willow saplings growing roughly in a square and its roof and walls had been thatched by interweaving leafy willow boughs over a framework. Last summer it had been almost invisible, but now, brown and dried, it couldn't have been more conspicuous lit with neon.

Thad dropped on all fours and wiggled through the low door. "Sugarpuss! Stop eating the walls!" He snapped away the white nose poking through the thatch.

"Kenny's not here yet," said Marcy.

"He must be. His canoe is pulled up," Betsy said.

"Walla walla woo hoo!" A whoop rent the air as a brown figure swooped from the mulberry tree, landed on Betsy, and tumbled her to the ground. Jip barked furiously and jumped into the fray.

"Hey, stop it!" Betsy thrashed and kicked herself free.

Kenny rolled over and over on the ground and sat up, grinning. "What a lookout! I saw you coming and heard every word, only I thought Jip was going to give me away at the start. Good old Jip! You wouldn't tell on a pal!" He tweaked the lop ears.

Betsy glared. "You're acting more like Tarzan than an Indian chief. And that reminds me. Don't you think maybe it's *my* turn to be chief this year?"

16

Kenny's eyes bulged. He straightened his headdress and planted his feet wide apart. He puffed up his chest till his chin nearly touched it.

"Mutiny!" he spat.

"You can't scare me," said Betsy.

"You can't be chief," protested Kenny. "I'm a boy. I'm oldest. And whose canoe is it? And whose great-great-grandfather was half Indian, anyway?"

"Yes," said Betsy, "but without us you wouldn't have anybody to be chief over."

Kenny slitted his eyes.

Betsy shrugged. "I'll make a bargain with you. I don't particularly want to be chief. But Thad has to be a brave this summer. He's tired of being the papoose."

"When I'm ten," Thad said quickly. "I'll stay a papoose till I'm ten in July."

"And I get to wear all the feathers I want," Betsy went on.

"How about Marcy?" Kenny grumbled. "I suppose she wants to be a brave, too. What a tribe! No squaws — no papooses — just four chiefs!"

"I'll stay a squaw," Marcy put in. "Except on raids or hunting trips. Then I'll switch, like last year."

"That's all," said Betsy. "Take it or leave it."

Kenny's scowl relaxed into deep thought.

"Sure," he said finally. "I planned all along Thad'd be a brave this year. We'll have a big ceremony on his birthday and then send him off into the woods alone for a day, so he can prove he's a man. And I don't care how many feathers you wear. Now let's get on with heap big powwow."

17

The tribe crawled into the wigwam, their backs crackling the fringe of dry leaves over the door, and seated themselves in a cramped circle. Jip lay looking in. His pink tongue dripped pearled threads of saliva. Sugar munched on thatch, like Hansel and Gretel on the gingerbread cottage.

"Ugh," grunted Chief Thunder Cloud, starting the ceremony.

"Ugh, ugh, ugh," chanted the others.

The chief shut his eyes and raised both hands. "Great White Spirit," he intoned, "hear-um us. We are wronged. Palefaces come from-um East. Build dwellings on Happy Hunting Grounds. Raise-um tents. Fence land. Cut down-um trees. Chase away game. Indian starve. Indian mad! Indian declare war. Send-um thunderbird to help Indian. Send-um victory. Help-um drive paleface away. Ugh!" Thunder Cloud lowered his arms.

"Ugh," amened the tribe.

"Well, braves," said the chief, "we-um ready now for war powwow. Who has-um plan? Brave Owl Eyes? Squaw White Feather? Papoose?"

"We could stage a massacre," the papoose suggested hopefully.

"Not first!" cried Owl Eyes.

"Besides, we don't have anybody to massacre," the chief said. "They aren't here yet."

"Aren't here yet!" chorused the tribe.

"I thought it was funny we hadn't seen them," White Feather said. "When will they get here?"

Chief Thunder Cloud shrugged.

"Well," said Owl Eyes, "it's really a good thing. Look at

18

this wigwam! It sticks out like a sore thumb!" She tore a withered branch from the roof and dead leaves showered down. "The scouts'll spot us the first time they come past. We'll have to rethatch."

"Let's enlarge it," added the papoose. "I don't remember that it was so crowded last year."

"We've all grown," Owl Eyes said. "Especially you."

"And we need to put by a stock of supplies," White Feather considered. "In case of seige."

"Are these old bows and arrows good enough?" asked the papoose.

The chief nodded. "Besides, I have-um good boughten one. But need-um tomahawks for scalping."

"I'm going to fix up some new feathers," Owl Eyes declared.

The papoose brightened. "I got a real Indian beading set for Christmas, and I'm going to make some decorations to go on my headdress, when I have a headdress. I'll have one when I'm a brave, won't I, Owl Eyes?"

"Yes," said Owl Eyes with a glance toward the chief.

"We have to find war paint," White Feather said.

The chief peeked through a hole at the mulberry tree. "Mulberries make-um best paint. I know! Let's have-um war dance tonight!"

"Oh, no!" cried the papoose. "You don't do that till you're ready to sally forth to battle. It gets you all in a frenzy for blood and scalps."

Owl Eyes went on. "And we'd have to get firewood and paint ourselves up and —"

"Okay," said Thunder Cloud grumpily. "It was a bum idea."

19

"It was a good idea," said White Feather. "We'll do it later."

"We'll need a flag," Owl Eyes said with inspiration, "on a willow pole, with the tribe emblem on it."

"What is our tribe emblem?" asked the papoose.

"For that matter, what's our tribe?" said White Feather. They all looked at Chief Thunder Cloud.

He shrugged. "Last year we were just Indians. No particular tribe."

"But we can't stage war unless we're a tribe," frowned Owl Eyes. "In the history books it's always the Crow against the Blackfeet, or something like that."

"Well, what can we be?" the chief asked.

The older Indians looked expectantly at the papoose.

"What *are* some tribes?" Owl Eyes asked. "You studied them last in school."

The papoose looked thoughtful. "There are the Seminole," he said slowly, "and the Navaho, and the Hopi —"

"But those are so far away!" White Feather objected. "Aren't the Seminoles in Florida, and the others out West somewhere? We ought to be a Wisconsin tribe. Woods Indians. Didn't you learn their names?"

"The Winnebagos," said the papoose promptly, "and the Chippewas up north, and the Potawatomi here. I noticed on the map."

"Potawatomi!" White Feather cried. "That's a beautiful name!"

"Sort of long to print on a flag," worried Owl Eyes.

"We'll just make the letters small," said White Feather. "Oh, let's be Potawatomi! They were the ones who actually lived on this lake —"

"Pot-a-wat-o-mi." Owl Eyes dripped the syllables off her tongue. "Suits me. And the thunderbird can be our emblem."

"Okay," agreed the chief. "What else?"

"Let's think," said the papoose.

White Feather looked out through the sparse thatch. The sun was down behind the hill now, and the shadowed swamp a darker green. On the far shore trees were flame-tipped. Even as she watched, they blackened like the wicks of blown-out candles. Then everything was in shadow. The breeze died. The lake was calm, dimpled with fallen insects. A fish flopped, and widening circles showed where a midge had danced too close to the surface and made a mouthful for the hungry bass.

"Well," said Owl Eyes finally, "maybe we've figured enough for now. Tomorrow we'll start rebuilding, and by the time we're done, maybe the Boy Scouts will be here."

"Powwow over, then," Chief Thunder Cloud said. He held out his clenched fist. "Ugh."

"Ugh, ugh, ugh!" the Potawatomi chorused, piling their fists on top of his. They dropped their arms, crawled outside, and stretched.

"Maa?" Sugarpuss peeked from behind the wigwam, her head bobbing as a brown leaf disappeared inside her mouth.

"Yes, maa!" The chief rubbed her knobby forehead. "You old goat! What would anyone want a goat for?" He pushed through the willows to the narrow beach and climbed into his canoe.

"Can we ride home with you?" the papoose asked wistfully.

21

Thunder Cloud hesitated. "I can't take all the livestock —"

"That's all right," White Feather said quickly. "I'll walk home with Sugar. She's never ridden on water, yet. Look out!"

She caught the goat around the belly as she tried to spring after Owl Eyes into the canoe. Jip and the papoose scrambled in last. White Feather gave them a push off. The canoe sliced back, making a V-shaped ripple in the still water.

"Dig in, papoose!" cried the chief. "Have-um forgotten how to hold paddle after landlocked winter?"

"Beat you home!" called Owl Eyes.

White Feather nodded agreement and brushed through the willows to the clearing. She stood a minute by the wigwam, crumbling a brown leaf between her fingers, and then sat down. The grass was damp on her bare legs. Sugarpuss nibbled a fallen mulberry, and came and lay beside her. Her flank was warm and coarse. White Feather pulled her cylinder ears gently. The goat gave a little burp as her cud rose into her mouth, and began chewing.

Over the lake a tiny wisp of wind stirred the mirror calmness, and the sky glowed orange beyond the far ridge of black trees.

Behind her the swamp came to life. She heard a splash, maybe a turtle, and nearby the great galumph of a frog. Another frog answered, and then a whole chorus chimed in from every bank. The crickets' high cry pulsated. A fish plopped out in the lake. She heard a faint shout calling her, but she didn't answer. A June bug bumbled by her ear.

She sat contentedly. This was the moment she had been waiting for — all day, all winter! To be by herself, surrounded with the sight, and feel, and sound, and smell of the Sky Blue Water. There had been an interval like this last year, when she hadn't really seemed *here* till she'd reviewed everything and put it all in a careful row in her heart, and then another time with the pain of saying good-by. All winter, when she was falling asleep at night, she'd picked first one thing about the lake, and then another, to think about, like selecting one crystal from her rock collection, examining it carefully, and then replacing it.

But now she was here, and the same frogs were gunking in the swamp, and the same crickets shrilling — or if not the same, at least so nearly like as to be identical. Last year and all the other years overlapped and swam together, at the beginning of this year.

Now across the lake appeared the yellow rim of a full moon, the lord that all the golden light was heralding, and at his arrival a golden carpet was thrown across the water for him to walk down, straight to the wigwam in the willow patch.

Marcy smiled. "Let's go, Sugarpuss," she said softly, standing up, "or the others will be back to look for us." She stretched in the dark and laughed out loud.

Back again! Last week, school! This week, the lake! Already

last week seemed years away, and her happiness almost unbearable. The whole summer stretched gloriously before them all, like the golden path from her feet to the moon. Some dark eddies swirled into the gold and made it narrower — that was the war, and the Boy Scouts, and other unknown dangers they would meet. But the golden path wriggled past the dark spots and flowed bright and sparkling to the very end. That was how it would be.

Marcy reached her hands high over her head and looked up at the sky. It was framed in a black willow fringe. The brightness of the moon had extinguished all but the bravest of the stars that had come out so valiantly not fifteen minutes before. She felt almost part of the sky, as if her feet weren't really on the earth at all. She stood poised there, stretching exultantly.

"Great White Spirit," she whispered. "Thank you."

Chapter

3

THE SUN slanting across the lake the following morning reflected on a thousand tilting mirrors and filled the cool willow thicket with dappled green light. In the clearing the Potawatomi were already hard at work, ripping the crackling thatch from the wigwam.

The papoose stubbed his toe on a stone, bent, and chucked it into the swamp.

Thunk! A black scar marred the smooth green surface.

Plop! Another jagged spot appeared, beside a floating board.

"I scared a turtle!" the papoose exclaimed. "And I didn't even see it! That's what happens to eyes in the wintertime. I know! Let's go on a turtle hunt in the Lily Pond this afternoon!"

"Last year we caught seven in half-um hour," grunted the chief. "In-um Turtle Swamp. Ought to go there."

"A *turtle hunt?*" Owl Eyes exclaimed. "With the palefaces practically attacking?"

"Not a turtle hunt, but maybe some things *are* more important than the wigwam," mused White Feather. "Like exploring paleface territory, before they get here. I bet *they* own the Turtle Swamp now!"

"We can't do everything at once," said Owl Eyes. "I haven't even run down the shore path in the other direction yet, or gone out in the boat —"

"Or walked around the lake," added the papoose. "We usually go the first day. Cabbage! Can we still walk past the Boy Scout camp?"

Thunder Cloud snorted. "The shore path is free — and if it isn't, we'll wade!"

Owl Eyes frowned. "We'd be *fine* Indians to go off without any base of operations. Why, the palefaces could claim this spot!"

"She's right," said Thunder Cloud. "We'll scout tomorrow."

"They won't be here that soon," Owl Eyes said confidently. "And this work'll go quick. We can use the old framework."

The papoose rattled it. "They could bust it in a minute."

"Nothing out of willows will be strong enough," White Feather commented. "We'll have to depend on camouflage."

The papoose crept behind the wigwam, hanging on saplings as water oozed around his toes. "Say, these trees are placed just right for another room!"

"But we'd be sitting in the swamp!" said Owl Eyes.

"We could build the ground up a little. Besides, if we ever didn't want anything, we could poke our hands out and drop it in the swamp, without even leaving the wigwam!"

"Ugh!" Thunder Cloud lopped a little willow from the middle of the proposed room.

"Wait!" said Owl Eyes. "What do we want such a big wigwam for?"

"Prisoners!" the papoose cried.

Owl Eyes nodded. "Well, okay. We'll need a lot more thatch and poles and bark, then. Chief, you go behind the swamp and get a load. It'll expose the wigwam if we cut them all from here."

"I'm going," Thunder Cloud said irritably. "Come on, papoose."

Jip raced up, wet and black to the elbows, and loped after them.

White Feather watched them out of sight. "You boss the chief too much. He doesn't like it."

Owl Eyes tossed her head. "Somebody's got to boss him. Think of going on a *turtle* hunt!"

"That was the papoose's idea."

"Yes, but the papoose is only *nine*." She took the butcher knife. "I think I'll cut a door through to the new room."

White Feather picked up the felled sapling and tore the bark carefully up the trunk. It came off in a long wet strip, pale green and smooth on the underside, wide at the bottom and then narrower until it ended up near the leaves in a little curl. She hung it on a cross pole of the framework.

27

"Bark is perfect, isn't it! It's easy to tie when it's just peeled, but when it hardens, it'll never come undone."

"Best of all, it's not paleface rope," Owl Eyes said.

White Feather nodded. "We must live off the woods and lake as much as we can."

Owl Eyes made a face. "The Boy Scouts will be as bad as the Girl Scouts — compasses and cook kits and a little book to tell them just what to do."

"They're soft," agreed White Feather scornfully. "They probably have to wear shoes."

"And go to bed when taps blows."

"And swim inside of ropes."

"I hate paleface civilization!" Owl Eyes cried. "Next they'll buy *this* swamp, and cut down our willow thicket."

"We can still be Indians."

"On our own pier, I suppose! The Potawatomi Reservation! Oh, I *hate* the Boy Scouts!"

A cry sounded. "Walla walla woo hoo!"

"The papoose," said Owl Eyes. "They're on their way back!" She snatched a bark strip from the goat and tied a pole in place.

"The framework's not neat like a garden trellis," White Feather commented.

"It's more like a real Potawatomi wigwam. Maybe they built one on this very spot! It's a good place."

"Walla walla woo hoo!" The hoot was very near. Jip trotted up. In a moment Thunder Cloud and the papoose arrived, panting and sweaty, sweeping the path behind with a great broom of willows.

"Ugh," greeted Chief Thunder Cloud.

"Look at our travois," the papoose gasped proudly.

They dropped their load and flopped on the grass. Sugarpuss wandered over and tugged at the chief's straw-colored hair. He thrashed out and she sprang back with a blat.

The papoose moved his white arm alongside Chief Thunder Cloud's. "You sure are tan. You look like an Indian already. I bet you don't lose much tan in the wintertime."

"Ugh. Don't. On account of my Indian blood."

White Feather looked at the reclining chief. He wasn't the only one who resembled an Indian. "Have my braids grown?" she asked.

He squinted his eyes and measured a space with his thumb and forefinger. "Oh, about that much."

"Hey, come and help, you drones," ordered Owl Eyes.

"Ugh," murmured Thunder Cloud. He propped himself on an elbow and began to strip bark.

Conversation lagged as the Potawatomi worked steadily. Slowly the new framework grew, a hefty web among the trees.

A honk and a splutter broke the noontime quiet. The chief sprang to his feet and cupped his hands to his ears.

"Bugles! The Boy Scouts! Battle stations!" He swung up into the mulberry branches.

The others burst out laughing.

"Come on down," the papoose chortled. "That's only Janice."

The chief swung down sheepishly.

The bugle blasted again and they saw Janice picking her way through the trees like a long-legged bird with a silver bill. Jip bounded to greet her.

29

"Down, Jip! Down! You're all dirty!" Janice held her bugle aloft. "Hello. Lunch is ready."

She had on a scarlet sunsuit. Red-lacquered toes peeped between white sandle straps. Her black hair curled around her ears like a fuzzy cap, and her face had the first faint flush of sunburn. She raised the bugle to her lips.

"Not again!" Kenny clapped his hands over his ears and writhed on the ground.

Janice smiled down on him. "Hello, Kenny."

"Ugh," muttered Kenny. He began vigorously slicing thatch.

"Look at our wigwam," Betsy invited.

"Haven't got much done, have you?"

"Well, we only started this morning," Thad said indignantly.

Janice patted the framework. "It's nice. Will you invite me down when it's done?" A breeze ruffled the trees. She wrinkled up her nose and looked distastefully around. "It smells down here. There's a dead fish somewhere close. And look at that icky green swamp! How can you stand to be practically wading in that scum all day?"

"We *like* it here," said Thad.

"Besides, it isn't scum," Marcy said. "When you look close, it's tiny green floating plants. Algae. It isn't icky at all."

Janice shrugged. "When there are so many *nicer* places to play —" She glanced toward the lake and the white of the new pier caught her eye. Her face lighted. "Aren't you excited about the Boy Scout camp? I wonder when they'll get here! It's going to be oodles of fun, don't you think, Kenny?"

"Don't know," muttered Kenny.

Janice smoothed back her hair. "Maybe they'll teach me some bugle calls. Well, come on, kids."

"Put the bark in water so it won't dry out," Betsy instructed.

"Ugh," said Kenny.

"Ugh," replied the others. They left the willow patch and filed along the shore.

"What does 'Ugh' mean, anyway?" asked Janice.

"Anything. Anything you want it to mean."

"I don't believe the Indians really said 'Ugh.' "

"What did they say, then?" demanded Thad.

"I don't know, but not 'Ugh.' That sounds silly."

"I suppose our words sounded just as silly to them," Marcy said. "Come on, let's hurry."

After lunch the tribe met back at the clearing. Owl Eyes

sniffed. "Janice was right. There *is* a dead fish somewhere."

"Ugh," said Thunder Cloud. "Wasn't so bad this morning."

"The sun was making it worse, but our noses were used to it."

"Papoose, find it and bury it," ordered the chief.

"Wait! Leave it!" White Feather darted out of sight among the willows. "Come here!" The rest followed her voice and found her part way around the edge of the swamp, where the trees grew shorter and finally ended. The receding water had left a flat patch of steaming black earth, with needly shoots of marsh grass poking up. Hundreds of tiny green frogs squeaked and plopped into the swamp.

"Look!" said White Feather. "For supplies, in case of siege!"

"I don't see any supplies, except frogs," said the chief.

"We have to grow them, like the Indians did. A garden!"

"What would we raise?" Owl Eyes dug a dubious toe in the earth.

"Maize! Indian corn! Even the woods Indians raised Indian corn, and they put a dead fish in each hill for fertilizer."

"Where we get-um maize to plant?" Thunder Cloud asked.

"There's an ear at our cottage, hung on a nail by the husk."

"It's been there for years," said Owl Eyes. "It won't grow."

"Didn't a lotus seed found in one of the mummy tombs grow?" said the papoose.

"We shouldn't stop thatching," said Owl Eyes.

"The Pilgrims didn't wait till all their houses were built," White Feather objected. "They planted right off, and then worked at other things while the gardens were growing."

32

"You and the papoose plant, then," decided Owl Eyes, "but we'll keep on, on the wigwam."

"Get the corn, papoose, and I'll get the fish!" White Feather galloped off toward the shore.

The carcass was not hard to find. A big one, it lay half out of the water. Flies walked over the shriveling scales, and a red eye had fallen down inside the head.

Wrinkling her nose, White Feather slid the chief's paddle under it and bore it to the garden. She returned for another she'd noticed down the beach. By the time the papoose arrived, she had collected a sizable heap.

"Pe-yew, what a stink!" the papoose exclaimed. "Here's the corn."

He tossed her the ear and she cradled it in her hands. It was knobby and irregular, with red and purple and black kernels scattered along the crooked yellow rows.

"It's too pretty to plant! But maybe we'll grow lots like it."

The papoose scooped a hole in the damp earth. He lifted a small dry fish on the paddle and dumped it in. White Feather shelled four kernels of different colors on top, and the papoose patted the dirt over in a small mound.

"That's right, in hills the way the Indians did," said White Feather.

Before long there was a row of heaps bordering the swamp.

"This soil is awfully rich and black," said the papoose. "I bet there's millions of dead fish decayed in it already. The maize ought to grow like anything."

"Twelve, thirteen, fourteen," counted White Feather. "Fifteen hills. That's enough. Sugar, keep out of the garden!"

33

They picked their way along the swamp to the higher ground of the willow patch, stopped at the lake to rinse their hands, and returned to the clearing.

By now the wigwam framework was crisscrossed with willow poles, some still with bark on, others stripped and gleaming white. Willow thongs bound every juncture firmly. Owl Eyes and the chief were weaving thatch in and out.

The papoose put his bare foot gently on the ribs of Jip, stretched out in the shade, and rubbed the spot that made the dog's hind leg scratch in the air, as if after an imaginary flea. Jip woke up, looked reproachful, and moved to another spot.

"I'm parched," said White Feather. "I'm going for a drink."

The goat trotted after her mistress. Beyond the clearing the path snaked levelly through a tunnel of bushy willows. When it turned toward the swamp and sloped up, Marcy could glimpse blue water behind. Then it straightened and followed a ridge through a dense jungle until the trees thinned and stopped. The sun shone hot.

"This is Snake Grass Hill," she announced. "See? Snake grass." She pulled a long spear from among thousands of others. It was dark green, almost blue, with minute flutings, and smoky black rings where the horny segments met. She popped it apart at each joint and held out her hand. Sugar nuzzled her palm, ate a segment, and turned away.

The hill bristled with snake grass, from the shore to the marshy grass and cattails that marked the end of the landlocked swamp. Marcy stood still, watching the vibrant green surface. Only a wild storm could disturb its calm and stir up the black waters underneath. Red-winged blackbirds trilled

34

their joyful "Coch-la reeee!" as they swung on the cattails.

It would be fun to be a dashing redwing — but she'd prefer being a little brown mate sitting on her nest in the cattails, just above the water, enjoying the fun going on above while her breast kept warm the ugly babies growing in the shells. Perhaps if she looked hard she'd see one sitting patiently! She stared till the green and brown blurred before her eyes.

No, they were too well hidden — no — but what was that? In the spot where she had been looking a form came into focus — a big brown-streaked bird standing on stilt legs among the cattails! The long neck stretched up; the head and bill pointed at the sky; and it was still as a statue. It blended perfectly with the swamp pattern.

She held her breath. Sugar stirred. Never moving her eyes, Marcy reached out a restraining hand, but the goat sprang into the snake-grass spears, making them rattle. The bird gave a startled *qua*, flapped over the reeds, and dropped out of sight among the cattails on the far end of the swamp.

Sugar ambled unconcerned down the hill toward the picnic tables and stone fireplaces of the public beach. Marcy followed.

"I wonder what he was," she mused out loud. "Some sort of heron, maybe."

The pleasant grove was deserted. Sundays, there were sometimes half a dozen cars, and raucous people who brought radios and left garbage littered around, and screamed in the water, so that they could be heard all over the lake.

She left the path and climbed down the low bank. Close under it a spring trickled. A red tile pipe was sunk around it, so that the sides were smooth and clean. On the side nearest

35

the lake the tile was cracked. Water overflowed and meandered down a tiny grass-lined stream to meet the lapping waves.

She squatted. Soggy leaves layered the bottom of the spring, around the edges of the tile. A leopard-spotted frog was stretched out with his humped nostrils barely above the surface and his long webbed toes dragging on the salt-and-pepper sand. She scooped her hand under him. He came to life and with strong strokes dived up and down. Her hand chased, fingers widespread, till she caught him and tossed him on the bank. He hopped away in kangaroo leaps.

She strained the roiled water and shook the brown clinging leaves onto the grass. Then she sat back on her haunches, waiting for the water to clear. Sugarpuss tiptoed up, sniffed, and daintily drank, using her lips like a straw.

Marcy pushed the goat away and watched the black specks tossed round and round as they tried to settle on the bubbling sand. Round and round — round and round — she blinked and became aware of her reflection on the surface of the pool. Bright sky was mirrored there, and a puffy cloud. The branch of an overhanging oak framed her solemn face. Her feather stuck over her head, and watery braids fell up to meet the real ones.

The girl in the spring was an Indian maiden, hot from running. Enemy Indians were chasing her, and she came darting through the willows to crouch by this secret spring. She must run on or she would be taken captive and carried away from the Sky Blue Water. But her feet were leaden. Perhaps they'd race by on the bank above and not notice her! She bent even lower while the enemy braves ran silently by. Were they gone? Was she safe? When night came, she could go creeping back to her wigwam. Her brave would be there — just returned from the hunt — not knowing where to look for her. He was tall and lithe, with a single red feather in his hair. No, he would come in pursuit of the enemy warriors, and pause here for a drink (he knew about it too) — and see her kneeling here, and come softly through the grass — and she'd see his reflection above hers in the water —

A shadow fell into the pool. She rocked forward, startled. The square-pupiled yellow eyes of the goat gazed up through the spring.

"Sugarpuss!" said Marcy in disgust. She shoved the goat away again, lowered her head till she met her own lips, and drank as the goat had done. The water was icy. She stood up and started down the beach, away from the willow patch. A few fishing boats, motionless as gulls, rode the ripples that began near the middle of the lake.

She stopped at the edge of the public beach. Here, their former wild lands adjoined, separated only by a deep red-stained trench, the outlet for an egg-shaped bog filled with rusty bushes and cattails. The bog looked solid enough, but every bush was ankle-deep in coppery water. Grassy hills crowned with trees sloped down to its edges and the tangled fence of the public beach drifted aimlessly away along one side.

White Feather balanced her way across the board bridge and stood daringly on Boy Scout land. Ahead were alien hills that once were theirs. There was the peak of a tent — the knob of a flagpole. What if someone spotted her, standing on enemy territory?

She whirled, her heart pounding, and raced back along the path. Sugarpuss grabbed a final tuft and sprang after her. They galloped without stopping past the beach, over the hill, and through the thicket to the clearing.

Chapter

4

THAD TRAMPED UP THE HILL behind the cottage. A bunch of letters was in his fist. "Cabbage! I don't see why we have to go for the mail!"

"It's our turn," panted Marcy, giving Sugarpuss a helping shove. At the top she took a deep breath. Climbing the hill always seemed like coming into a different world: the trees ended and the landscape flattened into commonplace farmland, where nobody seemed to know the lake existed, in its hollow behind the screen of leaves.

"That farmer's corn is way high already," Thad pointed out.

"We only planted ours yesterday. It'll be ripe before fall."

"But what if the palefaces siege us sooner than that?"

"We'll have to have more supplies, for an emergency."

A garbled note burbled up the hill and then rang clear. A higher one fizzed into a burp, and then stopped abruptly. Thad cocked his head. "Janice is improving."

"She ought to. She practices all the time. Come on." Marcy walked with one foot placed directly ahead of the other. She was the captive maid, and she must appear unafraid before her captors. She held her head high, so that the white feather rode proudly, and her braids hung straight.

A gap in the trees exposed the Boy Scout pier, a quarter way around the lake. Antlike figures hurried to and fro.

"Look, they're putting up a raft! They're counselors, don't you suppose?" said Thad. "Kenny paddled close this morning early, and said the tents are still empty."

"He doesn't think the scouts'll be here today," Marcy said. "There's the swamp down there."

"Walla walla woo hoo!" yelled Thad.

"Walla walla woo hoo!" Two small figures waved from the willows.

"Busy thatching," said Thad.

The road dipped and the bank on the right formed the rim of the Sunken Forest, in whose windless center grew trees whose tops were on a level with the edges.

"You don't *really* think somebody lives down there, do you?" Thad asked.

"I don't know. *Somebody* answered once when we called 'Hello-o-o there!' "

"It might have been an echo." He peeked over the bank into the gloomy depths. "Ish! People have been dumping garbage."

"Palefaces," Marcy sniffed.

40

Ahead, Jip, with little yips of excitement, was burrowing into a cut-back gravel bank.

"The Buffalo Burying Ground," said Thad. "Do you think he's found a buffalo?"

Marcy stooped. "Here's a stone just about right for a tomahawk!"

"You're lucky!" Thad began to search. "Here's a good arrowhead stone. Oh, here's a tomahawk for me. How do you make one, anyway?"

"You bind the heads to a stick with willow bark, I think."

"At the museum this spring a man chipped a rock till it was sharp as a knife, and I ran my finger over the edge when he wasn't looking, and it cut just like a razor. I bled and bled. It looked easy; I think I'll try it." He loaded his pockets with stones. "Maybe this is where the Potawatomi got their arrowheads. Was this gravel pit here then?"

"Sure — the glaciers made it, just like they made the lake and the Sunken Forest."

"They did! How did they?"

"Well," said Marcy, "all those ice chunks were heavy, and dug into the ground. And when they got about this far in Wisconsin, they started to melt, and just like when a snowman melts, there's always a little pile of junk left — especially if you rolled him over a driveway — these glaciers left junk like gravel, and one big chunk of ice made the lake —"

"And we swim in melted ice?"

"Well, Daddy says springs in the bottom keep it full."

"But then the Sunken Forest didn't have any springs, so it all dried up and trees grew!"

41

"That's right."

"Maybe there's still a little ice in the bottom of the lake," Thad conjectured. "That's why it's so cold."

They passed the road to the public beach and hurried to the highway. Cars streaked past like great silver-trimmed fish. Marcy herded the goat into the ditch, and Thad hopped along the hot shoulder to the row of mailboxes. He ruffled the letters to mail.

"Here's two Janice wrote, to her boy friends! Let's open them!"

"How would you like someone to open *your* letters?"

"I never write anything I'm ashamed of. Not like Janice. She always puts her hand on her paper if you peek over her shoulder." He poked the letters into the box, fastened the catch, and raised the flag. Then he flopped in the grass beside his sister and Jip.

He plucked a grass blade. "Do you have a boy friend, Marcy? Is Kenny your boy friend?"

"No," said Marcy emphatically. "I mean, he's my friend, and he's a *boy,* but he isn't my *boy friend,* if you see what I mean."

"Uh huh."

"I have lots of boy *friends,* only to have fun with, and play with. Not like holding hands and all."

"But you will when you're grown-up, like Janice is."

"Maybe," said Marcy uncomfortably. "That's a long time away. Even Betsy doesn't have one yet."

"Me neither," said Thad. "Being nine is just right. But ten will be better, because then I can be a brave and get a head-dress and a name, and spend all day alone in the forest."

"Ten was a good age," Marcy agreed. "I always liked ten. But you'll like eleven, too."

A red gasoline truck toiled by, and a whole string of impatient cars behind it.

"There's a car with a New Jersey license," Thad noticed. "And look — that one's from California! What do you suppose they're doing way up here?"

"Maybe they came here for a vacation, just like people here go out West."

"If we sat here long enough, I bet we'd see cars from all the states. They don't know it, but they're passing the best place of all, right here! I'm sure glad we aren't going anyplace."

"Me, too," Marcy said.

"Jip has hair between his toes." Thad lifted a limp paw. "And his pads are all cracked and leathery. I wonder if my feet would get that way if I went barefoot all the year around."

"Probably, except for the hair."

Thad rose to his knees. "Look at all those chickens over there! Cabbage! Do you think anyone'd mind if I gathered some feathers for my headdress?"

"Go ahead," said Marcy.

"Here, keep my stones. Come on, Jippy." He crossed to the farmyard, scattering squawking fowls, and disappeared behind the house. Before long he emerged.

"They had *turkeys,* too!" he shouted, waving twin feather dusters. "And a little kid had boxfuls of feathers, and let me take all I wanted, so I got some for Betsy, too." He approached her. "And here's a white one for you. I figured you didn't want more or we'd have to call you White Feather*s.*"

43

Marcy plucked it from the bouquet and held it before her like a taper. "It's *perfect*."

"And the lady said they sell eggs and fryers, to tell Mother. Isn't the mail here *yet*? Cabbage! We'll *never* get started on our scouting expedition!"

"Listen!" Marcy silenced him. "Do you hear something?"

"Singing! From those open trucks!" cried Thad.

Three trucks rumbled up, jammed with dozens of uniformed boys, hollering and singing:

> "Forty-nine green bottles
> A-hanging on the wall,
> If one of those green bottles
> Should chance to take a fall,
> There'd be forty-eight green bottles . . ."

As the last truck roared past, one boy leaned over the end and waved. "Hi there, local yokels! Get a horse!"

The Indians stared after them, dumfounded. Then they turned slowly to look into each other's wide eyes.

"Local — yokels!" gasped Marcy.

"Why, it's —" began Thad, and they finished together in chorus: "the Boy Scouts!"

Later, back in the thicket, Owl Eyes peeped through the branches toward the camp. "Look at them! It's like uncovering an anthill. The ants grab up those white eggs and dash every which way!"

"They can't all fit in those four tents we can see," said White Feather. "There must be more back in the hills."

44

"Ugh," said Chief Thunder Cloud glumly.

"At least they know more bugle calls than taps," the papoose said. "That'll give Janice some new ideas."

"Too bad about our expedition," Owl Eyes said.

"They're running to the dock with towels and things," observed White Feather.

"They've uncovered the tag board," said the papoose.

"Swimming tests," grunted the chief.

The papoose sighed. "Lucky stiffs, with that three-decker raft!"

"Look how white they are!" Owl Eyes said scornfully. "And don't they splash! As bad as the public-beach palefaces!"

"Hey!" cried the papoose. "They're opening the boathouse!"

Chief Thunder Cloud whistled. "Look at the canoes!"

"Bright yellow!" exclaimed the papoose. "And rowboats, too."

Owl Eyes flounced around. "I don't want to watch those stupid scouts! The problem is, what do *we* do next?"

The rest swiveled reluctantly.

"Ugh," said the chief. "The wigwam's done."

In the swamp a frog jumped. Up the hill came the sharp caw-caw of a crow.

"Well, I don't see what we're sitting around for," the papoose said. "Let's start our war!"

"Tonight?" said Owl Eyes dubiously. "We aren't ready."

"Sure we are. We'll have a big fire —"

"And a war dance!" cried White Feather.

"And then a raid!" finished the chief.

"Maybe we *ought* to strike right away," said Owl Eyes

slowly. "If we wait, they'll be so settled in, that we'll *never* rout them."

"Hot cabbage!" The papoose kicked his feet in the air. "I'm going to wear gobs of war paint!"

"Ugh!" Chief Thunder Cloud ordered. "Braves! Gather wood!"

Before long the bonfire at the entrance to the thicket was a huge bristly heap. It was largely old thatch and dead branches, but the top was crowned with half a cork life preserver and ribbons of sand-caked seaweed draped like tangled hair.

"Do we have a war dance every time we have a raid?" asked the chief.

"No," said the papoose. "Do you think the Indians came running back to dance before every little skirmish? They'd never've gotten any warring done!"

"What sort of raid should we have tonight?" asked White Feather.

Owl Eyes pondered. "We can't afford to lose any braves."

"The chief has his boughten bow and arrows," said the papoose, "and we have our homemade ones."

"I have it!" Owl Eyes cried. "We'll land after dark, and creep to wherever they are; they're bound to have some sort of shindig the first night — and we'll shoot an arrow with a threatening note into their midst! You'd shoot it, of course, Chief Thunder Cloud. Our arrows always go crooked."

Thunder Cloud straightened his shoulders. "Ugh. Lose-um one arrow. But — worth it."

"Okay," Owl Eyes ordered. "White Feather, you write the note. Chief, bring the canoe. Papoose, we'll make tom-toms from that old inner tube in the dump. And meet back here at dark!"

"PALEFACES — LEAVE! OR ELSE! The Potawatomi declare WAR!" In the gathering dusk White Feather crouched by the cellar doors and whispered the dire message which she had written on a curl of bark and bound around the chief's sleek arrow. She touched her cheek where jagged red smears of war paint made the skin feel puckery, and rubbed a mosquito from her leg with one foot.

Behind the doors, from her bed among the oars and fish poles, Sugar blatted plaintively and with a nicker settled down to sleep.

At the camp a bugle sounded faintly. The shadows deepened over the lake. A breeze sprang up and sent a little rough patch of water hurrying toward shore. White Feather shivered, but not with cold.

"Time to go," she whispered. She slunk to a nearby tree, then to a bush, and in little spurts progressed toward the thicket. Ahead she saw the papoose drop on all fours. Behind, a twig snapped. She froze into the lilac bushes. Owl Eyes pressed through the hedge beside her and glided on. Out on the lake a dim cigar shape trailed a silver wake, but made no splash.

At the thicket the wake curved toward shore. Two forms from beside the black brush heap pulled the canoe up on the sand; a third shadow stepped out.

"How!" Chief Thunder Cloud saluted softly.

White Feather joined the circle.

"How," the tribe replied.

"Are all-um Potawatomi here? White Feather — light-um fire!"

White Feather knelt by the brush pile. She scratched the match across a stone. It grated, caught. She held a cupful of warm light, until the stick was brightly burning, then touched it to the dry thatch.

The leaves flashed, glowed red for an instant, and then dropped from the branches like scorched tent caterpillars falling from their burning nest. There — a twig caught. Orange tongues licked along, gaining strength, and leaped to another twig.

White Feather gazed into the fire. It was so sunlike, so hot, so alive! No wonder early men worshiped it! But the Indian didn't worship fire; he worshiped the spirit, the creator of fire —

"Great White Spirit," she murmured, "thank you for fire — fill us with fire —"

She stood, and looked at the others. Light played over the yellow war paint of the chief, and his red breechclout flamed around his waist. The gleaming wood of his unstrung bow was a thin shaft of fire. Jagged orange streaks stretched Owl Eyes' mouth to her ears, while the papoose's face was a smoldering mulberry color. In every eye a flame danced.

"We really are filled with fire!" she whispered.

The flames leaped hungrily toward the stars. Yellow smoke billowed from the shriveling seaweed. Across the lake the horizon brightened.

Chief Thunder Cloud lifted his bow high. The tribe knelt.

"Great White Spirit," he intoned. "God of Fire. God of Indian. We dance-um war dance for you. We build-um fire for you. Guide us safely in-um war canoe over black waters. Send us good fortune on-um raid. Let us cast-um fear into the hearts of palefaces. Let us drive-um palefaces from Happy Hunting Grounds. Ugh!"

"Ugh! Ugh! Ugh!" chanted the warriors.

"War!" The chief raised his bow higher.

"War! War! War!"

"Blood!"

"Blood! Blood! Blood!"

"FEAR!"

"FEAR! FEAR! FEAR!"

The papoose struck an oatmeal box with a padded stick. *Thump,* thump, *thump,* thump!

Chief Thunder Cloud began hopping up and down on the sand in time to the tom-tom, bending so his chin almost touched his knees. Owl Eyes caught up a dishpan drum, stretched tight with inner tube, and pounded it with her hands. Its deep voice mingled with the little oatmeal drum. BOOM, BOOM, thump, thump, BOOM, thump, thump, thump.

White Feather started to dance around the fire, doing the Indian step Mother had taught them that afternoon. Toe, *heel,* toe, *heel.* Owl Eyes, still drumming, joined the dance.

"Ai, yi-yi-yi, ai, yi-yi-yi!" the papoose chanted in singsong. Thunder Cloud war-whooped. "Oh-wah, oh-wah, oh-wah!"

Crackling flames cast the great shadows of swinging arms and swaying feathers on the willows. It seemed that Indian spirits were dancing along with them! The drums beat faster;

49

the whoops grew louder. White Feather clenched her teeth to keep from bursting with excitement.

At the peak of the dance the chief stopped and brandished his bow. "Papoose! The knife!"

The papoose whipped a butcher knife from his belt. "Indians must pledge! Blood brothers to the death!" With a flourish he sliced a small scab from his knuckle and passed the knife to the chief.

White Feather's knees went watery. The Blood Brother Ceremony! They'd talked of doing it before, but never had the courage! The chief was giving the knife to her now. She selected a finger, winced in apprehension, and pulled the knife across it. A stinging line of red appeared.

Owl Eyes snatched the weapon. "Ready, tribe?"

Four painted arms met like the spokes of a wheel.

"Blood brothers to the death!" declared Owl Eyes.

"Blood brothers to the death!" the tribe chorused. They pressed their bloody wounds together.

"The magic words!" cried White Feather. "Wa-ka-pot-a-mi!"

"Wa-ka-pot-a-mi!"

"Kat-a-hop-o-mi!"

"Kat-a-hop-o-mi!"

"Pot-a-wat-o-mi!"

"Pot-a-wat-o-mi!" Bloodcurdling whoops rang out.

"Our common blood is now mingled in each other's veins," stated Owl Eyes. "If one falls, we all feel the blow."

"The fire dies," the chief declared. "Off to war! Blood! Scalps!"

"Scalps!" whooped the tribe, and charged for the canoe.

"Silence!" breathed the chief. He and the papoose paddled with swift, powerful strokes.

The waves slapped the canvas sharply, like the echo of a tom-tom. On the beach the fire flickered low, and firefly sparks circled skyward. The lopsided moon cast a path that traveled with them and lit up their painted faces.

White Feather dragged her bleeding finger in the water. Her flushed frenzy was gone; now she felt cold and tense as the peaceful hills of the camp loomed up. She fingered the blood-daubed arrow.

On the far shore lights twinkled. No one in those cottages knew that on this gentle night a war canoe was gliding to attack the paleface settlement. She looked at Chief Thunder Cloud's grim face. Owl Eyes' back against her own was taut as a bowstring. Were they all feeling the contrast, too?

The canoe slid into the shore shadows beside the boathouse, and the Indians crept out. Owl Eyes tiptoed to the edge of the building and darted through the moonlight to the black shadow of a tree. A pause, and the papoose followed. One by one the tribe zigzagged up the hill toward the deserted stockade.

"Tents that way," hissed Owl Eyes.

"Look!" whispered the papoose. "There's light reflecting in those trees beyond that ridge!"

"Ugh! Quiet! Skulk!"

White Feather's legs ached from running crouched over, and her heart pounded with dread. She fell on her stomach, wiggled up the rise, and peeped over.

Before her was a kettle hole, a hollow like the Sunken Forest, but much smaller. A fire blazed at the bottom and rings of

52

seated scouts circled up the hill. Beside the fire stood a grownup, talking.

". . . eight, nine, ten . . ." White Feather started to count the enemy, but her numbers were drowned by the thump of her heart in her ears.

"I bet they never heard our drums at all," Owl Eyes breathed.

"Shhh!" Thunder Cloud rose to his knees.

"And Strong-Heart came to the land of Little-Faith," droned the grownup, telling a story. The fire spat like a bursting balloon. The chief flopped flat. He looked warningly at his tribe, then slowly rose again.

"Go on," urged the papoose.

Thunder Cloud lifted his bow. The firelight rippled over his bare chest and glanced off the polished shaft. He looked every inch a chief.

White Feather gave a terrified shudder — and then giggled. The palefaces, if they looked up, were the ones who should be frightened!

The chief placed the nock of the arrow on the string. The message made the middle bulge — would the arrow swerve?

"And then Strong-Heart said to the old man —" continued the storyteller.

"Easy," whispered Owl Eyes.

Thunder Cloud nodded grimly. A muscle in his cheek twitched. He drew back his elbow; the bow bent. The string creased his nose and chin.

"Twang!" The bowstring snapped straight as the arrow shot away.

Thunk! It landed. White Feather did not see where.

For an instant startled faces were upturned. Suddenly the papoose let out a war whoop and leaped into sight, waving his bow. White Feather fled, her heart icy with panic.

She plunged over logs and through brambles. Branches snatched at her headband. A sneaker came loose; she grabbed it off and hopped on, barefoot. She came to the long hill beyond the stockade and sped down it with giant strides to the boathouse dock. Running feet pounded behind her and Owl Eyes raced up. Thunder Cloud braced the canoe.

"Where's the papoose?"

"Wait for me!" He galloped into the moonlight and plunged for the canoe. Four frantic pairs of hands pushed off; then two pairs wielded paddles, and two scooped the water with cupped palms. A gap widened.

"Safe!" White Feather leaned back in relief. Safe afloat! And the war had begun!

Chapter

5

FOR DAYS the tribe were tensed for action. They waited and watched, and argued about just where the arrow had landed. They worked on large rubber slingshots. They cached a sack of last year's acorns in a keg in the mulberry tree. They stitched headbands. White Feather started the flag. The papoose chipped some crude tomahawk heads, and the chief bound them into split-stick handles with willow thongs. And nothing happened.

Daddy came up over the week end, bringing groceries and milk and a batch of Indian books. On Sunday the family rowed across the lake, and Sugarpuss nearly capsized the laden boat, taking a drink over the gunwale. At Almost Island

Mother fried chicken and a little fish that Thad caught, and they swam and sunned. After the picnic the tribe hurried back to the wigwam. But still the scouts had not retaliated. Owl Eyes smoldered, and laid plans.

Today, however, was too sultry even to think about war. Overhead a few clouds lay in hot yellow masses, their edges melting into the blue and mingling with the sky on the horizon to form greenish haze. Not a breath of wind sandpapered the water. Bugs and leaves drifted, barely moving. Even the dust lay undisturbed on the surface where it fell.

Marcy knelt in the bow of the old gray rowboat, her weight lifting the stern. Her chest leaned on the triangular seat that covered the prow, while her head poked out over the water and the tips of her pigtails grazed the surface. On either side her arms hung limp, the elbows bathed in lukewarm water but her hands in the cooler depths. The sun beat down hot on her back and glanced up from the water into her face.

A bugle spat staccato notes across the lake. Now the enemy would have to get up from rest hour and start doing things. She was glad she wasn't a Boy Scout. She didn't want to do anything at all, except drift.

She paddled a bit with her hands, staring down. The water was a little over her head. Bright green eel-grass fingers combed the slant sunbeams in undersea rhythm, and now and then parted to reveal a mossy rock. Little fish darted among the thick fronds. The bottom sloped down and the rich grass swept up like Rapunzel's hair. Pale green strings of a different sea-weed unwound themselves from the bottom and spiraled toward the surface. They grew closer and closer together, till she could see nothing but their winding threads. Soon they would reach the surface, but now they just grazed her fingers. She pulled one — it was slimy — and watched while it slowly unwound, floated to the top, and stretched out in the sun.

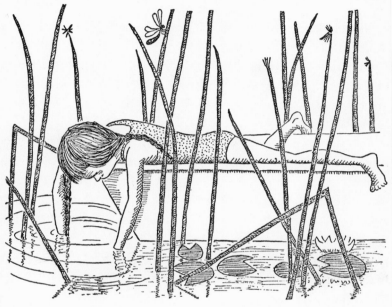

She glided over a new flower bed. Deep down, luxuriant seaweed crowded and shoved for space to grow. The broad leaves seemed made of crepe paper, pulled ruffly at the edges, and the colors ranged from deep rust to the most delicate shades of pink, all with a blue-greenish watery tinge. A turtle swam lazily above the dense weeds. She pictured herself in his world — paddling through the seaweed forest, a lush garden of the sort that must grow in steamy, tropical jungles, and yet cool and quiet, swaying gently in the current breeze.

Wild flowers, she mused, grew all jumbled on a hill — but seaweed seemed almost to have bounds. Who were the underwater gardeners? Who laid out the kaleidoscope of flower beds?

She paddled parallel to the shore, following the seaweed belt past the row of docks, past the pasture where lambs could be heard baaing in the woods, and headed in to the reedy shores of Juniper Knob.

Greenish fuzz clung to the sloping bottom, which showed through in brown untidy patches. A few skinny tongues of eel grass waved. Clams lay with their mossy backs hunched out of the sand.

She slid over a waterlogged rowboat, and shuddered. Anything unnatural in the water gave her a creepy feeling of almost violent horror: snags, and tree trunks, and barrels, but most of all boats. Seaweed grew through the slats of this derelict, and spiral-domed snails crawled along its sides. A little fish swam nonchalantly from under a sagging seat. And there — beyond the boat — tadpoles? No, a whole school of tiny black bullheads, herded slowly along by a brownish father bullhead! There must be hundreds in that inky mass! She longed to dip out a handful, but each whiskered baby had a spiny stinger on his head for protection. And she did not want to cause a panic, either, to find out whether the story were true — that if one strayed out of line, the father would eat him!

She let the bullheads move ahead and then veered into shore with a hard stroke of her hand. The boat swished to a stop among the reeds that pushed their strong, straight stalks up between the bright pebbles. Minnies no longer than her fingernail flitted to and fro, their bodies transparent and all their little red and blue insides exposed. Underwater insects bumbled around the hollow stems. Every depth of water, she mused, was a little world in itself, but from two to six inches in clear, reedy water was undoubtedly the most fascinating. Everything was so miniature. Tiny snails, tiny fish, tiny bugs, with only now and then a giant something making a startling appearance. Shallow water even had its own snake — seldom noticed — but there was one, black, and properly named a hair snake, slowly twining itself in a fantastic knot around a reed!

She leaned back on her knees and stretched. The air over the water had its own world of life, too. Midges danced, and gossamer-winged damsel flies, with long abdomens striped black and bright blue, clung delicately to the reeds.

She shoved out and back-watered slowly till the bottom was out of sight. One lone spray of spindly seaweed reached vainly for the surface. Now there was nothing, only sunlight sifting down long ramps until it was swallowed in darkness.

"Into the water," she murmured, making a poem.

> "Into the water,
> Slanting down — down — down —
> The sun's rays thrust like an arrow.
> They are stopped by shields of dancing green
> Before they pierce to the blackness below."

She stirred. Her body was stiff and her cheek ached where it had lain so long on the edge of the prow. Needles of sun pricked her back. She laid one leg along the gunwale and brought the other up beside it, so that she was lying precariously on the edge of the boat. She leaned her weight toward

59

the water; the boat tipped; she rolled over as easily as though she were in bed, and splashed in like a log.

Delicious coolness closed over her. She sank through colder and colder layers, making no effort, until her body paused, hung suspended, and floated slowly back toward the little shimmery mirror far above. She sighed out a trail of silver bubbles which streamed upward and popped free before she arrived. She surfaced, took a breath. She hung in the water like a partly waterlogged stick, her nose barely out and her feet dragging in the cold pockets. The boat, several yards away, swung slowly round and round.

She watched a hawk tilting motionless on the wind. She felt akin to him. They were both freed from the ground, buoyed up — they did not belong to the earth! He was part of the sky, and she, of the lake. With her eyes on the level of the water she could survey the whole shore, and see just what the lake saw. It was *her* watery body lapping at every inlet! She *was* the lake!

A rumble of thunder rolled ominously in the distance.

She bobbed erect. At the same instant the trees on the shore gave a little sigh, and a gust of wind tousled the lake's calm. Then everything was the same as before — except for a purple-black cloudbank with pale gray edges that suddenly chinned itself up over the trees.

"Oh-oh!" said Marcy. She swam to the boat, grabbed the gunwale, and rolled her dripping body into the bottom. She sprang up, wringing out her pigtails, and flopped on the prow.

Her aimless paddling had brought her a third of the way across the lake, and she had no oars. She took a bearing on the dark patch of trees that hid the cottage and vigorously turned the boat till it pointed the right way. The momentum of the elevated stern swung the boat on around, and she paddled fiercely the other way. Then, both hands churning like paddle wheels, she moved briskly off toward home.

The wind began again in a great gust and the lake changed to choppy, triangular waves. The gale gave the rowboat a long boost, then paused, shifted, and buffeted it from the side. Doggedly, Marcy tried to keep on course. One moment, she'd be paddling toward the public beach; the next, the bow would be swinging upshore in a half circle, past the thicket and cottages to the pasture and Girl Scout camp. She dug her aching arms deep in the waves.

A shadow engulfed the lake. She glanced up. The black clouds had tumbled one on top of the next until they'd put out the sun. Above the trees behind her a horizontal flash of lightning quivered. The last fishing boats were just scooting to safety. She was alone on the lake.

The wind howled with new fury and whitecaps sprang up. She leaned back, weary. The boat was streaming straight toward the Red Bog, like a milkweed pod puffed across a puddle. There was too much weight up above, and the sides acted as a sail. She grabbed the loop of the anchor chain and slipped into the water. She lay on her side, her back to the storm, and took long strokes toward home.

Ah, that was better. Her body was like an anchor, and now the boat followed her obediently. She measured her headway by some trees on shore. She was making progress! She felt charged with energy and excitement.

Thunder rumbled again, a long roll of kettledrums. Light-

61

ning trembled on the horizon. The whole sky was black now, except for an absurd ridge of bright blue above the swamp. Then even that was gone. But the wind shifted slightly; it was with her now. Home looked closer. She would make it!

She laughed out loud with the joy of adventure, and a wave slapped her mouth. She hung on the chain, gasping and choking.

"Here she is! Nearly drowned!" Sharp fingers dug into her armpits and dragged her from the chain. She was hauled roughly over the high gunwale of a white boat. She sprawled on the rounded bottom.

"You gave us quite a start when you disappeared!" a different voice bawled over the wind. "Got her boat, Jerry?"

"All okay, Red! Full speed ahead!"

Marcy scrambled to her knees and stared into the freckled face of a redheaded Boy Scout. Twisting around, she saw that a black-haired one held the chain of her rowboat, which was bucking and pitching like an angry goat.

She jumped to her feet and stamped a dripping foot. "Leave me alone! I didn't ask you to rescue me!"

"Sit down, you little fool!" Red barked as she dived for the gunwale. He stabbed the water with the oars. The boat sprang ahead and she was flung to the bottom. The scout Jerry pinned her down with his foot.

"You'll tip us over! Don't you know better than to stand in a boat? And don't you know you shouldn't be out on the water in an electric storm?" With each statement Red dug the oars into the waves, shooting the boat forward in jerks.

Marcy shook Jerry's foot off her back and huddled on the

bottom, refusing the seat he offered. She sensed him tense behind her, waiting for her to spring again. Well, she wouldn't give him the satisfaction.

"And without any oars in your boat!" Red continued. "You'd make a terrible scout! Our motto is 'Be Prepared'!"

"I wouldn't be a scout for a million dollars!" Marcy bellowed, and burst into tears. At that instant the sky opened up. Great drops pelted down, beating the waves flat and cratering the surface. The lake turned gray-silver. Drops splashed up, so that it seemed to be raining two directions at once; one could not tell where water ended and air began. Even the wind could make no headway against the vertical force of the rain. Marcy's tears streamed down unnoticed, and she saw with grim delight that the boys were drenched.

"Left a little!" Jerry yelled.

"How do *you* know where I live?" Marcy choked.

"Oh, we've noticed you kids," Red puffed. The thunder clapped again and drowned out all conversation.

Marcy crouched with clenched fists. The disgrace of it! Towed home by the palefaces, lectured like a baby! She'd been on this lake five summers; she could take care of herself! Now these scouts, here less than a week, were rescuing *her*. She was their *good deed* for the day!

The dock loomed out of the rain. The boat scraped the supports.

"Got it!" Jerry grabbed a post.

Marcy sprang into waist-deep water and snatched her boat.

"Marcella Richards! Aren't you even going to say 'Thank you'?"

Janice was on the pier in her new plaid raincoat.

"No!" Marcy screamed. "Rescuing people when they don't want to be rescued!"

The scouts, wet and embarrassed, braced their boat against the dock.

"I have to apologize for my little sister," Janice called over the storm. "We're really very grateful — we were so worried! She's awfully rude, but you know little sisters —" She smiled.

Thunder burst like a bomb overhead and a jagged streak of lightning pierced the lake. Everybody ducked.

"Wow! Was that one close!" yelled Red.

"Oh! You can't row back in *that!*" Janice squealed. "And you're soaked to the skin! All for that ungrateful little monster!"

Marcy poked out her tongue and wrathfully secured the boat.

"Come up to the cottage," Janice urged. "I'll get some towels — we can fix some hot cocoa — you *can't* go back till it lets up!"

The boys looked sheepish. Their olive uniforms were plastered to them like gloves. They grinned foolishly at each other.

"Well —" said Red. "It *is* pretty bad — can't even see the camp —"

"Toss up the anchor, mate!" Jerry called.

Marcy plowed through the muddy waterfall cascading down the steps.

"The tribe is at Chief Thunder Cloud's," called Janice sweetly.

Marcy sprinted down the path. She splashed sheets of water

with every step, and long grass whipped her mud-spattered legs.

"Just wait!" she gasped. "Just wait till they hear what's happened *now!*"

Behind her, laughing in the rain, the enemy tramped up to the cottage.

Chapter
6

THE RICHARDS FAMILY were lolling on the pier, sunning after a swim.

Thad looked toward Kenny's deserted dock. "I wonder where he went," he said for the hundredth time. "Here it's almost suppertime."

"He knew we wanted to have a powwow, too," Betsy said.

Janice carefully pushed back her cuticles with a little knife. "Are you kids still mad at the Boy Scouts for saving Marcy? That was two days ago! Why don't you grow up? I thought they were awfully nice, especially Red."

"That's your opinion," sniffed Betsy.

"Listen!" said Mother. "I always like it when the Girl Scouts come back. It's so pleasant to hear their singing."

From the mess hall atop Juniper Knob sweet voices drifted across the water:

> "Tell me why the stars do shine,
> Tell me why the ivy twines,
> Tell me why the sky's so blue,
> And I will tell you just why I love you."

"What a gooey song," said Betsy.

Marcy wrinkled her nose in agreement. Earlier, bright-colored caps had dotted the twin piers, and a new bugle mingled its notes with those of the Boy Scouts' across the lake. But the tribe didn't care about the Girl Scouts. They were trying to figure a way of getting even with the enemy! And they couldn't do anything till Kenny got home.

Marcy lay watching the water clear. On the underside of the slatted pier, drops from wet bathing suits gathered into pearls and splashed into the lake. Goggly fish darted around the swimming area.

Betsy, lying on her stomach, languidly raised her legs and crossed them, swishing them past Janice's nose on the way.

Janice held her scarlet-tipped nail-polish brush poised. "Mother! *Look* at Betsy's toenails!"

"Uh?" Betsy glanced back. "What's the matter with them?"

"Why, I've never seen such curly yellow hooks! It's disgusting! How do you ever expect any boy to look at you, when you —"

"I don't. I have warts, too." Betsy waved a hand.

Janice recoiled. "Your toenails — they look as if they've never been cut!"

Betsy smiled at her horny toes. "They haven't."

Mother's head snapped erect. "Why, Betsy Richards, they have too! I cut them for years, but I certainly thought you were old enough to do it for yourself by now! Of course you cut them!"

"No, I don't," protested Betsy. "They wear off."

Janice held out her scissors. "Here! Mother, make her cut them!"

"Why should it bother you?" Thad asked.

"I'd be ashamed, Betsy," Mother said. "Cut them at once!"

"Well, I'm not going to do this very often!" Betsy grumbled. "Only once every thirteen years. Oof — there's a tough one!"

"Hey!" Thad exclaimed in delight. "A fish just swallowed one of your toenails, Betsy! Oh — he spit it out. I'll bet it surprised him!"

Betsy hunched eagerly to the edge of the dock. "Where? Which one?"

"It's sunk now. Throw in another."

Betsy snipped. A little fish darted up, grabbed the nail, and flashed into deeper water. He stopped, seemed to reflect, then disgorged the morsel. A second fish flipped in to grab it but was muscled out by a larger one. The big fish braked to a stop and tried to turn his mouth inside out. His eyes bugged.

"He can't get it out!" shrieked Thad. "Serves him right, the greedy pig!"

"It'll probably poison him," commented Janice.

"Drop in another," Marcy urged. "They're all waiting!"

"Can't. No more toenails."

"Asparagus," mourned Thad. "Just when it was getting funny!"

"How about this?" Betsy gouged a hunk out of a sticky bar of soap, rolled it into a pellet, and dropped it in the water.

A fish snapped it and spit it out. Another grabbed and discarded it, then a third. After each expulsion the pellet sank a little lower, and a fish on a deeper level shot forward to taste it, with a look of solemn surprise. Finally the pellet lodged on the bottom and rocked gently back and forth.

"My turn!" cried Marcy. "Look — they haven't learned yet!"

"Why don't you get them some bread?" Mother suggested, but moved over to watch the sport.

"That one's grabbed the same pellet three times!" Betsy declared.

"He can't believe it!" Janice, too, was hanging over the edge.

Mother looked up. "Now isn't that pretty!"

"What? Where?" Four heads bobbed, to see red and yellow canoes streaking the middle of the lake. Orange paddles flashed in the sun.

"It's the Boy Scouts," said Thad.

"*And* Girl Scouts," said Betsy.

"Their boating periods must be at the same time," Marcy said. "Right after their suppers. Now isn't *that* convenient!"

"It's disgusting!" Betsy exclaimed.

"There's one of those guys who 'rescued' me." Marcy glowered. "See him, the red-haired one, alongside that boatload of girls?"

"Hasn't he ever seen females before?" Betsy sneered.

Janice's face was stricken with dismay.

"Walla walla woo hoo!"

"There's Kenny, back from town." Thad jumped up. *"Finally!"*

"Call us for supper, Mommy," said Marcy. The tribe hurried off the pier. Kenny was standing at the top of the long flight of cement steps that led to his cottage. His back was to the sun and his arms folded. He, too, was watching the colorful regatta.

"How!" Thad shouted.

Kenny raised an arm in greeting as the tribe panted up the hill.

"What took you so long?" Betsy demanded. "You knew we wanted to have a powwow."

Kenny's eyes narrowed enigmatically. A faint smile curled. "Ugh!" He wheeled and strode off.

"Isn't he maddening?" Marcy whispered.

They followed the chief behind the cottage to the garage. He stood back to let them pass, the little smile still playing around his mouth, and threw his hair out of his eyes with a jerk of his head.

They stared.

There, fastened to the trailer behind his grandfather's car, lay a gleaming yellow canoe!

"But —" said Marcy.

"Why, it's —" began Betsy.

Thad ran his finger along the gunwale. "It's the *old* one, *painted!* I can tell by that gouge we made last year!"

"Ugh," agreed Kenny.

Marcy looked puzzled. "But how — so quick —"

"We took it to a garage and they dried it under all those hot lights," Kenny explained.

"Why, it's just like a Boy Scout canoe now!" Thad marveled.

Betsy patted the shiny new finish. She darted an approving look at Kenny. "Well done, Chief!"

Kenny's chest swelled. "Ugh," he murmured.

"Let's go out now!" Thad cried. "They're all in the middle, making simpy eyes at the Girl Scouts. Won't they be mad when they see us lakers in a yellow —"

"No! We should keep it secret!" Marcy protested.

"Till we figure out the best way to use it," Betsy said slowly.

"Ugh." Kenny nodded.

"Betsy! Marcy! Thad!" A yodel sounded through the trees.

"Supper," said Thad. "But do let's go out after dark! Nobody'll see us then."

"Okay," Kenny agreed.

By the time dishes were finished, it was almost dark. The tribe carried the canoe down to the lake and slapped it in the water. It floated like a regal yellow pond lily. They climbed in and the canoe slid away from the pier. Kenny stroked toward Juniper Knob.

Betsy looked over at enemy territory. "How can you fight a war if the other side doesn't *do* anything?" she cried in vexation.

"They did something to *me*," Marcy said darkly.

"Yes, but they might have done that without *knowing*."

"They knew," said Thad. "Remember they said to Marcy, 'Oh, we've noticed you kids'?"

71

"Then why don't they attack us back?"

"Ugh." Kenny shook his head.

An offshore breeze rippled the water. Marcy shifted so that the center rib cut her in a different place. The water slipping under the canvas cooled her bottom.

Across the lake a few lights winked on. Kenny guided the canoe over the wooden bobbers into the calm black space between the Girl Scout piers. The white slide on the nearer one loomed ghostly, its steel lip grazing the water.

"What are we doing here?" Thad whispered. "The Girl Scouts don't allow even their own boats in the swimming area."

Kenny pulled off his shirt. "I'm going for a swim. Haven't been in all day."

"Hot cabbage!" said Thad. "Can we too, Betsy?"

Betsy looked around cautiously. "Well, there's nobody about — and it's been a while since supper —"

"At least an hour," said Thad promptly.

"Let's," said Marcy.

They climbed out. The chief had on trunks underneath, but in the darkness the rest stripped to underthings. They stowed their clothes in the canoe.

Thad scampered up the ladder and pumped the hand pump briskly. It let out wounded squeals.

"Shhhh!"

"I can't help it!" he called in a hushed voice. "It squeaks!"

"Pour some water on it!"

"I have to *get* some, first!"

Water gurgled up the pump. He splashed some on the plunger and the squeak diminished. A river flowed down the slide

72

and he scooted down with it. He hit the water, disappeared, and bobbed to the surface.

"Hot cabbage! That's wonderful!"

"*Shhhhhh!*" shushed the tribe, ranged up the ladder.

Across the lake a bugle burbled out the notes to assembly. The last note trailed off into a miserable honk.

"Bugler must be sick," said Betsy. "And he's repeating it! Cabbage, once is enough!" She pumped vigorously and disappeared with a splash.

Then it was Marcy's turn. She sat in the icy flood and swooped down. The black lake loomed up; she shut her eyes and plunged under. Cold shocked all over her. She swam frantically and hauled herself up on the dock, where the breeze instantly raised goosebumps on her flesh. But she felt like shouting with delight.

When she was halfway up the ladder again, Kenny clutched her ankle. "What's that?"

The four froze.

There was a crunch-crunch on the beach and giggles rippled across the water. "Who's there?" demanded a girl's voice, guardedly.

Betsy tiptoed for the canoe. Kenny climbed down the ladder.

"Nobody here but us chickens," he squeaked in a high voice.

The giggles peeled again.

"No swimming without a lifeguard!" a different voice shrilled. "Don't you know it isn't swimming hours?"

Kenny mimicked the voice. "Don't you know little girls like you should be in bed?"

The girls laughed loudly and tramped onto the dock. Marcy crept to the canoe. Atop the slide, Thad shoved off and hit with a splash.

"Oooh!" squealed the girls. They advanced cautiously and stopped a short distance away.

"What naughty boys, swimming on our docks," the first girl said. "What would your camp director say? We could report you!"

"Isn't that too bad?" Thad piped from the canoe.

"They think we're scouts!" Marcy whispered in delight.

"Well, keep your head down and shut up!" Betsy growled.

"Watch out or we'll report *you!*" mocked Kenny in the same high voice. "Why aren't you up playing drop-the-handkerchief with all the *good* little scouts?"

Snickering, the girls shoved each other forward. The boards shook.

"Elephants," whispered Betsy.

"Oh," said the first girl, "we felt like going for a walk. Besides, Annette lost her ring here this afternoon, and we have to look for it." Both girls bent and studied the dark pier, stifling their giggles.

"What are your names?" blurted the one called Annette.

"I'm little Georgie Vashington," said Kenny, "and my friend here —"

"Is the cherry tree!" supplied Thad.

The girls shrieked and clung to each other.

Marcy nearly choked. "They think that's funny!"

Betsy pinched her. *"Shut up!"*

The girls took a step toward the canoe. "We heard more of you than two. Who are all those?"

"Old moldy mummies!" said Kenny hastily. "We're tomb robbers! Whooo!" He jumped at them.

The girls giggled and scampered back a few steps.

"We're Potawatomi Indians on the warpath!" piped Thad.

75

"Oh, you are not. You're just Boy Scouts. We probably met you on the lake this evening."

"We'll be boating tomorrow," said the other. "We could meet you somewhere."

"A date?" asked Kenny. "How about the pasture stile at sundown?"

"Wait till they start making eyes at *me*," Betsy threatened. "*I'll* give them a surprise!"

A brisk crunch sounded on the beach.

"*Girls!*" a sharp voice rang out. "What are you doing out there? Who are you talking to? Come off that dock this instant!"

As Kenny dived for the canoe, a beam shot from shore and spotlighted the girls. They squealed and raced headlong into the glare. It covered them until they leaped onto the shore and then swept back over the lake, fastening on the retreating flank of the yellow canoe. Marcy and Betsy, huddled in the bottom, squeezed each other in damp excitement. Thad and Kenny bent their backs and paddled furiously.

". . . and stay away!" the voice flung after them. The beam trained on them till they were out of range.

Marcy sat up. "Are we safe?"

"Ugh," said Kenny smugly.

"They never suspected who we were, even when I told them the truth!" boasted Thad. "Imagine us, Boy Scouts!"

"I nearly choked, trying to keep from laughing!" whooped Betsy.

"And the way Kenny answered!" shrilled Marcy.

The canoe wallowed while the tribe got rid of pent-up glee.

"Are we *really* going to have a date with those girls?" Thad asked suddenly, his voice edged with horror.

Kenny snickered. "Ugh, no!"

"Thank goodness!" Thad was relieved. "I never had a date before."

Still chortling, they pulled on their clothes. Marcy wrung her braids over the side.

"Where next?" chirped Thad. "It's still pretty early."

"Boy Scout camp?" suggested Kenny.

They paddled the width of the lake and paused beyond the raft.

"Look," said Thad. "Flashlights bobbing down the hill."

A light went on in the boathouse.

"Why all the activity?" asked Betsy. "Now they're shining lights on the water. Somebody drowned?"

"I don't like the looks of it." Kenny paddled for the middle.

Behind, lights went off at the beach and flashlights flickered back up the hill. Nearby, the creak of rusty oarlocks betrayed some night fisherman.

Nobody felt like going home just yet. Marcy tried to pick out the Little Dipper. She leaned back on Betsy and could tell by the vibrations that her sister was humming to herself. The stars rode on the ripples, disappearing into troughs and appearing again on the crests. Faint shore noises sounded. The four tents visible from the lake lit up, like Thad's cheeks when he closed his mouth over a flashlight. Taps blew and one by one the tents went black. In the opposite hills the Girl Scout bugler repeated taps like a faint echo.

"Well," said Kenny, "it's getting late. Let's shove."

77

"Let's," agreed Betsy. "My bottom's itchy."

Marcy squirmed. So was hers.

They slipped toward shore. The cottage's dim light shone clearer and clearer on the trees. The canoe gently grazed the pier.

"Hello." Janice's voice came low. "Where've you been?"

"Oh, around." Thad climbed out. "What are you doing here?"

"Sitting. I was out in the boat awhile." Her voice was tight, and a little strange. She leaned forward and looked intently at the canoe in the starlight. "Say — I thought your canoe was green, Kenny."

"Painted it."

"When?"

"Today."

"What color?"

"Yellow."

"Aha!" Janice's shout was triumphant. "You kids weren't swimming at the Girl Scout piers tonight, were you?"

"What business is it of yours if we were?" Thad demanded.

"What do you know about it?" asked Betsy coldly.

Janice was silent for a minute. "Well, I overheard the Boy Scouts talking about it."

"But how did *they* know?" Betsy shrieked.

"Calm down. They didn't." She paused again. "But I happened to row in close to shore — beneath the hill there — after I blew assembly on my bugle —"

"We heard a rotten bugler," said Thad. "We should have known it was you."

78

"And all the scouts assembled, right in the middle of some game, and were awfully mad —" Janice giggled.

"But why? I thought you liked the Boy Scouts," said Betsy.

"Boy Scouts!" spat Janice. "Didn't you see them this afternoon in the middle of the lake?"

"Did they know it was you?" Betsy asked.

"Red — the red-haired one — might have. He gave me a lesson on the different calls, the afternoon of the thunderstorm. Anyway, I just drifted awhile, and some counselors came pounding down the hill and turned on the boathouse light and said —"

"Couldn't they see you?" Thad interrupted.

"The rushes hid me — and they were jabbering about a yellow canoe, and one said, 'They're all here,' and another said, 'They must've got back awful quick,' and another one said, 'That's funny, the bottoms are all dry,' and they tramped out on the pier and shone lights around. Then they came back and one said, 'I don't think she saw a yellow canoe at all,' and another said, 'She was positive over the phone,' and then they talked about the slide and that something must have been planned with some girls — and that's all I heard. They were too far up the hill."

Betsy hugged herself. "We fooled them! Hot spit!"

"Was the slide fun?" Janice asked a trifle wistfully.

"Aw-awfully!"

"Thad! Your teeth are chattering! You get right up and into dry pajamas," Janice ordered. "All three of you."

"Janice?" said Betsy. "You won't tell?"

"Not if you don't tell on me."

"Cross our hearts, hope to die, by the blood of the Potawatomi," said Betsy. "Better lie low with that garbage scow tomorrow, Kenny."

"Ugh." Kenny pushed off. The canoe glinted golden.

Betsy started up the steps. "Blowing assembly was a real stroke of genius!" she said enthusiastically. "Janice would make a good Indian if she weren't so grown-up."

"With that and the swimming we got the palefaces mad *twice* tonight!" Thad chattered. "Hot cabbage, what a war!"

Marcy looked back. "You go on," she said. "I forgot to tell something to Janice." She turned. Janice sat looking out over the lake.

A lump of pity swelled in Marcy's throat. Poor Janice. She was so alone. There was nobody her age to play with here; she must get awfully bored. And the tribe never asked her to play anymore.

She took a step and then paused. Maybe Janice didn't want company. Sometimes people liked to be left by themselves. You could only know by a funny feeling inside yourself, and that wasn't always right.

She stood for a long moment watching her sister, and then padded quietly up to the cottage.

Chapter

7

ALL THE NEXT TWO DAYS the Potawatomi feverishly prepared to be attacked, for as soon as the Boy Scouts found out there was an alien yellow canoe on the lake (and it could not lie forever under a canvas on Kenny's pier) the war would really be on! Red had paddled over to see Janice and mentioned the mystery — that the staff was puzzled and was going to talk to the boys at their next council meeting. That council was tonight. The Potawatomi, determined to find out how much the scouts suspected, sat in the clearing, waiting for suppertime and dark.

Willow branches had been planted around the wigwam; if they took root, they would help camouflage the already withering thatch. The chief had found a tin box in the dump and secured it high in the mulberry tree. It was filled with cookies and other dry supplies, pilfered from their cottage shelves. Inside the wigwam Owl Eyes had hacked a hole through soil laced with orangy willow roots and sunk a potato-chip can. When the lid was covered with leaves, it formed a secret icebox. Water seeping around it kept it cool.

Along one wall White Feather had stacked "squaw wood," small twigs for kindling. And she'd built a fireplace in the middle of the clearing, a hollow between two flat stones.

The dump supplied chipped dishes, bent pans, and jelly glasses. These, scoured out with sand, were stacked in a box inside, along with paper, pencils, and crayons. The box was also White Feather's desk.

She poked her head outside. "How do you spell Potawatomi?"

"P-o-t —" began Owl Eyes. "Oh, ask the papoose."

The papoose, crouched over his loom, threading beads on a needle, pulled in his tongue and frowned. "Cabbage, you expect me to know everything! We never had to *spell* it."

"Chief?"

"Ugh," shrugged Thunder Cloud.

White Feather sighed. "What a tribe!"

"How's the flag coming?" asked Owl Eyes.

White Feather displayed it. A large blue thunderbird with pointed beak and beady eyes spread his wings over a square of white. In one claw he clutched crossed arrows, in the other, a tomahawk.

"I have to print the letters in a circle around the edge,

there're so many," she said. She flexed her fingers and took a fresh grip on the flat-ended crayon.

Chief Thunder Cloud rolled a lazy eye at the papoose's beadwork. "Going to get that done in time to sew on your bonnet?"

"Sure — it's almost two weeks till my birthday — my brave day, I mean — and Owl Eyes promised to fix the headband and feathers."

A mulberry plopped onto the chief's chest. He popped it in his mouth. "These'll be gone by then. What'll you eat?"

"When?"

"On your brave day."

"Can't I take food?"

"No," said Owl Eyes. "You've got to live off the land for a day, like a real Indian."

"And do a deed to prove you're worthy to be a brave," said Thunder Cloud.

"We'll have a big ceremony when you get back," White Feather said, "and you'll tell about it, and then you'll get your headdress — that is, if you're worthy enough."

"Cabbage! None of *you* had to be worthy. You just started *out* being braves."

"I'll go on your brave day for you," said White Feather.

The papoose hastily reconsidered. "No, I'll go myself."

The chief's attention strayed to the goat. He mimicked her chewing. She stopped, swallowed, and waited. A bulge traveled up her throat and popped into her cheek. She began chewing again.

"What does she do that for?"

83

"Chewing her cud," said Owl Eyes.

"She swallows grass whole," the papoose explained. "Then she burps it up and chews it later. It must be nice, always to have something to chew in your spare time."

"She's got three or four stomachs," said Owl Eyes.

"Ugh." The chief gazed thoughtfully at Sugarpuss. "What does it look like?"

"What does what look like?"

"Her cud."

"I don't know," said the papoose. "I never looked."

The boys exchanged glances. The papoose laid down his needle. Thunder Cloud crept on all fours toward the goat, who chewed placidly at them.

"Grab her throat so she can't swallow," said the papoose.

"Hey!" protested White Feather.

The boys lunged.

"Maa-*aa*-aa!" Sugar gave a strangled blat and tried to struggle away. The papoose forced her jaws apart.

"Aa-*aa*-aa!" screamed the goat, jerking her head. A little green wet ball fell out. The boys released her and she bounded off, her tail flat against her back.

The papoose poked the ball with a twig. "It looks like what you spit on your plate after you've chewed and chewed real stringy string beans."

Jip stepped up and sniffed it indifferently.

"Nothing but grass," said the chief. "Phew."

"Well, what did you expect? Marshmallows?" White Feather thrust him a cup. "Go pick some mulberries. Poor Sugarpussy!"

The boys guffawed and scaled the tree. White Feather kindled the fire, then uncovered the icebox and lifted out bread, bacon, lettuce, and green onions. Owl Eyes filled a pan from the lake and made room for it on the flames. Alongside, bacon strips turned transparent on a sheet of tin.

A mulberry splashed in the pan and giggles sounded overhead.

"Throw soup, if you want to throw," White Feather called.

The lid banged. "Soup ahoy!" A silver package hurtled down and narrowly missed the fire.

White Feather peeled a twig and turned the bacon. She poked a finger in the warming water where green specks went round and round, then emptied the packet. Tiny noodles and what looked like colored sand sank to the bottom; green and red flakes of dried vegetables floated. She stirred the soup with the greasy twig.

85

Tonight she was the squaw, preparing a strengthening meal before the braves went forth to battle. Maybe this soup would give one brave the final energy to stagger over the Red River, and she would help him home, and bathe his wounds . . . but how silly! She'd be one of those braves herself! It was confusing to be both brave and squaw.

The boys climbed down with a cup of oozing mulberries. Owl Eyes finished laying out the dishes and reeled in a willow thong from the swamp. On the end was a quart of milk, green-blotched with algae. White Feather slopped soup into the bowls and served bacon with the twig, as though lifting angleworms from a bait can. Sugar grazed her way back. Jip sat alert, ears forward, eyes beseeching.

The papoose slurped his soup. "Except for the sand, the lake water adds flavor."

"It should," said Owl Eyes. "It's full of invisible plants. What whales eat."

White Feather looked out over the choppy water. It was flecked with foam and the shore before the thicket wore a long, sudsy curl. Overhead the trees kept up a constant murmuring. "Scout rowboats are out, but no canoes," she observed. "It's too rough."

"Do you think they suspect we're coming?" asked the papoose.

Owl Eyes frowned. "If they got our arrow, they might. But they can't be sure about the yellow canoe, or Janice blowing assembly."

"First she's friendly, then she's not," said the papoose. "If she's really on our side, maybe she'd spy for us."

"I wouldn't trust her," said White Feather. "She's like those half-breeds who used to be on whichever side would pay the most."

The Indians finished their meal, cleared up, and changed to long trousers and sweat shirts. The papoose took home the dog and goat. The siren called all scout boats in, and at the signal the spies crept over Snake Grass Hill and through the trees to where the Red Bog separated enemy territory from the public beach.

Shrill peeping filled the bog. A faint white mist rose from the rusty vegetation, and bats swept out over the darkening lake. Far in the camp, a bugle called assembly.

The Potawatomi crouched on the hillside, watching the ridges of the tents beyond the rise. Scouts appeared on a far hill and vanished in the woods. A wisp of cloud across the lake lost its rose color, became blue, then dark blue, then purple.

"Now," said Chief Thunder Cloud.

White Feather felt a pinch of excitement in her stomach. One by one the Indians crossed the board and followed the edge of the bog deep into the camp. They dogtrotted through the sparse spears of knee-deep grass thrusting up through the spongy turf, then cut up the hill through the trees to the kettle hole. It was deserted.

"They must not be meeting here," the papoose whispered.

"Easier to check on-um arrow." The chief led the way to the bottom and darted the flashlight around the burned area of the fire.

"I told you, it's gone," Owl Eyes said. "They *must* have it!"

Thunder Cloud doused his light and blacker darkness returned. The four clambered back up to the ridge.

"Spread out and look for their campfire," ordered Owl Eyes.

The chief struck a harkening pose. "I hear-um singing!"

"Well, let's go, or we'll miss what they're saying about us!" Owl Eyes plunged ahead. The tribe followed the faint voices down a snarled hill and through a deserted tent area, until a glow betrayed the council. The scouts sat facing a blazing fire at the foot of a slope. The bay gleamed beyond. Their leader was speaking.

The Indians wriggled forward till they were squatting a few yards behind the last row. They poked their heads out of the grass like pheasants in a hayfield, and listened.

A grass spear tickled White Feather's nose and she controlled a sneeze. The breeze bore back snatches about the ideals of scouting, about what the boys should get out of their camp experience. Nothing yet about the Potawatomi. The boys shifted. White Feather did, too.

She straightened her cramped legs and looked at the stars. She traced out Draco the dragon, a constellation she had just learned from one of the books Daddy had brought. She really should learn what constellations the Indians had; they must have had their own names.

At length she sat up. Asparagus! Red had said the scoutmaster would talk about the yellow canoe and the mysterious Potawatomi who were disturbing the camp. Why didn't he?

She felt sorry for the scouts, having to listen to all this

junk. But *she* wasn't a scout! Why did *she* have to endure it?

"Is that fat pig going to talk *all* night?" whispered Owl Eyes.

"We've missed it, I know we have," said the papoose. "They wouldn't leave an unpleasant subject till last."

"Let's go," White Feather hissed, "before I scream."

"Ugh!" The chief held up an arresting hand and pointed. The speaker was sitting down, and a young man in khaki shorts was now beside the fire. The wind carried his voice.

"When I behold . . . heavens . . . work of Thy fingers . . . moon and stars . . . which Thou hast ordained . . . what is man . . .." He moved, and the fire lit up a long, slim object on a tripod beside him.

An electric thrill jolted White Feather. A *telescope!* The fiercest longing she had ever felt gripped her.

"Cabbage!" muttered Owl Eyes. "A star talk! Well, we've missed it."

"Ugh. Follow me." Chief Thunder Cloud crept away.

"Wait!" White Feather grabbed Owl Eyes' sweater. "We can't leave now. It's a telescope! A *telescope!*"

"So what? Come on."

"I — we can't!" cried White Feather, but the rest were gone. With a despairing look at the gleaming tube she crawled reluctantly after them. Woods closed in; the tribe stood and walked freely.

"Well, doesn't that frost you," said Owl Eyes. "Janice was wrong. They didn't talk about the yellow canoe at all."

"Why wouldn't you stay?" White Feather reproached passionately. "I wanted to look through the telescope!"

"A Boy Scout with pigtails?" Owl Eyes was scornful. "Besides, Indians didn't use telescopes."

"That's because they didn't *have* them," the papoose chirped.

Owl Eyes turned on him. "Sure, the palefaces brought lots of wonderful things, but wasn't the Indian happier when he could look at the sky out of his own two eyes, anywhere on the lake he wanted? He didn't have three-decker rafts, either, but he could swim anywhere without being chased off. And don't forget the bad things — the firewater, and guns, and fences. And the palefaces tricked and cheated and killed the Indians, and the Indians accepted their ways and got soft. We have to be hard! If we give an inch, we're lost!"

White Feather sighed. "Okay," she said meekly.

"Ouch!" the papoose yelled.

"Shhhhh!"

"I can't help it; I tripped over something. Here — an arrow. I broke it."

"An arrow! The chief's?"

Thunder Cloud flashed his light on the splintered stick. "Wrong-colored feathers. Ugh! Look!" He spotlighted a target fastened to a pile of straw bales. "Archery range."

"Bum shots," sniffed Owl Eyes, feeling the bull's-eye. "Palefaces!"

"I'm going to save this." The papoose tucked the pieces in his belt.

They crossed the range and found a path. Over a woody ridge the hill sloped down to the four tents by the lake.

"Cabbage, what a dull evening!" said the papoose.

90

The dark shape of the first tent loomed up. "I wonder what they're like inside," White Feather mused.

The tribe stopped as if a single Indian. Without a word they turned and glided under the tent flap. Inside they huddled in the center of the wooden floor. A smell of mildewed clothes, sweat, and insect repellant hung over everything.

"Here goes the light," breathed the chief. He sent the beam scurrying like a mouse into every corner and then switched it off. The brief view revealed a counselor's cot and four untidy double-decker bunks. Clothes were strewn about and suitcases with spilling contents crammed under the beds. A wet bathing suit stained the floor. Orange crates bulged with comic books. Tennis rackets were propped in the tent frame, and the new canvas was already marred with scrawled names.

"Fools' names and fools' faces," quoted Thad.

"Phew!" said Owl Eyes. "We could show them a thing about housekeeping! Look at those beds!"

"Why don't we fix them up?" yipped the papoose.

"Ugh!" The chief balanced the flashlight so that its beam on the orangy canvas was reflected throughout the tent and ripped off the nearest blanket.

"Hurry!" Owl Eyes urged. "And if you hear anything, run like mad!"

The four jerked the beds apart, folded each top sheet so that the scout could get in only halfway, and then remade the bunk.

"Not too neat or they'll suspect!" hissed White Feather.

The papoose waved a striped shirt. "I'm knotting their pajamas!"

"All done?" Thunder Cloud panted after a moment. "Let's go!"

They slid out the flap, listened intently, and glided to the next tent. There the same frantic activity was repeated.

In the last tent White Feather paused. "How will they know it's us? Maybe they'll think some other scouts did it!"

"Fix a message," said Owl Eyes. "They've got to know they're being warred against. I can short-sheet alone as fast as the boys."

"We're tired, that's why," puffed the papoose.

White Feather looked around, then swung to an upper bunk and lifted a hurricane lantern from a nail in the ridgepole. She swiped her finger inside the sooty chimney and printed in greasy letters on a hanging mirror, PALEFACES! LEAVE! OR ELSE!!!

"Sister Ann, Sister Ann, is there anyone coming?" called Owl Eyes.

White Feather peeked. "Not yet." She snatched the papoose's broken arrow. "We'll leave this too! An arrow's our symbol!"

"That's mine!" roared the papoose.

"Oh, let her have it," said Owl Eyes.

White Feather found a half-written letter, scrawled *Watch Out for the Potawatomi* over the writing, and with the broken arrow, spiked it onto a partly sucked orange. She balanced it on a banjo case.

"Listen!" hissed the chief. He tackled the flashlight.

The papoose jerked a blanket taut over an unmade bed and crept with the rest to the tent flap. Lights were bobbing down the hill!

The tribe scuttled across the trampled grass to high weeds. Beams from flashlights swung in wide arcs and sliced across their bodies as they stood up and raced down the shore path. They leaped the Red River and stopped, gasping, at the safety of the public beach.

"We finished all but two," panted the papoose. "I never made so many beds so fast in all my life."

"My arms are killing me," groaned the chief.

Owl Eyes sank onto the grass. "Let's stay here a minute. I want to hear the anguished shouts of discovery."

In the hollow the four tents glowed like a row of Halloween pumpkins. The night resounded with shouts.

"The trouble is," the papoose said, "you can't tell if they're anguished shouts or just ordinary shouts."

"We'll know," said Owl Eyes confidently.

Taps caught the tents still alight, with flashlights bobbing outside like yellow chicks around fat mother hens. Each hen hastily clucked her brood under her wings, and one by one the tents disappeared. By the end of the bugle call, all was dark.

There was a moment of silence. Then a shout, and a cry of rage. Flashlights spilled outside again. One by one the four tents lit up.

"Hot spit!" Owl Eyes rolled on the ground in a paroxysm of mirth. "We did it! We did it, tribe!" Her face grew fierce. "And *this* time they won't be able to ignore that there's a *war* on!"

Chapter

8

A WEEK after the short-sheet raid an acorn bouncing along the roof woke Marcy before dawn. For a moment she drowsily watched a fat spider spinning his web between the rafters, and then sat up straight. Where was the dreary drum of rain? Or the drip of water from the eaves? She peeked out under the canvas.

Hurray! The rain was over! It was going to be a nice day at last!

In the wet brush birds sprang and bickered. The lake had a meringue of mist, and clouds still in their pink cotton pajamas lay slivered in the pale sky. The world was fresh and gleaming. She had to be out in it!

She pulled on her clothes and picked her way over the pans

that were scattered in the zigzag aisles between the humped cots.

Jip's tail beat a soft tattoo. She held open the screen while he stretched deep to the floor and curled his pink tongue. Beneath the cottage Sugarpuss nickered. She hurried through the wet grass and unlatched the doors. The goat rose stiff-legged from her hay bed, sprang over the sill, and stood sniffing delicately.

Marcy tiptoed down to the lake, past the handkerchiefs of spider webs that draped the grass with lace, and onto the pier, where water-pearled strands sagged between the poles. She sat down and dangled her feet in the water. She was just in time for sunrise.

Behind her the birds fell silent. Chipmunks stopped chipping. Even the insects suspended their hum. The whole world was hushed in readiness.

Across the misty lake the horizon brightened, in a great crescendo of light. At the very peak of brightness the first golden ray dazzled through the vapor. The sun had risen!

The world came alive again. The birds' twitterings mounted to a raucous pitch, chipmunks scolded, a woodpecker drummed a tree, and from the bog a pheasant berk-berked. Mist began to rise now, in great streamers from the surface. Marcy twitched away a little fish nibbling her toes, and stretched her arms high in a glad welcome.

Sunrise was like sunset, only just the opposite, wasn't it? First darkness merging into lighter dusk, and then the colors getting brighter, and finally daylight and the sun. Like running a movie backwards.

She watched a dragonfly, a tiny metallic helicopter, hover over her knee and then dart away. She shook her head. No, they weren't really alike at all — because the feelings were so different! Sunset was tiredness; drowsy chuck-chuckings in the bushes, the fretful blat of a goat. And the day's happenings were like fishing lines, with their hooks and leads and colored bobbers all in a tangle inside of you. But sunrise was a stretching and singing time! The day ahead lay like still water, and you felt eager to slip in and start paddling — or sometimes, to jump with a splash right in the middle! There was a whole *day* of difference between sunrise and sunset!

She wiggled joyously. And today was a free day and a fresh day — today anything might happen!

It had been a bad week for war, with company and rain all the time. It was the palefaces' turn to do the warring, anyway; that was the trouble, and they went on ignoring the Potawatomi. As Owl Eyes said, how could you wage war if the other side wouldn't fight?

The Indians had found other things to do, until the rain had started — a steady drizzle from a leaden sky that lasted for days.

The living room of the cottage was filled with the woodsy steam of wet logs, sputtering in the fireplace. Meals were strange inside, with the lights on. The grown-up company played bridge and the children played Monopoly and Parcheesi and every variety of cards. They wrote letters and read all their library books, toasted marshmallows, made up secret codes — and when the living room grew too cramped to stand any longer, they spilled out on the leaky porch to make chilly caves of the cots. But it was dreary there and they soon crowded back to jostle in front of the fire.

When quarreling developed, the grownups forced them to climb into icy bathing suits and go for a dip, or to don slickers and take a soggy walk. The rowboat filled up with rain water. Sugar refused to step through the open doors of her bedroom till hunger drove her, and then stood mournfully beneath the eaves and nibbled the sparse vegetation there, or pressed against the screen door, her wattles adrip, and blatted to get in. Jip lay under Janice's bed, dry and bored.

The rain stopped a few hours on the evening of the Fourth, long enough for the scout piers to explode in fountains of colored lights. Roman candles blossomed above the black water, and skyrockets rushed skyward, burst, and drifted down in a million needles of red. As the sky closed in and the rain began anew, the Potawatomi gasped and realized they'd been enjoying the paleface holiday that spelled Indian doom — but it was too late to undo their pleasure.

Evenings they played word games with the grownups, and when they finally crawled into their clammy beds, Janice told marrow-chilling stories, accompanied by the drip of rain.

But today the rain was over, and company gone! The sun which yesterday had been a white ghost peeping through a ragged shroud of clouds now poured its honey over everything. Snowy pollen from the spiral seaweed hitched slowly on a windless current.

What time was it? Five? Six? She left the pier and started down the slippery path, past the jungle and Fisherman's Rest and the steaming stump at the foot of Kenny's hill. She herded

Sugarpuss past the trim flower beds of Heaven's Annex, tramped along the green lawns of the cottage row, and slipped between the fence poles into BOATS FOR RENT. She threaded her way among the ropes stretched from unpainted boats to a motley array of cement-bucket anchors and climbed the stile into the pasture. She trod the turf carefully, avoiding sand-burs and cow pancakes.

Up in the woods treble and bass bleating sounded. Sugar blatted in response as a flock of sheep burst from the trees. The leader stopped and stared while the others crowded around him.

"Walla walla woo hoo!"

Kenny in his canoe glided into the reeds. "Hop in."

She captured the goat and plunked her in, then the dog, and shoved off. The sheep bolted to the vacated shore and thrust their black muzzles into the water.

"What're you doing out?" Marcy asked.

"Stretching."

She nodded. The chief too had been like a caged animal.

They paddled past Juniper Knob toward Almost Island. The channel into the lily pond yawned invitingly and they slipped in. On the placid surface lily pads lay like green dinner plates, jeweled with drops. A water lily opened its fragrant white cup to the sun, and yellow pond lilies thrust up gnarled fists.

Kenny steered down a black aisle of open water, dipping shallowly so as not to stir up the silt. The aisle narrowed until pads were brushing the canoe. Marcy scooped up the twisty brown shell of a floating snail and pressed its foot with her thumb. The snail shriveled back.

"Ugh." Kenny jerked his head toward the island. His eyes gleamed.

Amid the thick cattails a knotty white tree trunk sprawled sideways, and on top, basking in the sun, were half a dozen turtles.

Like a cat after a bird, never flicking her eyes, Marcy leaned over the bow. Kenny poled cautiously shoreward, pushing on nearly solid vegetation. Lily pads folded under the bow with glugs and bubbles. Marcy tensed to spring.

The biggest turtle plopped into the water. Another followed. Kenny jabbed the paddle deep in the muck and the canoe leaped forward. The remaining turtles flipped off the log.

Marcy grabbed at a disappearing hump. "I — can't reach — wait!" She looked down intently, snatched a lily pad away, and thrust her arm in to the elbow. Her fingers closed over the shell. She brought up the turtle, dripping seaweed and still swimming in the air.

"Nice going." Kenny jerked the canoe backwards till it floated free. Marcy rinsed her prize and examined him. His flat underplate was salmon-pink and divided into sections; his larger-sectioned hump was green-black. His nose was pug, with two tiny nostrils on the flattened end, and his mouth had a little hook in the horny upper lip. His sloe eyes were black and expressionless. He twisted his smooth striped head, pulling the loose neck folds taut, and clawed the air.

"Poor little turtle," crooned Marcy. "Don't be afraid. We'll let you go soon." She held him back for the goat and dog to sniff, then set him on the bottom before her. He scratched his way clumsily forward till he jammed in the bow.

"See any more?" asked Kenny.

"We've probably scared them all now."

Across the lake the Boy Scout bugler blew reveille, and a moment later the crisp call was repeated on top of Juniper Knob.

Kenny backed the canoe. "Let's try the Turtle Swamp."

As they re-entered the lake, fishermen were rowing to their chosen spots. Wind ruffled the bright blue water. They zagged rapidly across and slid behind the point just as bright caps

100

appeared on the Girl Scout piers and, nearer, Boy Scouts came racing for their morning dip.

"Just in time," said Marcy. "Have they seen this yellow canoe yet?"

"Hope not." Kenny paddled through the slough entrance.

"Isn't it funny how on such a little lake all three swamps are different," Marcy remarked. "Ours behind the thicket is like a green rug, and no boats ever get into it. And the lily pond's like a shallow lake, and this one's sort of between the two."

She surveyed the snail-nibbled lily pads and the masses of green algae that held prisoner the crescent-moon bellies of dead fish.

The canoe slipped into the farthest recess of the swamp. "That's queer," said Kenny. "There are usually loads of turtles."

"You'd think they'd want to sun, after all that rain."

Kenny spat in the water in disgust. "No point sitting here. Go see if the coast is clear."

He steadied the canoe while Marcy climbed out on enemy territory. She walked along the brackish bayou, through rank grass and scrubby poplars and willows. In a moment the lake sparkled before her. Not an enemy was in sight.

"All at breakfast," she murmured. She turned back, but detoured as a hill of new earth caught her eye. She rounded the heap and stopped, rigid with shock.

Before her gaped a pit full of turtles! There were some big as pie plates, others small as half dollars, and every size between. They crawled in the ooze, or clawed against the steep sides and tipped over backwards. Some were only humped islands in puddles of muddy water.

"Kenny!" she screamed. *"Come here!"*

Kenny, with the animals, came bounding. He skidded to a stop before the teeming hole and stared, goggle-eyed.

"So *that's* where they disappeared to!" he blazed.

"It's the palefaces, capturing our game! Betsy's right! We might just as well be on a reservation!"

Chief Thunder Cloud squared his shoulders. "Work for-um Potawatomi," he said grimly, and clambered into the pit. "Palefaces steal-um land, but we won't let-um steal our game!" He picked up a turtle. "Here, squaw! Put-um in war canoe!"

"Shouldn't we let the poor things go?"

"Here? For-um palefaces to catch again? You got sickness-in-the-head!"

Marcy pulled out her jersey to make a basket and walked rapidly to the canoe with a slithering load. The chief followed with an angry snapper held well away from his body.

In a few trips the pit was emptied. Thunder Cloud climbed out with the last turtle, his legs and clothes caked with mud and a long muddy streak across his cheek. White Feather grabbed a stick and scratched on the smooth table of loam that the rain had washed from the mound, "TURTLES ARE POTAWA-TOMI GAME!" She brushed the dirt off a soggy feather, wedged it in the end of her stick, and thrust the makeshift arrow in the ground. She scampered after the chief. The canoe resounded with thumps and scratches as the prisoners clam-bered over each other and clawed up the sloping sides and fell back.

102

"What about Jip and Sugarpuss?" she asked. "Do we dare let them run home through the paleface camp?"

"Hmmm." Thunder Cloud frowned. "We'll squeeze 'em fore and aft, and that'll leave the middle for the catch."

"There's that one snapper —"

"Hang your feet over! Maybe he'll give old nanny-puss a bite if she gets nosy!"

White Feather climbed dubiously into the bow and balanced the craft while the chief crammed the struggling goat between her knees.

"Hold tight!" he panted. "Come on, Jippy!"

A moment later the yellow canoe slid innocently into the lake, Sugar blatting tragically at her wavy reflection.

"The palefaces'll think we *are* sick-in-the-head!" giggled White Feather. "All crowded up with our feet over, in an empty canoe!"

"If they only knew our cargo!" the chief chortled. He puffed out his chest. *"The Potawatomi have struck again!"*

Chapter

9

THE NEXT EVENING the Indians were lolling around a racing circle of bark laid on the grass. Turtles being turtles, the tribe was giving only half attention to the rocklike racers within.

"Cabbage, I bet the palefaces were mad when they found their pit empty yesterday!" Owl Eyes exulted for the thousandth time.

The papoose lay half out of the wigwam, trying to concentrate on *Hiawatha,* one of the Indian books Daddy had brought for him to study for his impending brave day. He looked up hopefully. "I bet they're planning an attack right now!"

"We've been waiting all day," grumbled the chief.

Owl Eyes prodded a turtle shell. "Myrtle! Get moving!"

"Old Snapper has it in the bag," said Thunder Cloud complacently.

"There goes mine," said White Feather as the littlest turtle poked out its blunt nose and waddled briskly toward the swamp.

"She's stopped right on the edge," crowed the chief. "Wake up and give her a bite, Snapper! Oh-oh, the papoose's is moving."

"Is he?" The papoose slapped his book shut. "I know what we could do with Janice — let her be Old Nokomis. She was Hiawatha's grandma."

Owl Eyes frowned. "Why do we have to do anything with Janice?"

"That red-haired scout was over again today," said Thunder Cloud.

Owl Eyes shrugged. "I s'pose he'll put up even with Janice, now that Girl Scouts seem to be taboo. Look, Myrtle's opened her eyes."

"Maybe we're taboo, too, and that's why they don't fight back," suggested White Feather.

"Snapper's starting!" yipped the chief. "There, he's over!" He snatched the fierce turtle as it plunged for the swamp. "The winnah!"

Owl Eyes glared into Myrtle's shell. "I'll hide you back in the chief's rowboat, with all the others!" she threatened.

Jip growled and the hair along his backbone bristled. Sugarpuss stopped chewing her cud. Her ears popped up like a rabbit's.

105

The chief looked at the animals, then crouched and pressed his ear to the ground. "Footsteps! *The attack! Cover!*"

In an instant the thicket looked deserted.

White Feather, behind the mulberry tree with the goat, caught a flash of color through the willows. She flattened against the trunk. A panting figure jogged into the clearing. A Boy Scout!

"Walla walla woo hoo!" Chief Thunder Cloud plummeted from the tree and tumbled the enemy to the grass, slapping a hand over his mouth. White Feather lunged. Owl Eyes and the papoose sprang from the wigwam. Jip barked, and Sugar poked a cautious head from behind the tree.

"Quick, rope!" cried the chief.

The papoose produced a bundle of wet willow thongs.

The scout jerked his head free. "Let me go! Let me go!"

"Shut-um up or we'll scalp you!" the chief warned.

"You don't dare! Let me up! Let me go! You'll be sorry! Who do you think you are?"

"Ask-um no questions!" Thunder Cloud held the prisoner in a clam-tight grip while Owl Eyes bound him firmly. He was thin and sandy-haired, and every freckle on his nose stood out like a polka dot. White Feather felt sorry for him. He didn't know they wouldn't scalp him. Her own scalp prickled. Neither did she!

Owl Eyes finished and the scout flopped on the ground like a fish out of water. Sugarpuss stepped up and breathed in his face.

He wet his lips. "What are you going to do?" he asked in almost a whisper.

106

"It depends," said Owl Eyes. "Why were you running through our thicket?"

"What's that paper in his pocket?" the papoose interrupted. He snatched it and read aloud, " 'Black feather, live clam, white oak leaf, small —' "

"Let me go!" the boy pleaded. "We're having a scavenger hunt and I have to run to the Girl Scout piers to get the signature of one of our counselors — he's standing on their dock — and I'm our team's fastest runner —"

"Ugh! How many teams?" demanded the chief.

"Four. We —"

"All with-um same lists?"

"Yes. Oh, please let me go! We were way ahead!"

"Chief!" Owl Eyes cried. "That means there'll be three more through here, any second!"

"Ugh! Pitch-um in wigwam!"

"You'll ruin our scavenger hunt! Our team will lose!"

"*No* teams get-um signature! Chief Thunder Cloud has-um decreed!"

White Feather took the prisoner's red neckerchief and gagged him. They dragged him, squeaking, to the wigwam and then melted into hiding again.

"Papoose, shut up!" Owl Eyes hissed.

"That's not me, that's the prisoner!"

"Well, shut *him* up!"

White Feather strained her ears. More footsteps! She tensed. A moment later another breathless boy burst into the clearing.

This time the tribe dropped silently from ambush, trussed and gagged the startled scout before he could cry out, and

108

rolled him into the wigwam, where the papoose put on the finishing touches. They glided back just in time to turn and leap onto the third runner.

"More rope!" the chief ordered, his knee in the back of the struggling boy.

White Feather hopped in a frenzy. "I hear whistling!" They hastily packed the bound scout beside his campmates and leaped for concealment.

The last scout strode into view. Inside the wigwam a warning of grunts rang out and a foot burst through the shuddering thatch.

"Cut it out!" shrilled the papoose.

The whistler stopped abruptly under the tree.

"Walla walla woo hoo!" Chief Thunder Cloud sprang. White Feather grabbed the feet and hung on like a terrier. In a jiffy the last scout was writhing on the ground. She caught a glimpse of his face and started. It was Jerry, the one who had hauled her from the lake!

"That's all," panted Owl Eyes. "I'm pooped!"

"Now we got-um, what we do with-um?" Thunder Cloud said.

"Question them!" Owl Eyes cried promptly. "We'll find out *now* how much effect we've had on them, and after tonight we ought to see some *action!*"

The tribe dragged the earlier victims forth and arranged them all in a sprawling row beneath the mulberry tree. The papoose brought out headdresses and weapons, and the Potawatomi decked themselves.

White Feather watched the scouts. Above the bright gags,

each pair of eyes was different. The first scout still showed fright. The second's eyes were hostile; the third's, darting and crafty. The fourth — she looked closer — *Jerry was laughing!* He caught her eye and winked. She fixed her face in a stony stare. When she peeked again, he was watching Owl Eyes. She took the chance to observe him more carefully than she had that day in the boat. He wasn't any older than the chief, probably fourteen, too, with straight black hair and a nose that turned up. His mouth was covered, but his black eyes were still laughing, and they made her uncomfortable.

The chief paced back and forth, examining the prisoners through narrowed eyes. The feathers of his headdress spilled down his back and flopped in rhythm. He stopped in front of the crafty-eyed scout and leveled a finger at him.

"Ugh! Will question lardy paleface first. Promise not to holler when we remove-um gag?"

The scout looked slyly at his companions and nodded.

White Feather loosened the gag. The scout thrust his double chin high and screeched, "Help! Help! Help! He — !"

The chief clapped a hand over the bellowing mouth. "Hear-um *that?*" he asked in a shocked voice.

The tribe nodded solemnly. Thunder Cloud's eyes roved down the line and fastened on their first prisoner. "Freckled paleface, recite-um scout laws."

The papoose slipped down the gag. The scout's eyes bulged and he looked ready to cry. "A — a scout is trustworthy —"

"Enough! Tribe, is lardy scout trustworthy?"

The Potawatomi shook their heads gravely.

"Toss him back. Can't do-um business with a liar." The

110

chief squinted at the second scout, whose wrists were red from working the bindings. "Skinny paleface, if you value-um scalp, don't get-um Indians mad!"

The second scout stared insolently while the papoose undid the neckerchief. "Go ahead," he sneered as soon as the bandage dropped. "You kids won't get away with this. What do you want to know? You can't keep us here all night. You can't —"

"Mouthy, isn't he?" Chief Thunder Cloud chucked him under the chin with his tomahawk handle. The scout shyed and nearly tumbled from his knees.

"Paleface looking for trouble," said the chief. "Speak-um when spoken to. Stay-um healthy."

The scout lunged forward and spit in the chief's face. The tribe gasped. The other two prisoners made muffled noises.

Thunder Cloud's jaw tightened. The slobber rolled down his cheek, but he did not wipe it off. Owl Eyes hastily regagged the scout.

The chief turned slowly back to their first prisoner. "Freckled paleface, continue with-um scout laws."

"A scout is trustworthy, loyal, helpful, friendly, courteous —"

"Stop! Tribe, was skinny paleface *courteous?*"

The tribe shook a solemn no.

"Or *friendly?*"

No.

"Ugh. Drag unfriendly, discourteous paleface away!"

"You guys aren't friendly or courteous, either!" shrilled the freckled scout, getting bolder.

The chief stared at him coldly. He jerked his cheek against his shoulder and wiped off the spit. "You-um right. But we

111

don't recite-um laws that say we are. Now, you want-um talk so much, tell me —"

"I won't! I won't tell you anything, not even if you torture me!"

"Clammed up," said the papoose.

"Pitch him," advised Owl Eyes. "Let's try this last one."

White Feather met Jerry's eyes again and she felt another twinge of foreboding. Chief Thunder Cloud fixed him with a calculating look. Owl Eyes slipped the gag.

"Hail, great chief!" said Jerry.

The chief opened and shut his mouth like a fish.

"Paleface comes in peace. Paleface did not know he was trespassing on Indian territory. Paleface sorry, wishes to make amends."

Thunder Cloud stood agape.

"Savvy, big chief? Understand-um English?"

Owl Eyes jumped into the void. "Indians not peaceful! Palefaces steal Happy Hunting Grounds, build camp, swarm over Indian lake. Indians *mad!* Indians on warpath, drive palefaces from Indian territory!"

"Owl Eyes!" gasped White Feather.

"I don't care! It's time they knew there's a war on!"

Jerry whistled softly through his teeth. A knowing look dawned on his face. He tilted his head, trying to make out the letters on the limp flag. "Indian tribe *Potawatomi,* maybe?"

"Ugh!" Chief Thunder Cloud recovered his voice.

"Potawatomi make short-sheeting raid on Sleepy Hollow — eight, ten days ago?"

"Ugh."

112

Jerry looked incredulous. "And — oh, no! — but tell me — did Potawatomi steal palefaces' turtles yesterday?"

"Potawatomi freed Indian turtles," Owl Eyes corrected.

Jerry's look traveled from Indian to Indian. He smiled and shook his head dazedly. "Ugh! I mean, gosh! Do Indians know how much strife they're causing among the palefaces?"

"We are?" the papoose exclaimed with delight.

"Sleepy Hollow boys mad about short-sheet raid; raid Ridge. Then Ridge boys mad; raid back. Then Ridge turtles disappear. Ridge boys dump Hollow boys' suitcases in the lake. Hollow boys . . . But a Boy Scout is loyal. Must not reveal to Indians the civil war in paleface camp." He grinned. "But some scouts are puzzled. They say, 'Which are the Potawatomi? Is Hollow Potawatomi? Or is Ridge Potawatomi? Why both Hollow and Ridge sometimes leave message calling themselves Potawatomi? It doesn't make sense!' "

"I told you! They *have* noticed!" Owl Eyes cried in triumph.

White Feather watched uneasily. Jerry's eyes were still mocking.

"Head paleface tell-um camp, no play-um with Girl Scouts," Jerry went on. "No play-um with lake kids. Stay out of trouble. Stay friendly. So, palefaces friendly to Indians, don't want war."

"Palefaces steal land, then say they don't want war!" said Owl Eyes scornfully.

"How about palefaces buy-um land from Indian?" Jerry suggested. "Reach-um in pocket, little Indian, find-um treasure."

The papoose, dubious, tried to shove his hand in. "Your

113

pockets bend the wrong way," he complained. He grappled around and drew forth a scout knife, a ball-point pen, and a silver rosary with black beads.

"Reach around my neck," Jerry instructed.

The papoose fished down his shirt. Jerry ducked out of a yellow and blue lanyard with a police whistle on the clip and a thin silver chain with a Saint Christopher's medal.

Jerry cocked an eye at the assembled heap. "Pretty. Shiny. Indians look good in-um. Palefaces give-um all in payment for land."

"Remember Manhattan Island, Owl Eyes," White Feather warned.

Owl Eyes kicked at the pile. "Keep your beads and trinkets! Indians happy only when they have back Happy Hunting Grounds!"

"Indians not so dumb as they used to be," mumbled Jerry. "Palefaces can't be peaceful, smoke-um calumet with Indians? Indians live in peace in thicket, palefaces live in peace in camp?"

"No!" the tribe chorused.

"All right. Palefaces will have to subdue Indians —"

"See?" said Owl Eyes. "They mean to put us on a reservation."

The sharp triads of a bugle sounded. Muffled shouts and thumps came from the wigwam.

"Assembly," said Jerry. "Calling all in on the scavenger hunt. We'll be missed and a posse will come to rescue us."

"What are we going to do with them?" Chief Thunder Cloud asked.

114

The papoose looked hopeful. "Keep them all night?"

"We'll have to let them go," said Owl Eyes. "But one at a time, at the public beach."

"Scout's honor, we won't counterattack," said Jerry. "Tonight, anyway."

"Scout's honor of-um other three . . ." murmured Thunder Cloud.

"Leave them bound. I won't cut them loose till we get to Sleepy Hollow — that's where the four tents are. You can keep my feet bound, too. We can all hop."

Owl Eyes nodded. "I'll trust you. Tribe, line them up!"

They lugged the prisoners from their jail, set them on their feet, and tied them to each other in close formation.

"Promise to keep your word?" Owl Eyes asked Jerry.

"I'll shake on it, if you'll untie me. It's an old paleface custom to show you aren't hiding any weapons."

At Owl Eyes' nod the papoose sliced Jerry's bonds. He stretched, rubbed his bruised skin, then scooped up his possessions from the ground. He grasped the papoose's hand and shook it gravely. He shook with the chief and then White Feather. His grip was firm and friendly. Owl Eyes extended her hand. Jerry took it, but instead of shaking it, he held it close to his eyes, examining it in the failing light.

"Warts," he said.

Owl Eyes flushed and snatched her hand away.

"Palefaces have-um stinging medicine that takes away warts, over at camp. Let-um Indian use it, if she's brave enough."

"I don't want your old medicine," Owl Eyes declared

115

angrily. "I like my warts! Now march, and don't try any tricks!"

Jerry twitched the lead thong. "Come on, settlers." The procession hopped off. On top of Snake Grass Hill the Indians stopped.

"Farewell," said Jerry cheerfully.

The tribe watched the scouts lurch and stumble until lost in the gloom of the public beach, and then turned back.

"What a night!" declared Owl Eyes. "We sure put a hole in *that* scavenger hunt! And what do you think of that black-haired scout? Hot spit, but he'd make a good Indian!"

"Ugh," said the chief dourly.

White Feather grinned. The chief was mad because he'd been out-Indianed by a paleface. Then her grin faded. Why wasn't *she* as jubilant as Owl Eyes? It was that same paleface, bothering her. He knew who she was, yet he didn't mention it. He knew Janice, too. He knew lots more than he let on! Should she warn the rest? What could she say?

They paused in the clearing and the papoose crawled into the wigwam. "I've got to get my book."

"I'll take the turtles," said the chief. He and Owl Eyes picked up the pail and went on ahead. The goat followed.

White Feather listened to the papoose scrabbling around inside.

"Hey!" he exclaimed, muffled.

"What?"

"Nothing."

"Hurry up," urged White Feather. "They've all gone on without us."

116

"Just a minute," said the papoose. He emerged, tucking in his shirt and looking very sly.

"What took so long? Couldn't you find it?"

"Oh — yes." He flashed *Hiawatha*. "It was dark, and I had to hunt." He grinned, and held his arm against his T shirt. "Come on, Jip, let's run!" He galloped off ahead.

"Now what's he acting so funny about?" said White Feather to the empty thicket.

Chapter

10

IT WAS TWO DAYS LATER, the evening before Thad's brave day.

"We'll have a big feast ready when you get back tomorrow at sunset, so all you'll have to manage is breakfast and lunch." White Feather pulled a blanket taut over a pile of willow boughs.

"I won't starve," said the papoose mysteriously.

"Well, there's —"

"Don't tell me anything! I want to do it all by *myself!*"

"Okay." White Feather felt the bed. "There. Will two blankets under you be warm enough? And two on top — and Jip, of course."

The papoose crawled onto the bulky pile and lay with his eyes shut. "It's springy but not very soft." He bounced off. "Are you *sure* Owl Eyes will have my headdress done in time?"

"She's still got all day tomorrow."

"I can hardly wait to see it," sighed the papoose.

"Now do you have everything? Raincoat? Dog food? What's that book?"

"Just something to read." The papoose shoved it under the branches.

"You'll be plenty busy without *reading*," White Feather said as he crawled out the door. She looked around with satisfaction. The wigwam seemed very lived-in, with weapons and Indian garments hanging on the walls, and the willow bed filling the main room.

She lay down, squirming till the branches settled themselves comfortably under her.

Her heart beat faster. In her imagination night blanketed her; starlight pricked through the thatch. Tomorrow was her brave day, and White Feather must go alone into the wilderness! What would be his brave deed? Rescue the captive maid and carry her back to the Land of the Sky Blue Water? Tears would course down the wrinkled face of the old chief, and he would put his hand on White Feather's shoulder and say, "Brave White Feather shall have my daughter as his squaw, and be chief of the Potawatomi, as I am old and weary with many wars —"

"Here come the others," called the papoose.

White Feather blinked regretfully back to reality.

The two older tribe members threw themselves on the grass.

"I don't believe they're going to do anything again *today*," Owl Eyes exclaimed in disgust.

"Ugh." The chief plucked a grass blade away from Sugarpuss.

"You'd think they'd fight back after being captured — but I s'pose they aren't *allowed* to." Owl Eyes was furious.

"We've wasted two days just guarding the wigwam," said White Feather. "It's getting boring."

"That Jerry — you'd think *he'd* do something." Owl Eyes shrugged. "Papoose, are you all ready? Remember, you can't eat any of the stored food."

"And make-um deed plenty brave," advised the chief.

The papoose frowned with annoyance.

On the ripply lake yellow canoes fanned out from the Boy Scout shore. Opposite them a similar phalanx of red canoes streaked the water. Behind each group advanced the slower rowboats.

"Boating period!" Owl Eyes raised on an elbow. A gleam came into her eyes. "Let's *us* go out!"

"In-um canoe? You crazy?"

"Why not? If they don't know about it by now, they ought to! What's the use of having a canoe if you never use it except before reveille or after dark?"

The chief nodded thoughtfully.

"*We* can paddle among the Girl Scouts!" Owl Eyes went on. "Nobody makes *us* obey any rules. We can have fun rubbing it in!"

"Okay, let's!" whooped the Potawatomi and, glad of action, galloped down the shore path. They whooped at Janice, wading beside the Richardses' pier, clattered onto Thunder Cloud's dock, threw back the canvas, seized the gunwales, and slapped the craft into the water.

"Hurry up!" ordered Owl Eyes. "So they'll see it's us, before their all-in siren."

"We'll just go for a friendly paddle in the middle of the lake," said the papoose. "The lake's free."

The tribe climbed in. The animals crowded forward expectantly.

"Shove back the pests!" Thunder Cloud pushed off. Sugarpuss flicked her tail and wandered from the pier, but Jip sat down on the end and eyed them reproachfully.

The canoe sped quickly toward the middle. The tribe's laughing voices rang over the water. They pretended to ignore the other yellow canoes.

"See them stare," chuckled Owl Eyes.

"Hey, there's a couple canoes at our dock, there with Janice," White Feather whispered. "I see Red and Jerry and some others."

"Jerry?" Owl Eyes squinted hard through her glasses. *"That* bag of wind! What does he hang around Janice for? She's old enough to be his grandmother!"

"Old Nokomis," commented the papoose.

"She says she despises the Boy Scouts, but you notice she's always around when they're boating," said Owl Eyes.

"Cut it," warned the chief. "Ugh."

A red canoe slid by their bow. The paddlers, alike in white blouses, green shorts, and orange neckerchiefs, stared at them with aloof curiosity.

"It must be awful to get to go out on the lake only in boating periods," the papoose said loudly.

The scouts' eyes widened. The pigtailed girl paddling stern swept awkwardly at the water.

"Hey, girlie," Chief Thunder Cloud called, "you're in a canoe, not a kitchen! Don't they teach you nothing at that kindergarten but how to hem hankies?"

The girl flushed, and stabbed with her paddle. It turned on edge and sliced the water so rapidly that she tottered on her seat.

The tribe snickered. The other scout flashed them a baleful look. "Don't pay any attention to them, Martha. They think they're smart."

The chief slanted his paddle into the water at right angles to the gunwale, the blade flat. With a sharp thrust he shot it under the surface.

The girls gasped. Thunder Cloud smiled blandly. Three or four seconds passed, then the paddle sped up again on the same path it had traveled down. He opened his hand and caught the dripping handle as it boomeranged back.

The girls' eyes bulged. The chief shrugged, twirled his paddle, and took a stroke.

"Look!" giggled White Feather. "They're trying it!"

Out of the corners of their eyes the tribe watched the pigtailed scout try to repeat the trick. She shot her paddle into the water and waited expectantly. But her push had not been even; the paddle leaped out of the water behind the canoe, flopped flat, and floated there.

The scout in the bow tried to back the canoe, but did not

122

know how. The craft wallowed helplessly around in a circle while the pigtailed scout, her face red, strained toward her paddle.

The Potawatomi rocked their boat with raucous laughter. The chief and Owl Eyes shot their paddles deep into the water, again and again, and they jumped back like glinting fish.

Just then a yellow canoe slid between them and the craft in distress. A Boy Scout retrieved the paddle and held it out to its owner.

"He's doing his good turn for the day!" Owl Eyes simpered loudly.

"The little gentleman!" Chief Thunder Cloud shouted. "Why doesn't he teach her how to use it?"

"He doesn't *know* how, that's why!" bawled the papoose.

"You can't expect Boy Scouts to know anything!" the chief sneered.

White Feather clutched the gunwales. "Tribe! Look! All those yellow canoes!"

"There's one on our starboard — and one behind!" yipped the papoose.

Owl Eyes twisted, alarmed. "We're almost surrounded!"

"Ugh!" The chief shot the canoe for the one open spot in the narrowing circle. A scout canoe glided across the gap.

Thunder Cloud braked. "Trapped!"

The Indian canoe drifted while the grinning scouts tightened their ranks. Red canoes hovered outside the yellow ring, like timid does watching their bucks with fascinated but terrified eyes, at any moment ready to break and flee.

123

"I don't like the looks of this," murmured the chief. "Can't even get up speed to ram them."

"There's nothing we can do. We're helpless!" White Feather cried.

"Absolutely helpless!" echoed the papoose, pounding a thwart.

"Oh, no, we aren't!" Owl Eyes swung her paddle in a wide arc. It spanked the surface and a sheet of water splattered into the faces of the boys in the nearest canoe.

It was the blast for battle. The scouts' grins disappeared, they grabbed their paddles, and in an instant the Indians were being deluged from all sides.

"Owl Eyes!" howled the papoose, clasping his hands over his head like a small monkey. "Haven't you got *any* sense?"

"You've done it now!" cried the chief. He and Owl Eyes splashed grimly but could not make a dent in the watery onslaught. It was like spitting into the wind.

White Feather cowered, drenched. Water sprayed from every direction, blinded her eyes, clogged her ears, and streamed in rivers off her chin. Behind the wall of water the Boy Scouts shrieked with glee.

"I'm drowning!" The papoose paused from his feeble splashes to shield his eyes and stare into the canoe. "Truce! Truce! They're swamping us!"

"Well, bail!" the chief ordered through gritted teeth.

"We haven't any bailing cans!"

"Use your shirt!"

The papoose peeled his shirt and plunged it under the water in the canoe. He slopped it over the gunwale and wrung. White

124

Feather cupped her hands and frantically scooped. It was no use; water splashed in faster than they could bail.

"Stop, Owl Eyes!" White Feather screamed. "We're too full, we'll tip!"

Heedless, Owl Eyes swung again. The canoe wobbled sideways and shipped water.

"Balance!" cried Thunder Cloud as everyone leaned the other way. The canoe rolled back and shipped water on the other side. They all threw themselves against the farther gunwale, but the weight of the lake was already pouring in. The canoe slowly sank, right side up.

"Keep low!" shouted the chief. He and Owl Eyes slid off their seats. The water swirled around the tribe's shoulders. They clung to the sides and let the water support their weight, balancing to keep the craft from rolling over. Only the canoe tips showed above water, like sharks' fins, alternately as the canoe teeter-tottered slowly back and forth. The paddles floated free.

The scouts jeered and whistled through their fingers. Their uniforms were spotted and their hair clung damp.

The tribe sat dignified and precarious, ignoring the catcalls. "They're wet, too," the papoose murmured. "But they sure got us!"

"Ugh," agreed the chief. "They sure did."

Owl Eyes turned carefully. Her eyes glittered behind her spattered glasses. "This is more like it! They're fighting back! Hot cabbage, will we make them suffer for this!"

"Ugh. Have to get to shore, first."

"Why? Let's swim! Make them think they threw Br'er Rabbit in the brier patch! That'll stop their gloating!"

"Okay," said the chief.

He leaned to the side, and as the canoe rolled slowly over, they all glided out. The canoe's ribbed back humped out of the water. The Boy Scouts hooted.

Owl Eyes trod water and removed her glasses. "Here, Chief, put these in your zipper pocket." The papoose and White Feather retrieved the paddles and stowed them under the seats.

"Now — have fun!" ordered Owl Eyes.

The papoose shinnied astride the canoe. "I'm king of the mountain!"

White Feather gave him a push. "You *were!*"

"Let's make it go round and round and scramble over the top!" gurgled the papoose, with an eye toward his audience.

"Let's trap air under it and come up underneath and shout!" howled the chief.

"Laugh!" whispered Owl Eyes. "They're still watching us!"

"Whoopee!" shouted Thunder Cloud. *"We* can *swim* off *our* canoe!"

The tribe frolicked amid the taunts and insults of the enemy until the all-in siren screamed. The yellow circle fell apart like a shaken kaleidoscope.

"Toodle-oo, kiddies!" caroled one of the boys.

"Sorry we can't watch you baboons longer!"

"But we *dassn't* be late!"

"See you in our nightmares!"

White Feather glimpsed Jerry's laughing face on the edge of the armada. Beyond, Girl Scout canoes skimmed for home like dry leaves before the wind.

127

"Jump and play!" ordered Owl Eyes. "Till they're all ashore!"

"I wish they'd hurry! I'm frozen!" chattered the papoose.

"I guess they're far enough now," said Owl Eyes. "Let's shove."

They set off like tugs around an ocean liner.

"Say!" A thought struck the papoose. "How did they know we could all swim? They could've drowned us!"

Owl Eyes looked grim. "We'll get even!"

"Look on our pier — Mother and Janice and the animals!" White Feather giggled. "What'll we tell them?"

"The truth!" declared the papoose. "We were just innocently paddling and —"

Conversation broke off while they thrashed through the clinging tendrils of the seaweed belt. In a moment they could touch.

Thad took a cheerful offensive. "Hi, Mom! Hi, Janice! Did you see us swimming in the middle?"

"I should say I did," Mother said. "What ever possessed you to tip over the canoe at this time of day?"

"A little accident!" Betsy cried gaily. "Lift her, tribe!"

They hoisted the canoe upside down, heavy as rock with the combined weight of boat and water. Then the gunwales broke surface; air gushed in as water swooshed out; and the craft was light as a dragonfly. They held it high, flipped it, and smacked it on the surface.

"Accident!" said Janice scornfully. "It was deliberate."

"We were just paddling innocently around —" Thad began.

"Innocently! Mother, the Boy Scouts tipped them in!"

"We tipped ourselves in!" the tribe shouted indignantly.

"Well, I couldn't see for all the splashing. But they swamped you, and I told them to go ahead, that you could all swim —"

"*You* did!" Betsy's voice was shrill with fury. "Why, you traitor!"

"We'll never let you be Old Nokomis now," Thad vowed blackly.

"I never said I wanted to be."

"But why?" Mother was bewildered.

"It served them right! They deserve even more! They've been heckling the poor Boy Scouts something awful, all summer —"

"Poor Boy Scouts," mimicked Betsy.

"— with all their stupid Indianing, and the scouts finally decided to get even." She laughed. "The way they surrounded you, and you didn't even suspect! I nearly died! But, Mother, let me tell you the awful things they've been doing —"

An indignant babble rose from the water.

Mother covered her ears. "I don't want to know! I trust Betsy not to let the tribe do anything harmful. You haven't, have you, Betsy?"

"*Mother!*"

"All right! Just don't let things get out of hand. If they swamped you, you probably deserved it. Now they're even — and if I were you, I wouldn't give them any more reason to —"

"It was fun!" Betsy interrupted. "And I don't see what business it is of Janice's —"

"But, Mother! Don't you want to hear —"

"No," said Mother firmly. "Let them fight their own battles, so long as no one gets hurt. Betsy, Marcy, Thad — it's almost dark; get into dry things. And, Thad, if you're sniffling, you can't sleep out tonight! Kenny, you're soaked, too."

"Ugh," said Kenny from a respectful distance. He handed over Betsy's spectacles, slid, dripping, into the canoe, and paddled off.

Mother followed Thad toward the cottage.

"Traitor," snarled Betsy, climbing out of the water.

"Tattletale," added Marcy. They dribbled up the path and joined Thad, who was giving himself a vigorous rubdown on the darkening porch.

"Garbage!" whispered Betsy. "What a sister!"

"We'll just have to treat her like a paleface," chattered Thad.

They fell silent as Janice marched past into the living room.

Dressed, Thad tiptoed to the icebox. "Now I'm just going to have a little snack before I go to bed. There's no law against that, is there?"

"Not at all," said Betsy.

He wolfed down a carrot, a peach, and a slice of ham, and took a long glug of milk. The living-room windows made wide rectangles of light on the porch. He looked in at Mother reading in the old plush rocker, and Janice lying on a cot, her nose buried in a magazine. Moths zoomed and dipped around the lamp.

He padded into the living room and stood at Mother's elbow until she looked up from her book.

"Well," he said, "guess I'll be on my way. See you tomorrow night."

"My little papoose," smiled Mother. "You'll be a ten-year-old brave when you return. I won't dare to baby you any more."

"Well, maybe just once in a while," said Thad.

Mother patted his bottom. "You'll be warm enough?"

"I'm all set." He stood there. "All set," he repeated.

"We'll have a birthday cake when Daddy comes — and keep Jip with you all the time — and don't eat a thing you're not sure of — and leave a message tomorrow in the wigwam, so we'll know you didn't roll into the swamp."

Thad blinked rapidly. "Okay." He shifted his weight. "Well, I guess I'll be on my way."

"Good night," said Mother.

He kissed her on the cheek. " 'Night," he said huskily. He stood a minute longer, swallowing, then turned and hurried out the door.

"G'night, papoose," called Janice.

Betsy and Marcy followed him to the screen door. The dog and goat stood looking in.

"The Boy Scouts won't attack tonight, anyway," Betsy said heartily. "They got it out of their systems. So you needn't worry about *that*."

"I'll go around the house with you," said Marcy. "I have to put Sugar to bed."

They circled to the basement.

"Well, come on, Jip, old boy," said Thad. "Time to go. 'Night, Marcy." He flicked on his light and marched off across the grass, the dog trotting at his side.

" 'Night, papoose."

She sat down on the doorsill, her arm around the goat's

131

hairy neck, and watched the light bob down the path. The air was loud with chirping crickets. She looked up. A pale quarter moon floated in the sky.

The goat nuzzled her and she scratched the hard head absently. The moon blurred before her eyes and she felt a twinge of tightness in her throat.

"Great White Spirit," she whispered, "take care of him."

When she looked again, the light had disappeared into the dark. He was gone. And they were none of them papooses any more.

Chapter

11

"HURRY UP! He'll be here any minute!" White Feather's face as she squatted by the fire was as red as the sun that was resting like a squashed tomato on the rim of the hill behind the swamp.

"Don't rush me!" Owl Eyes cried. "Ouch! Now you've made me prick myself!" She bit off a thread and held up the headdress. "There, what do you think of it?"

"It's *perfect*."

Owl Eyes hid the bonnet in the wigwam. "He'll just *have* to have done a deed brave enough!"

The underbrush crackled. The Indians started up as Chief Thunder Cloud appeared with a bundle of wood. He dropped it by the fire and straightened to look at the red sliver of sun. "Where is he?"

"Don't ask *us*."

White Feather flipped the browning hamburgers. In the lake a milk bottle poked up its head like a turtle. Sugar wandered up and stretched her neck toward a bunch of grapes. The chief snapped her on the nose.

"Everything's done," White Feather said. "Why doesn't he come?"

"He'll be ravenous." Owl Eyes' voice had an edge of worry. "There's nothing to eat in the woods but berries."

"We knew he was okay this morning," said Thunder Cloud. "He left some sort of message."

They glanced at the edge of the path where little rocks were piled, tufts of grass tied, and pictures scratched in the dirt.

Tears flooded White Feather's eyes. The feeling that had been lying like a cold pancake in the bottom of her stomach mushed up to choke her. She blindly fed a stick into the fire. "Oh, why did we ever let him go?"

Behind them a twig snapped. They whirled.

"How!"

It was the papoose. His bare legs and feet were muddy. His grimy T shirt had a gaping hole burned in it. His eyes were gray hollows. But his sooty face was split by a wide grin.

"Thad!" the tribe shrieked in relief.

"You've been in a fire!" shrilled White Feather.

The papoose smiled evasively and set down a paper sack. "Now don't peek!"

The hamburgers spluttered.

134

"Ugh!" cried Chief Thunder Cloud. "On with feast! Papoose hungry after day alone in wilderness!"

"Oh, not so hungry," said the papoose.

"Well, let's hurry before I die of curiosity!" Owl Eyes shoved hamburgers onto plates while White Feather dug for the potatoes roasting in the coals. Their leaf wrappers were like charred paper.

"Say, where's Jip?" asked Chief Thunder Cloud.

"Home. I just left him off."

The chief arose and spread his arms. "Great White Spirit, we thank-um for papoose's return. We thank-um for thunderbird that guard-um papoose all day in-um wilderness. Witness now joyful Indian feast. Witness noble new brave at-um braving ceremony. Ugh."

"Ugh," chorused the tribe, and fell to devouring the feast.

"He doesn't act like a starving man," Owl Eyes whispered.

The papoose sat aloof in the place of honor. A puckish smile hovered on his face. He ate slowly.

The tribe waited impatiently. White Feather stacked every dish as soon as it was emptied. The chief heaped up the fire.

"Can't you hurry?" exclaimed Owl Eyes, exasperated. "I bet you're keeping us in suspense for nothing."

The papoose examined his fingernails. "Well, if you don't want to hear —"

"Ugh! Braving ceremony continues with papoose's story of-um brave day! Papoose, begin."

"And don't leave out a *thing*," White Feather prompted.

The papoose smiled at the eager circle, swallowed, and began.

135

"Hear, O Potawatomi, the tale of the papoose on my brave day. Well, last night my faithful dog Wag-tail and I came to the thicket, and it was awful dark, and — ah — the frogs were groaning —"

"Were you scared?" White Feather asked.

"Shhh, don't interrupt!" hissed Owl Eyes.

"A little bit," the papoose admitted. "So, well, I built a fire and — ah — read awhile —"

"Read!" exclaimed Chief Thunder Cloud.

"Oh, just a book I had along. Then we went to bed, and — ah — the fire died, and water slapped on the shore, and the wind was all rustly —"

"I don't see how you ever got to sleep," said Owl Eyes.

"Well, you don't notice after a while. I woke up once, awful cold, so I had Jip — I mean, Wag-tail — crawl in with me. And something screamed in the swamp, and a rowboat went by with creaky oarlocks — but I guess I went to sleep, finally, and when I woke up, it was morning."

"Oh," said Owl Eyes.

"Let's see, first I went for a swim. Say, you know, the bottom here's all covered with a sort of spongy fuzz. Why do you s'pose —"

"That doesn't have anything to do with your brave day," said Owl Eyes.

"Well, it felt funny. Let's see. And Jip — I mean, Wag-tail — waded in up to his knees and lapped —"

"No want-um hear about Wag-tail's brave day —"

"Well, he reminded me of breakfast!"

"Yes, breakfast!" The tribe leaned forward eagerly.

136

"So, I netted some minnies with my T shirt."

"You didn't eat minnies!" Owl Eyes cried.

"Cabbage, I'm not that dumb! I wanted them for bait."

"Catch-um anything?"

"Just a minute, I'm getting to it! Nothing bit, so after a while I fastened my line and went and dug up three — no, four — worms at the edge of the garden. You know, real wiggly skinny red ones, not like the regular sort. You know the sort that are there by the swamp."

"We know," said Owl Eyes. "Go on."

"So then I came back, and guess what? My line was zig-zagging every which way, and there was a big old bullhead on it!"

"No kidding!" The chief marveled. "So you had him for breakfast?"

The papoose flashed an annoyed look. "Wait till I get there! So — well, he'd swallowed my hook whole; bullheads always do. I wonder why? So I had to kill him to get it, and then I put a worm on — I didn't want to waste them after going to all the work of digging them, did I? And they kept squeezing up real fat, and then waving out real long — you know how they do, it's like trying to thread a needle when the thread keeps moving — and I cleaned the bullhead —"

"Who taught you how to clean a fish?" Owl Eyes demanded.

"Well, I had a — I mean, I've watched Daddy." The papoose smiled. "It *was* sort of messy. You know how slimy they are; you're s'posed to nail them down and pull off the skin with a pliers. But I decided to cook him with the skin on."

"Ugh," said the chief.

137

"And while he was cooking I caught a sunfish, awfully little after his head and tail were off, but it was too late to throw him back —"

"I should think so," White Feather commented.

"It's against the law to keep fish under the limit," Owl Eyes warned.

The papoose sniffed. "Paleface law. Well, the bullhead wasn't bad, but the little one was all bones, and I hadn't got all the scales off, and I sort of burned them because there wasn't any flour to roll them in like Mother does, or butter —"

"Ugh," said Chief Thunder Cloud.

"Go on," urged Owl Eyes. "You're so slow."

"You asked for the details," said the papoose with dignity.

"*Please* go on," begged White Feather. "Don't mind Owl Eyes."

"Well, I cleaned up the thicket and left you a message —"

"What *was* your message?" Owl Eyes interrupted.

"It was Indian picture language. I drew a sun to show it was a new day, and a fish to show I'd had breakfast, and an arrow to show which direction I'd gone, and I signed it with a papoose, and piled up some stones so you wouldn't step on it."

"Your papoose looked like a potato," said White Feather.

"I can't help it if you weren't smart enough to figure it out. Well, I got a drink at the spring — did I already say that? — and all the time I was trying to think what to do for my brave deed. And I went up past the Sunken Forest and I called, 'Hello, there!' like we do, and then I thought, 'I know! I'll go down and see if somebody really lives there!' "

"Oh, papoose!" shuddered Owl Eyes.

138

"What was it like?" White Feather asked breathlessly.

"Well, the main thing, I guess, was that it was so quiet. There wasn't any wind — no rustlings or anything — and the light came down all — well, dusty; and it seemed like I was the first one ever to be there. And the trees were spindly with leaves way up at the top — you know, like that seaweed must look from the bottom, that doesn't branch out till it's almost to the surface."

The tribe nodded.

"There was lots of dead wood and dry leaves, and Wag-tail and I sounded like elephants, even though we tried to walk quiet. You felt like being quiet, it was so quiet. You know, like in church —"

"Quiet," prompted White Feather. "Go on."

"Well, the ground sloped down steep — why do trees on hills grow straight up? I used to draw them slanted, but they aren't that way at all! Well, then I got to the bottom, and guess what? There was a little mushy pond with cattails and tufty grass, so there's a tip of the glacier left down there after all! And I shouted and walked all around and it really wasn't so spooky. It didn't feel like a brave enough deed. Well, then I started back up. And *all of a sudden"* — he paused dramatically — "I almost ran smack into the *biggest spider web I've ever seen in my life!"* He held out his arms. "It was as tall as I am, and this wide, and in the middle of it was an e-*nor*-mous *yellowback spider!"*

The tribe gasped.

"I jumped back, all shaky," he went on, talking fast, "and then I thought if I captured that spider, that'd *really* be brave.

139

So I blazed trees up to the dump, and punched some holes in a pickle-jar lid, and followed my trail back to the web. The spider was still there, doing a little dance, and I took the jar in one hand and the cover in the other —"

"Papoose!" White Feather squealed. "I can't stand it!"

The papoose licked his lips. "And I stretched out my arms, one on each side of the web, and whamo! I clapped the lid on the jar and there she was, running around inside like crazy!" He dug into his sack. "And here she is!"

A monstrous gold and black-velvet spider squatted in the jar.

"Ugh!" cried the chief.

Owl Eyes hugged herself in horror. White Feather shivered, but added fervently, "She's a *beauty!*"

The papoose, pleased, set the jar carefully down and continued.

"Well, I didn't want to carry my spider around all day, so I put her in that hollow up in the Chipmunk Tree, you know, where all the daddy longlegs are. And who should come past but Owl Eyes and Mother, coming back from the mailbox, and I bounced an acorn off Owl Eyes' head!"

"Why, you bum!" Owl Eyes howled. "That was you! I should have known it wasn't an accident!"

"I hid behind the trunk, nearly choking! And then I — um — no, then I thought I'd better think about dinner, and I found an empty can, for cooking leaves —"

"Leaves? To eat?" Owl Eyes wrinkled her nose.

"Sure. Let's see, I gathered dandelions, the little tender leaves, and milkweed shoots — and clover leaves — and plantain — you know, pig's ears — and cattail shoots — I got all muddy getting them —"

"And you *ate* them?" asked the chief incredulously.

"But how did you know they were good to eat?" Owl Eyes demanded.

"Any really *good* Indian knows what plants are good to eat."

"You could have caught some more fish," said White Feather.

The papoose frowned. "You don't like to have for *dinner* the same thing you had for *breakfast*. Well, I built a fire behind the bog and cooked my leaves, and they didn't taste too bad. I had salt from the wigwam. You know, salt's a nice stingy taste all alone — it makes your tongue puckered after a while —"

"Not much of a meal," sniffed Chief Thunder Cloud.

"Well, I'm not *through*. You guys butt in all the time!"

"Okay," ordered Owl Eyes. "Next one to talk is a big baboon — except the papoose, of course."

"Well, I decided to walk up to the highway, and across it there was a pasture with a cow — I mean, a buffalo. And without my spider my deed didn't seem as brave as it had; I didn't know *what* you would think was brave enough, so I took my can —"

"Oh, no!" Owl Eyes groaned. "You didn't *milk* her!"

"He's making it up!" said Chief Thunder Cloud.

"I am not! Well, she lowered her head at Wag-tail and pranced in a circle, but after I ordered him back, she began to eat again, and I grabbed ahold of a tit and squeezed it, and she kicked a little and switched her tail. Well, I tried them all and nothing would come out, but finally I noticed I was

141

squeezing the ends, so of course nothing would, so I squeezed at the top and stretched it and a little milk dribbled down! I held my can under her, and I had to sort of squat, and she kept walking and slapping me with her tail —"

"It's a wonder you got any at all," said Owl Eyes.

"Well, I finally got about a mouthful, and it was foamy and a little green — I hadn't washed my can — so I let Wag-tail drink it. Well, after that a — a bird came squawking out of some bushes along the fence, and I looked and there was an egg, so I built a little fire and cooked it."

"What sort of bird? One you'd ever seen before?" asked the chief.

"Well, they're sort of common around here; I can't quite remember the name."

"Papoose!" said Owl Eyes suspiciously. "Was it a chicken?"

The papoose grinned. "It might have been. I'm not quite sure."

"What if the farmer had caught you?" asked White Feather.

"How did I know it was his hen? She wasn't in his henyard! Well, let me see. Then I passed the Boy Scout camp entrance on the highway, and somehow my deeds didn't seem brave at all, and I thought, 'What's the bravest thing I can do?' and I answered, 'March into enemy territory,' and so I did."

The tribe leaned forward, pop-eyed.

"They could have massacred you!" squealed White Feather.

"There were some scouts at the end of a field," the papoose continued, "but they didn't pay any attention to me. Well, I went in the woods and there was a big puffball and I was still hungry —"

"It might have been a poisonous mushroom!" Owl Eyes cried, alarmed.

"It was too big. It says in my — I mean, I read somewhere that there's no mistaking a puffball. It was big as a volley ball, and there were littler baseballs and ping-pong balls around, and I broke open the big one and it was all creamy, no worms, so I ate some of it."

"Ugh," commented the chief.

"Well, I kicked the rest downhill, and then I came to a sort of hollow where there was a lean-to and a ring of stones for a fireplace, and wood piled up, and I thought, 'You Potawatomi won't believe I'm here; I better send you some Indian smoke signals.' Well, I made a big fire and threw on all sorts of green stuff and that made a lot of yellow smoke billow up. Then I took my T shirt —"

"So *that's* how it got burned," said Owl Eyes.

The papoose looked rueful. "I accidentally dropped it."

"We noticed some smoke, but thought it was the palefaces," said White Feather. "That was *dangerous* — they might have seen it, too!"

"As a matter of fact, they did."

"And they didn't stop you?"

"They helped." The papoose grinned. "A scout came up suddenly behind me and said, 'Are you a scout?' and I couldn't run, so I said, 'Sure —' "

"You lied," said Owl Eyes.

"I'm an *Indian* scout, aren't I? Well, he said, 'How come I haven't seen you around?' and I said, 'I just came.' I was afraid he'd recognize me from the swamping last night, but

143

just then another guy came up and I quick gave him the scout sign and that convinced the first guy —"

"How did *you* know the scout sign?" Owl Eyes asked.

"Oh, I just did. So they said, 'What are you doing?' and I said, 'Working on a merit badge, signaling,' and they said, 'Oh.' Then — let's see — they saw my T shirt was burned, so they got a gunny sack out of the lean-to and helped me send up some pretty good puffs!"

The tribe snickered.

"Oh, they asked earlier if that was my dog and I said he was a stray around camp; well, Wag-tail was snuffing by some boxes they'd brought and they called, "Here, Shep!' and 'Here, Rover!' and all sorts of names, but Wag-tail didn't come, and then one said, 'Here, Brownie!' and for some reason Wag-tail trotted right over, so they thought that was his name."

"Brownie!" the tribe whooped.

"But wait till you hear what comes next! After a while I discovered they were Sleepy Hollow boys, so I said I lived on the Ridge. They asked had I heard about the feud yet, and told me about the short-sheeting — I nearly busted out laughing! — and that they'd put cracker crumbs and frogs in the Ridge beds, and then the Ridge put dead fish in theirs — and it was a regular civil war — and then they discovered some lake kids had started it all! Well, I kept asking, 'Why?' and they said, 'Oh, some silly game they're playing' —"

"Hah!" snorted Owl Eyes.

"— and they told about the scavenger hunt and the turtles, and how they swamped us last night, and I said it serves us

144

right, but they shouldn't stop at just that, and they said they had lots of plans, but they'd have to do them on the sly because of their camp director. It must be awful, having a camp director bossing you —"

"Ugh! What if they'd realized who you were?"

The papoose smirked. "Well, I tried to sound them out on the plans without seeming *too* interested, you know, but they only talked about raids and things, nothing definite. And tonight we're safe because they're seeing a movie of the Boy Scout jamboree, except for the ones on the cookout. It turned out those guys were sent ahead to fix things up, and had the chow, but they didn't have much to do because the fire was already going, except they weren't supposed to have used matches. It was getting late and I was tying some knots in some vines, and wondering how to get away before the rest came, when one said, 'Why are you practicing knots? Aren't you Second Class already?' and I said, 'I'm practicing to tie up those lake kids when we catch them.' And they thought that was a good idea, and then I had a plan, so I said, 'Why don't you tie me up for practice, and see if I can get loose?' and they said, 'No, you tie us up first; that's more fun.' So I argued with them, but not too much, and we cut a lot more vines and two of us tied one guy up real tight, and while he was struggling, I tied the other one up."

The chief whistled.

"Well, when I saw they were good and helpless, I took some of their chow and they yelled, 'Hey, that's for tonight!' and I went on eating, and they began to get mad, so I gagged them

145

and told them to beware of the Potawatomi — and, oh, I brought these back." He dug again in the bag and produced two scout caps.

"Scalps!" cried Chief Thunder Cloud.

"I never knew you were so clever!" White Feather squeaked.

"I never knew, myself," the papoose said.

"Finish it!" ordered Owl Eyes.

"Well, I skedaddled and came out of the woods behind the bog, and got my spider, and then lay low in Thunder Cloud's garage till sundown. When I came past the cottage, Wag-tail wanted in. And that's all."

"What a brave day!" Owl Eyes murmured.

Chief Thunder Cloud stood up. He folded his arms and looked solemnly at the papoose. The papoose straightened up expectantly.

"Papoose, today you have-um lived ten summers. Today is brave day. You sleep-um in wigwam alone. You fix-um food from wilderness. You capture giant spider in-um Sunken Forest; you milk-um wild buffalo; you spy-um on paleface territory and by-um cleverness scalp two palefaces. Tribe, is papoose worthy to wear-um feathered headdress of brave? Is papoose worthy to be called by brave name?"

"Ugh, ugh!" Owl Eyes and White Feather chorused.

"What brave name is chosen for papoose?"

White Feather rose to her knees. "Oh, great chief, I have a name!"

"Speak, White Feather!"

"Would papoose like Crafty Fox?"

"Ugh! Is name okay with papoose?"

The papoose grinned widely and nodded.

"Papoose kneel-um, then."

The papoose leaned forward onto his knees, looking modestly into the fire while Owl Eyes fetched the headdress from the wigwam. The chief held it in the light. The papoose peeked up, and gasped.

The tribe grinned. The feathers of the bonnet were neatly graduated in height and bound into the headband with a fringe of fluffy chicken feathers. Tufts like small feather dusters fell on thongs at either side. The beadwork shimmered.

"Now you know why Owl Eyes is still wearing her old feathers," White Feather whispered.

"It's *beautiful!*" the papoose declared, his eyes moist and bright.

Thunder Cloud held the bonnet poised. The papoose knelt very straight.

"Great White Spirit, today you fill-um papoose with courage. Today, change-um from papoose to brave. Keep heart always full-um courage. Let-um no cowardly act spoil-um bravehood. Make-um ever worthy of being Potawatomi."

He looked down. "Thunder Cloud, chief of Potawatomi tribe, say from now on papoose will-um be called Crafty Fox. Remember, Indians, when you hear-um name, the brave deeds done on-um brave day. Then even in-um hundred moons will Potawatomi sit-um round council fires and repeat legend of Crafty Fox!" He lowered the headdress. "As-um brave, you wear-um feathers of brave, wear-um war bonnet. Stand up, brave Crafty Fox!"

Crafty Fox leaped to his feet. His eyes were sparkling. He touched the feathers with careful fingers.

"Ugh! Ugh! Ugh!" cried the tribe in applause.

"Ugh! UGH! *UGH!*" Grunts in grotesque echo of their own mocked them. The Potawatomi stopped in bewilderment and whirled. Out of every willow clump grinned a shadowy face!

"The palefaces!" yelled Chief Thunder Cloud. "At 'em, braves!"

The scouts poured from ambush. Reinforcements whooped up the path. Scuffles raged hand to hand. Sugarpuss blatted frantically. Shouting filled the thicket.

148

A shrill whistle blasted, and as quickly as the attack had begun, it was over. The palefaces turned and ran.

"We're routing them!" Owl Eyes cried exultantly.

The tribe chased the retreating forces to the edge of the public beach. The chief ran even farther. He came puffing back to the top of Snake Grass Hill, where Owl Eyes and White Feather were gasping and comparing wounds. "Where's Crafty Fox?"

He was answered by an anguished wail and pounding feet. Crafty Fox burst from the willows and skidded to a stop, screaming.

"What's the matter?" cried White Feather.

Owl Eyes shook her brother like a rag doll. "Shut up!" she shrieked. "Where have they hurt you? What have they done to you?"

"My headdress!" howled Crafty Fox. "They — stole — my — headdress!"

A horrified silence fell on the group. In that instant a muffled bleat sounded across the water.

The tribe stood dumfounded.

"What — where is —" stammered Owl Eyes.

White Feather recovered quickest. "Your headdress!" she yelped. "That's *nothing!* They've *kidnaped Sugarpuss!*"

Chapter

12

"IT'S A REAL WAR NOW! We can't expect to win all the time; it wouldn't be any fun if we did!" Owl Eyes' cheeks held little spots of red and her eyes glinted.

Crafty Fox and White Feather listlessly cleared up the rubble from last night's raid.

"If it was your headdress, you wouldn't be so happy," said Crafty Fox. "It wasn't your spider that got away."

Wag-tail thumped his tail sympathetically.

A tear dribbled off White Feather's nose.

"Ugh." The chief shrugged, not knowing whose mood to follow.

"Instead of moping, we should be making plans!" said Owl

Eyes. "Now, it seems to me we can either capture back our stuff, or get something of theirs so valuable they'll agree to trade."

"They haven't anything half so valuable," mourned White Feather.

Crafty Fox let out a strangled cry. "Look! They're carrying it on a pole! *My headdress!*"

"And Sugarpuss!" cried White Feather. "Look how they're dragging her along! They're choking her!" She whirled. "I'm going to go right over there and —"

Owl Eyes grabbed her flying braids and jerked her up short. "Don't be a fool! Then they'll have you, too! They *want* us to come charging over, but we won't fall into their trap! We've got to keep calm and outwit them!"

"Maybe they're returning our stuff," Crafty Fox said hopefully.

White Feather shook her head. "Why would they?"

"The headdress looks okay," said Owl Eyes. "And you can see Sugar's fine. Just as stubborn as ever."

"If they'd untie her, she'd follow right along," wept White Feather. "She just hates to be forced."

The procession, with Sugar as a balky caboose, paraded past the tents of the Hollow and on toward the Red River. The Potawatomi crept onto the shore to get a better view.

White Feather wiped her eyes. "They're turning around. I knew it! They were just rubbing it in!"

"No — wait —" said Owl Eyes. "There's someone coming on — he's lifting something — a truce flag! Quick!"

The tribe scrambled back to the thicket, pulled on their

151

Indian garb, and arranged themselves in a row, arms folded, just as a flash of white showed through the willows.

It was Jerry. He stopped a cautious distance behind the mulberry tree. "Hail! Will Potawatomi braves meet under white flag?"

"Ugh." Chief Thunder Cloud nodded.

Jerry advanced and planted his flagpole in the grass.

White Feather looked at him narrowly. He had the same laughing eyes! "Goatnaper!" she whispered through clenched teeth.

At Thunder Cloud's motion they all sat down around the trampled fireplace.

"Noble red-skinned brothers," Jerry began, "paleface settlers want peace. Plenty of room on lake for both palefaces and Indians. But Indians do not want peace. Send Crafty Fox into paleface land —"

"*Indian* land," corrected Crafty Fox. Jerry took no notice.

"— to scalp unsuspecting settlers. So, settlers raid Indians, carry off camp livestock and ceremonial headdress of brave Crafty Fox."

Crafty Fox sat straight, pleased to hear his new name so often on the lips of a stranger.

"Ugh." The chief nodded Jerry on.

"Settlers sue for peace. Suggest treaty terms. Will return Indian property unharmed when Indians pay the ransom."

Owl Eyes leaned forward. "And what is the ransom?"

Jerry fumbled in his pocket and brought forth two rolls of paper. "Paleface talking leaves." He unrolled one and read:

" 'We, the undersigned, hereby promise to return to the Potawatomi Indian tribe one ceremonial headdress and one white goat provided that by the evening of the next full moon' — that's next Thursday — 'the Potawatomi have delivered to us one hundred pieces of wampum, and the twenty-five turtles — ' "

"We can't," interrupted Crafty Fox. "We let them all go."

"Crafty Fox, shut up. Go on, Jerry," Owl Eyes ordered.

" '— the twenty-five turtles taken from the pit on Brownsea Island. The exchange will take place on neutral territory between the scout camp and Indian Thicket, with an equal number of unarmed scouts and Indians present. After the exchange, the settlers, to show their good faith, will forget past wrongs and make plans for a ceremony of smoking the calumet and burying the hatchet. Signed —' well, you can see the list of names."

He gave the paper to Chief Thunder Cloud and sat back, smiling.

"Indians must have council," Owl Eyes snapped. "Paleface, retreat beyond tree. Chief, give me the talking leaf."

Jerry sauntered off and stood looking away. He whistled softly.

The tribe bent their heads over the paper.

"But we don't *have* any turtles!" whispered Crafty Fox.

"You goon!" cried Owl Eyes. "Blabbing all our secrets! We can catch them back again if we want to."

"Yes," objected Crafty Fox, "but they're Indian game, and the scouts'll put them in their pit!"

Owl Eyes pushed up her glasses thoughtfully. "We all ought to agree to let turtles go after about four days, so there'll always be plenty to catch."

"What's wampum, exactly?" Chief Thunder Cloud asked.

"Indian money. Shell beads with a hole in the middle," said Crafty Fox.

"There are lots of clam shells in Oyster Inlet," said White Feather.

"And my granddad has a drill," the chief suggested.

Owl Eyes looked dubious. "Could we do it all in six days?"

"We could do it in *three*," the chief spat.

"Let's do whatever will get Sugar back!" pleaded White Feather.

"You'll get her back! But do we want to smoke the pipe and all? Why, this war is just beginning to be fun!" Owl Eyes

154

glanced suspiciously at the younger tribesters. "You *don't* want peace — do you?"

Crafty Fox looked uncomfortably at the ground.

"When they get taking goats —" White Feather said defensively.

"You mean you'd even *consider* it? After our war dance and blood-brother ceremony, and swearing to fight to the finish? You'd trade our hunting ground for a goat and a bunch of feathers? Fine braves *you* are!"

"It doesn't say we *have* to have peace," said Thunder Cloud.

Owl Eyes snatched the document and read it again. "You're right! It says the *settlers* will forget their past wrongs!"

"Once we get our stuff we could go right back to war," said Crafty Fox.

"But not before then," Owl Eyes warned.

"Ugh," nodded the chief. "Potawatomi show treacherous palefaces that Indian honest! Keep-um word when give-um it!"

"Getting the ransom might be fun," mused Owl Eyes.

"Then — ?" asked White Feather.

"Ugh. We-um sign."

Owl Eyes called back the messenger. "The Potawatomi accept your truce terms, with one amendment." She explained about the turtles.

Jerry nodded. "That's fair enough." He scribbled the clause on both sheets and held out the pen. "Now, please draw your marks."

The tribe looked at one another and then signed: a thundercloud, an owl's head, a white feather, and a fox — Crafty Fox lingered long over the first depiction of his name — then the chief returned one treaty to the messenger and placed the other in the wigwam.

Jerry wrenched his flag from the ground. "We'll parade Indian property every day so you can be sure it's all right."

"Say," said Crafty Fox, "what happens if we *don't* get the ransom?"

The messenger made a slitting motion across his throat. "Barbecued billy goat — and a nice feather duster for the lodge — I mean, the stockade!"

"You wouldn't dare!" shrieked White Feather.

"Calm down. He's just kidding," Owl Eyes said. "Anyway, there's plenty of time."

"Let's shake on the truce, then, paleface fashion," said Jerry.

Owl Eyes held out her hand.

"Oh, that reminds me." He pulled a small bottle from his pocket. "This is for warts. You daub a little on top of them every day and they gradually shrivel up. But it burns! Here, I'll —"

With a quick motion Owl Eyes slapped the vial out of his hand. "Paleface medicine!" she cried furiously. Her face was crimson.

Jerry's smile wavered. He saluted briefly, took his flag, and trotted off. White Feather, uncomfortable again, watched him go.

Owl Eyes stooped, stood, and threw something in the swamp. There was a plop, and a little black spot opened in the green.

"Owl Eyes!" cried Crafty Fox. "You might at least've saved it! Maybe *I'll* have a wart someday!"

156

Owl Eyes slid a hand into her pocket. "Who wants to go turtle hunting?" she said, tossing her head.

That afternoon the tribe split up: the elders to the Turtle Swamp and bay, and the two younger to Oyster Inlet. The bottom there was bumpy with half-buried clams. Empty shells lay open like iridescent butterflies.

"Take even broken ones," Crafty Fox instructed, wading as deep as his rolled pant legs would allow. "We can make wampum from bits."

"But not live clams; they're too hard to scrape out," White Feather decided.

Hunters now, they rowed on to the lily pond with their shell cargo. There, sun-glazed turtle backs glared from every log and hummock. By the time the pond was so roiled that no turtle would show his head for the rest of the day, eight captives were clunking over the clamshells, and Mother's faint yodel meant suppertime.

The tribe reunited at Thunder Cloud's pier. Owl Eyes lifted the catch into a huge bait cage resting half out of the water. "This will be a snap! You got eight and we got five. We'll get the rest tomorrow!"

The chief held up a big turtle with a peeling underplate. "Ugh! Old pal! Old Baldy! You get-um in lily pond?"

The Fox nodded. "We've probably caught most of these before."

Mother yodeled again. The Richards scrambled into the rowboat and skimmed for home.

Daddy had come, and Mother had served his supper early.

He was standing in his hip boots, gulping down a cup of coffee.

"Hey, Indians!" he called as they piled in the screen door. "I hear the Boy Scouts got your goat!" He laughed, choked on his coffee, and ended up coughing and stamping.

"It's not funny," said Marcy, but couldn't help laughing, too.

"*Kid*napers!" gasped Daddy. "They'll be begging you to take her back in a few days, and you'd be smart not to! Who's going fishing with me?"

"We can't," Betsy said.

Mother stood up. "I will. The children can do the dishes."

"Thad, there're some more Indian books for you," motioned Daddy. "One I read when I was a kid. Teach you how to skin a coon! Come on, Mommy!" He picked up his tackle box and rod and, pinching Mother to make her scurry ahead, departed toward the pasture.

"*Two Little Savages.*" Thad thumbed through the pages. "I wonder if it tells how to make wampum."

"Come and eat," said Betsy, her mouth full.

Janice sauntered around the corner of the porch and perched on the edge of the table. Her hair was up in pin curls.

"Ha, ha, you kids are really getting it now."

Nobody replied.

"How does it feel to be on the low end for a change?" Janice paused, then went on confidentially, "I know where they're keeping Sugarpuss."

"Where?" Marcy demanded.

"I thought that'd make you talk! Well, knowing won't do

158

you any good, because she's under guard day and night, but she's in a shed behind the mess hall. Or the lodge; it's the same building."

"How do you get so smart?" asked Thad.

"Oh, Red tells me. He's going to take me all around camp tomorrow, on visitors' day. He says maybe I can come to a secret council meeting sometime. He's a junior counselor and an Eagle Scout." She pulled out a bobby pin and rewound a curl. "I'll say hello to Sugar for you."

"Thanks," said Marcy icily.

"You know what?" Janice went on. "Jerry likes you kids."

"Well, we don't like him." Betsy shoved back her chair. "Come on, tribe." They paraded off the porch.

"Dishes!" yelled Janice. "I won't do them for you!"

"Nobody asked you to," Betsy replied.

The chief was squatting on a cement step with a doughnut clenched in his teeth. The shell he was drilling with a heavy brace and bit shattered just as they came up, and he swept away the pieces in disgust.

White Feather picked up a flake. It was a dirty mossy brown on one side, and the pearly pink of its other surface reflected in the setting sun like oil slick on water. She rubbed the edges on the cement till it was round and smooth.

The chief smashed another shell. "Garbage," he muttered.

Owl Eyes pounced on White Feather's fragment. "Try drilling this!"

"On something soft, so it won't shatter," suggested Crafty Fox.

159

Miraculously, the thin swirling bit ground slowly through the chip of shell. The tribe did a joy dance on the steps.

But it was tedious work. By dark there were only three finished pieces, a sizable mound of failures, and tribal fingers scraped raw.

"We'll have to work out a better way," said Owl Eyes, "or we'll never get done. Come on, kids. We've still got dishes to do."

After her chores Marcy drew up a chart and posted it by her cot.

DAYS OF TRUCE	HAVE		LEFT TO GO	
1ST DAY—SAT.	13	3	12	97
2ND DAY—SUN.				
3RD DAY—MON.				
4TH DAY—TUES.				
5TH DAY—WED.				
6TH DAY—THURS. (FULL MOON DAY)				
TOTAL				

She looked out over the porch ledge toward the pale hills of the scout camp. "Sugarpuss," she whispered, "you're still ninety-seven pieces of wampum away!" And with a sigh she went to watch Daddy clean fish.

The next morning Marcy and Thad went up to the feathers farm with Daddy to buy some chicken for Sunday dinner. They discovered an old grindstone down by the barn. A rusty can with a hole in the bottom hung above it, and the heavy stone spun round when they pumped the treadle. They sharpened a stick to the smoking point, and then the idea struck — couldn't wampum be smoothed on a grindstone? But the rest of the day was filled with family doings, so although the farm lady assured them it would be perfectly all right, they didn't get back to use it. The only progress on the ransom was three turtles Kenny caught.

But early Monday morning on his way back to work Daddy gave the younger members with their sack of shells a lift to the farm. In the afternoon the teams traded, and Crafty Fox and White Feather got to take the chief's canoe without the chief in it. The figures entered that night beside White Feather's bed, for the third day of truce, were four more turtles — three in the morning, one in the afternoon ("You scared them all away," the Fox accused the older tribesters) — and twenty-one pieces of wampum, complete with holes bored in the middle and strung on a stout string. Totals: turtles, twenty; wampum, twenty-four. Five and seventy-six left to go!

Tuesday was gray and the tribe did not need to check the turtle grounds to know that every humped back would be safely under water. They spent the day at the grindstone, growing expert at knowing which shells were too brittle, and

161

learning that the best beads were made from the thick shell near the hinge. With all but the treadler holding wampum against the wheel, they managed to complete forty-seven of the precious bits.

That night Marcy whispered into the dark, "Twenty turtles, seventy-one beads. We'll ransom you for sure tomorrow — unless it's a rainy day!"

It wasn't — it was blisteringly sunny — but when the turtle catchers came to relieve the wampum makers at noon, they had bad news.

"Ugh. No turtles," said Chief Thunder Cloud.

They'd combed the Turtle Swamp, the lily pond, and the bay, and then the reedy shore from the pasture to the Girl Scout piers, and even the rushes beside Almost Island, where Crafty Fox had once seen a turtle, but they'd caught only one.

The younger two had no better luck. Toward the end of the hot, tiring afternoon Crafty Fox spotted a wee one, paddling unexpectedly in clear water, and tumbled out of the canoe catching him. But that still made only twenty-two.

The tribe held gloomy council at the wigwam after supper, and watched the scouts marching the goat and bonnet up and down for the third time that day.

"Haven't they got anything better to do?" Crafty Fox raged.

"They're thinking we won't make it," said Owl Eyes. "Well, the wampum's done." She fingered the necklace of polished beads.

"What if there *aren't* any more turtles in the lake?" White Feather wailed.

"The chief's snapper is in there *someplace*," said Crafty Fox.

"Ugh. Still one untried turtle spot." The chief jerked his head toward the swamp.

White Feather's stomach lurched. Solid green hiding black water! Bottomless muck that would suck you down forever if you fell in! To portage a boat into the swamp was *unthinkable*. What awful dangers — snags, barrels, rocks — were lurking just below the surface? "Maybe it'll rain tomorrow," she whispered almost hopefully.

"It won't rain," said Owl Eyes quickly. "And we'll catch some, somehow, without going in *there*." She frowned. "We could petition for more time, but then wouldn't they crow over us!"

"Maybe your granddad would drive us into town," said Crafty Fox. "The dime stores usually have a tray of those little bitty turtles with flowers painted on their backs."

"Flowered turtles!" snorted the chief. "What would the pale-faces think of *that!* Besides, there's something wrong with our generator."

"We could hitchhike, maybe. If we don't tell Mother," Crafty Fox said.

"We still have till moonrise tomorrow. We'll think of something," Owl Eyes vowed.

Tears glistened in White Feather's eyes. "Maybe Sugar prefers the Boy Scouts now. She follows without being dragged any more. Maybe she won't even know me!"

"Sure she will," comforted Crafty Fox. "After Wag-tail was

163

at the vet's for two weeks he still knew me, didn't you, Wag-tail?"

"Goats aren't like dogs," White Feather sniffled.

Owl Eyes rose. "Well, let's go. No point sitting around here."

The lake was dark under a pancake of clouds, and a whitish light came in around the edges. It made everything look eerie. Little glimmers of heat lightning periodically glared on the horizon.

White Feather followed slowly behind the rest.

"Tomorrow — tomorrow for *certain*," she promised out over the lake. "Even if we have to hunt — *you know where!*"

Chapter

13

A TREMENDOUS CLAP of thunder slapped Marcy awake. She sat bolt upright as a fork of lightning riveted the lake. Her tooth-on-a-string was swaying wildly. In the next bright instant she saw Mother and Janice sitting up, too.

"Hurry!" called Mother. "It's going to storm!"

Marcy sprang onto the ledge and grappled with an awning. The wind whipped at her pajama legs.

"Ready?" called Janice from the other end. They jumped back to the floor and the pole fell, unrolling the striped canvas and spilling out surprised spiders. The wind flapped the sheet out. They caught the pole and hooked it at the sill, and the great curtain billowed like a viking sail. They scurried for the next one. Mother hurried around, placing pans under spots where leaks were known to be, and clearing books off the sills. Jip thumped a sleepy tail. Thad and Betsy flopped angrily in their sleep as their beds were hauled to narrow channels of safety.

The tethered wind pushed fretfully on the awnings; the boat clunk-clunked against the pier; thunder rolls died ominously, only to burst out again with fresh wrath.

"All shipshape!" Mother took a last look around. "Good night, girls."

Marcy paused with one foot in her warm cocoon. *Had she heard a blat?* Sugar was a mile away, but the wind was rushing from there, and she was deathly afraid of thunder! She always blatted with hardly a breath till Marcy crept under the cottage to cradle her trembling head. And now she was alone and frantic with fright!

Marcy snatched her sweater and slid silently out the door. Black trees mopped the sky. Thunder kettledrummed on the frothy lake, and flash-bulb lightning seared. Dust stung her ankles as she raced down the path. Any minute the sky would burst!

She dashed past ghostly cottages and along the soggy beach. In the thicket willows dipped and danced. She pressed her hand over the pain in her side, mounted Snake Grass Hill and sped across the public beach. She leaped the Red River and sprinted past the puffed and shuddering tents in the Hollow. Towels flapped frantically to free themselves from clothespins; spectral shapes strewed the grass.

A drop smacked her forehead as she plunged up the woods

166

path, and a sheet of water drenched her as she burst out onto the archery range. Her lungs ached to their very tips; she gasped and ran on. There was the stockade and the shed behind it! Goat screams were drowned in a din of thunder.

"It's me, Sugar!" She shook the door. It was locked. She grabbed a rock, smashed the hinge, so that the padlock fell to the ground, and threw herself in. The goat stopped in mid-blat as Marcy flung her wet arms around the trembling neck. Thunder burst again and rain drummed deafeningly on the low roof. The goat nickered, nuzzled her mistress, then knelt and began to chew her cud.

Marcy pushed the door shut and crept close to the warm goat, gently pulling her wattles and stroking her ears. The scouts had been good goatherds — the shed had a fresh grassy smell. She burrowed in the hay and yawned. Her heart pounded slower.

When the rain let up, she'd dash for home. Storms like this were over quickly; there'd be good turtling weather tomorrow. They'd catch those three, easy . . . and then Sugar would be ransomed . . . twenty-five turtles and one hundred pieces of wampum . . . Indian honor . . .

"I can't get 'em up, I can't get 'em up, I can't get 'em up in the mo-orning!"

Marcy sprang up horrified at the brisk notes of reveille right outside the shed. The goat nickered and struggled to her knees.

Marcy crouched rigid till the last sound faded away, and then peeped out. Hot sun beat on wet grass. A sign on a tree read EMERGENCY GONG, and from a limb hung a huge iron ring through which she could see the bugler trudging sleepily off.

She had to get away! She pulled the door wider. "Now, stay here, Sugar! It's only for the rest of today!"

But the goat, too quick, hopped the sill and gamboled over the grass. Marcy poked her head out and shrank hastily back. It was already too late! A boy in swimming trunks was trotting by.

"Who let *you* out?" he called to the goat. Marcy watched him pick up the padlock. "That's funny — hey, Jerry, the lock's off the door, but it's still fastened!"

Marcy crouched small and held her breath.

"Look, the door catch is broken," said a familiar voice. Then Jerry squatted and looked in. He was in trunks, too, with a towel flung over his shoulder. His eyes widened. Marcy glared.

He stood up and planted his legs in front of the door. "You go on. Maybe I can fix it."

"Well, hurry." The other scout's voice trailed off down the hill. Marcy sat numb with surprise.

Jerry knelt. "What are *you* doing here?"

She grinned feebly. "The storm — Sugar's afraid of thunder, so I came to keep her company — but I fell asleep —"

"Well, you can't stay here! Goat detail cleans up before breakfast. But you can't run — in those pink pajamas — with your hair — oh-oh, someone's going past." He turned around and sat with his back to her.

"I can tie my braids in a knot," Marcy whispered through the crack.

Jerry waited a second, then talked softly without turning his head. "I've got it! Stay hidden." He ran lightly off.

168

In the black shed just a thread of sunlight outlined the door. Marcy's pajamas felt damp and sticky. She frowned. It was bad enough to be at the mercy of the enemy without having him help her!

A white muzzle widened the crack.

"Sugar! Go away!" she hissed, then flattened as footsteps neared again.

Jerry whispered from outside, "Put these on and watch your chance! Good luck!"

A bundle was shoved inside. She unwound it. Trousers, and a hooded sweatshirt! She struggled into the clothing, rolling the legs and buttoning the hood firmly around her head.

She peeked out. A boy disappeared around the corner of the stockade and the coast was clear. She sprinted for the trees.

"Maa!" Sugarpuss lifted her head and galloped after her.

"No! Stay! Go back!" Marcy gave her a firm push. The goat danced sideways on her hind legs.

"If you come, it's your own free will! I can't help it if you won't stay!" Marcy glided into the trees. In a few moments she came out above the Hollow. Down the hill boys were washing at the pump. She felt her hood, hiked up the trousers, and sped down the path with Sugar bounding at her heels.

"Hey!" yelled a scout, his mouth foamy with toothpaste. "Where you takin' that goat?"

She passed the tents in a flash and pounded toward the Red River.

"It's one of those lakers, stealing her!" yipped another.

Bedlam broke out. Half-dressed boys poured from the tent

169

flaps, brandishing toothbrushes and towels. A bar of soap whizzed by her ear. She tripped, scrambled up, and raced on, hoisting her trousers in a frenzy of fear. She jumped the river and tore across the public beach. The scouts fell back, but their angry shouts followed her all the way to the thicket. Sugarpuss bounced along with carefree leaps.

She slowed down, until a new thought struck her. What were they thinking at home? Mother must be frantic! She put on a burst of speed and ran the rest of the way. She staggered up to the cottage and fell against the screen door. The goat, with dilated nostrils, puffed behind.

"I'm home!" she gasped.

Jip thumped his tail, but everyone else was still asleep. They had not even missed her.

But by breakfast her story had been told and retold — first to the family and then to Kenny, who put in an early appearance and quickly accepted an invitation to poached eggs and toast.

"That's the second time Jerry's rescued Marcy," Janice remarked. "I told you he likes you kids."

"Marcy didn't need rescuing either time," said Betsy. "She could have managed."

"Well, you kids broke the truce." Janice buttered another slice of toast. "You and your Indian honor!"

"It wasn't Marcy's fault!" yelled Thad. "She couldn't help it if —"

"She shouldn't have gone in the first place!"

"But she did!" Betsy cried. "And I'm glad, I'm glad! Now we don't have to accept their old truce terms. We don't have to have peace!"

Mother shook her head. "After all those frantic days of catching turtles and making wampum it does seem a shame."

"Say, what about my headdress?" Thad demanded.

"Oh, your headdress. I'll make you another one," said Betsy.

"I don't want another one. I want *that* one!" Thad thumped an eggy spoon. "Why didn't Marcy rescue my headdress while she was rescuing things? She just thinks about herself. Nobody thinks about —"

"But I didn't rescue Sugarpuss! *She rescued herself!*"

The screen door burst open and Jerry panted in, waving a white handkerchief. His chest was heaving and his hair clung to his beaded forehead.

"Excuse me — for busting in — 'lo, Mrs. Richards — but the guys are awful burned up — they say the truce is all off — and they're getting a gang up, to wreck your wigwam —"

"Ugh!" Kenny leaped up, overturning his chair.

"Let's go!" Betsy shrieked.

"If you can hold them off fifteen minutes," gasped Jerry, "they'll have to return — assembly —"

Marcy dived for the goat and pulled her onto the porch. "Mother! Guard her! And Jip, too!"

She galloped after the others, passing Jerry, who was trotting slowly, his shoulders sagging. Around the curve of the shore she saw a milling mob start across the public beach. Her throat caught. How could the tribe ward them off for even *five* minutes?

She panted into the clearing. War cries resounded from the far end of the thicket.

"Quick! Up here!" The tribe hauled her into the mulberry tree, and Owl Eyes thrust a bow and arrows at her. "Aim good, because we've just ours! The chief's and Crafty Fox's are at home!"

"We'll get 'em with slingshots!" cried the Fox. He poked hers in her belt, and the chief stuffed her pockets with acorns. She hooked her ankles around a limb and nocked her arrow just as the first wave of howling scouts poured into the clearing.

"Fire!" barked the chief. Bowstrings and rubbers twanged.

"Yeow!" The scouts whirled around. Another volley of acorns and arrows peppered them on the front side.

"Get the tree!" They shielded their faces and tried to storm the fortress, but the tribe stamped them down like pegs in a

172

pounding board. More scouts swarmed in and started to tear at the wigwam.

White Feather fired her arrows into the crowd. One or two hit with enough force to produce satisfactory yells, but most swerved or bounced harmlessly off. There was not enough power in her crude bow. She flung it away, grabbed her slingshot, and, bouncing up and down like a monkey on a stick, shot into the seething mob. She shrieked with glee at every yowl. The scouts snatched up the acorn missiles, but couldn't fling them back with the same deadly speed.

"More ammunition!" yelled Owl Eyes.

"Catch some!" the chief cried. "We're scraping the bottom of the barrel! Somebody's gotta go down into no man's land!"

"Ow!" An acorn nicked White Feather's shin. She fired her last nut blindly.

"I'm out of ammunition!" Crafty Fox cried.

"Prepare to fight on the ground!" ordered the chief. "Looks bad! We're outnumbered — but if we can hold 'em a few more minutes —"

White Feather glared helplessly down. They were lost! There wasn't a chance on the ground. Why didn't assembly blow?

"White Feather! Catch!"

She nearly toppled as a bulging kerchief hit her chest. She clutched it, and glimpsed Jerry's red face in the tides of battle. She pulled the knot open with her teeth, and gasped. Black walnuts! Twice as big as acorns! Twice as hard as acorns! And with a rough surface that could scrape the skin right off!

"Ammunition!" she whooped, and poured the nuts in the empty keg.

"Heavy artillery!" yelled Chief Thunder Cloud.

"Keep firing — ow!" An acorn hit Owl Eyes in the mouth. Enraged, she snatched up a walnut.

The first volley whizzed into the crowd. Scouts bellowed in pain.

"We're getting them!" shouted the Fox triumphantly.

White Feather let spin. A scout clapped his hands to his head and fled, howling.

A bugle sounded as another volley drove more casualties from the clearing. Those remaining suddenly realized how few they were.

"Assembly blew, didn't it?" one yelled. "Assembly!"

"Retreat, men!" The last few scouts stampeded down the path. The tribe tumbled from the tree and raced in pursuit, speeding walnuts after their backs.

"What a battle!" Owl Eyes cried.

"There were thousands of them," shouted Crafty Fox. "And four of us routed them all!"

"You mean five of us," said White Feather.

"Five?" Owl Eyes spun around as Jerry limped out of the thicket.

"He threw the walnuts up to me, just as we were losing."

Thunder Cloud stepped forward. "Ugh. Potawatomi thankum."

Jerry shrugged. His face was streaked and his uniform torn. Above one eye was a bloody bump. "I guess I didn't help much. Your wigwam's a mess."

He followed while the tribe hurried back to view the damage.

174

The clearing was a shambles, and the whole front of the wigwam was battered in.

"Our nice wigwam!" Crafty Fox wailed.

Owl Eyes made a hasty examination. "No, it's not so bad! Just the front gave way! We can fix it. But — if we hadn't been warned —" She looked sidelong at Jerry.

His face reddened. "Say," he blurted. "Your mouth's bloody. Here's a —" He stopped in confusion and jammed his handkerchief back in his pocket. "I mean — I guess I'm not a medicine man."

Owl Eyes touched her lips and looked at her crimson fingers. "I didn't even notice. My tongue's cut, too." She spat out a red drop.

"The tongue heals quickest of any part of the body," Jerry said. He noticed White Feather's bruises. "And the shin takes the longest."

"I sting all over," Crafty Fox announced.

"You don't know what stinging is till you've been socked by a jet-propelled walnut!" Jerry rubbed his forehead.

"Walnut," repeated Crafty Fox. "Walnut. Where did —" He stopped, looked peculiarly at Jerry, and started for the wigwam.

"You don't need to look." Jerry grinned, embarrassed. "They were your walnuts. Potawatomi walnuts."

"Ugh," said the chief. "Potawatomi no had black walnuts!"

"Yes, we did," said Crafty Fox. "Daddy brought them, and I hid them where I didn't think *anybody* could find them. For an emergency."

"But then — when *we* didn't even know —" Owl Eyes looked suspiciously from Crafty Fox to Jerry.

Jerry flushed deeply. "Once when you kids weren't here, I — well, sort of explored your camp a little."

The tribe stood shocked. White Feather knew they were feeling as she did now. Uncomfortable. Jerry was friendly and entered into the spirit of things — they should be grateful for his help — and yet — and yet —

"Well, that's okay," said Crafty Fox. "Where would we be now if you *hadn't?* And this *was* an emergency."

"Ugh," nodded the chief agreeably.

Jerry looked hopefully toward Owl Eyes. White Feather felt sorry for him. "Sure," she said. "We don't mind."

"Well . . ." Owl Eyes' voice was doubtful.

The hope in Jerry's face faded. "I have to go," he said. "I'm way overtime. I guess our tent'll get a demerit today. I didn't even get my bed made."

"Say, what will the others do to you?" asked Crafty Fox.

"Nothing. We got a demerit once before."

"No, I mean for siding with the enemy in the acorn battle."

Jerry shrugged. "I'll make out, I guess." He grinned, waved, and limped out of the thicket.

Owl Eyes looked after him thoughtfully. "He would have made a good Indian," she said.

"Well, why didn't you tell him so?" White Feather flared, and then nearly bit her tongue as the tribe stared at her in surprise.

Chapter

14

MARCY lay on the pier. Her braids, still damp from the morning swim, hung toward the water. Soon it would be an hour after lunch, and then, for the glory of the Potawatomi, the tribe would swim across the lake!

Janice and Gloria were going, too. Gloria had come to stay a week. She was between Janice and Betsy in age, but she stood and giggled with Janice on the pier when the yellow canoes flocked around.

Marcy sent a twitch down a string, and the floating leaf on the end jerked and scattered for a second the hundreds of shiny black waterbugs streaking around, each no bigger than her little fingernail. Sometimes they dashed into each other; sometimes they stopped abruptly and plowed crazily off in another direction. Some just went round and round, as if they had an itch and couldn't reach it.

She waited for one to climb on her leaf. She already had three, silvery underneath with their bubbles of air, zooming from top to bottom in her jar.

A bugle blew and scouts burst from tents in the Hollow, rest hour over. They were like waterbugs, too, spinning round and round in the same pointless activity. Why didn't they get busy on the war? A week ago today had been the acorn battle. If the Potawatomi had suffered such a defeat, they would have gained revenge long before now! A couple of times while they were repairing the wigwam Jerry had appeared and helped, but they hadn't liked to talk about the war. What if he were a spy? And if he weren't, shouldn't they despise him, a traitor to his own side?

And now they hadn't seen him for four or five days, for they had embarked upon new Indian activities. "We'll get soft, just waiting for the palefaces to do something," Owl Eyes had said. "We have to keep up our strength! Let's have Indian games!"

From Thad's books they learned to play hunting-the-deer, and quick-sight, and spot-the-rabbit. They set to work to make the rackets for lacrosse, the Indians' ball game. Exploring, they ranged far into the wooded pasture, following sheep paths and wagon ruts soggy with old leaves. Under spreading trees they discovered black pools where Jesus bugs skated, whose feet, dimpling the glassy surface, cast saucer-shaped shadows on the leaf-carpeted bottom. They found a bank of clay and built up bowls like braided rugs, drying them in the sun for use at the wigwam. All extra moments were filled with efforts to swim faster, dive deeper, throw farther, shoot straighter, and take swifter and more silent steps in stalking — all for the glory of the Potawatomi. Every day they bettered their old records.

And today was the *greatest* test of their strength — swimming the lake! Each Potawatomi had to uphold the tribal honor and prove himself strong and worthy.

"Walla walla woo hoo!" Thad, with Jip at his heels, tore down the path and flung an inner tube from the bank. It missed the boat and spanked the water. The waterbugs scattered in a flash.

"Is it time?" Marcy jumped up eagerly as Thad waded after the spinning tube.

Kenny bounded through the water from his pier, and the girls, with another tube, hurried from the cottage. Sugar trotted behind.

Marcy watched their approach. Gloria was pulling a green cap over her reddish hair. She had a matching swim suit, and was more grown-up-shaped than even Janice. Betsy was getting more and more grown-up-shaped too, she noticed with a pang. Last year Betsy had declared she was going to pound her chest to keep it flat, and had thumped vigorously every time she remembered, till Mother got wind and ordered her to stop. Marcy brushed her hand self-consciously across the top of her own suit. The family hadn't noticed yet, because she turned her back now when she was dressing on the porch, but she was aware of the tiny tepees that were beginning to thrust up on the flat plain of her own chest.

"We'll swim to Almost Island," Janice decreed. "The beach

179

is nicest there, and besides, the kids want to let their turtles go in the lily pond."

"Do you think Thad can make it?" Gloria tucked in the last copper curl.

"Sure I can!" Thad cried.

"Well, somebody has to row," Janice said. "Half can swim across and the other half back."

"More should swim across when the boat'll be crowded with turtles," said Marcy. "And then there's Jip and Sugar."

"Oh, leave them home!" said Janice. "Do they have to go everywhere?"

Kenny was anxious to be off. "Let the girls swim across, Thad, and we'll swim back."

"Well, okay," Thad agreed reluctantly.

"Start out, and we'll catch up after we get the turtles," said Kenny. The boys unfastened the boat, grabbed the oars, and rowed unevenly off toward Kenny's pier.

Marcy's skin prickled as she waded into the cool water. Almost Island looked a long way off. A mile. Could she make it? And what a disgrace to the Potawatomi if she couldn't!

Gloria giggled and bumped against Janice. She motioned toward the scout dock. "They'll see us go by!"

Mother came onto the pier. "Now, be careful, and if you get tired, hang on the boat. Don't be foolish if you can't make it."

"We won't!" Betsy plunged up and down.

"Or have Thad throw an inner tube. And watch him, coming back. The poor lamb thinks he can make it, but I wouldn't let him go any farther than halfway —"

"We won't. We won't," said Betsy, ready to go.

"Good-by, and good luck!" Mother waved them off.

"Ready, set, go!" Janice and Gloria dived from the end of the pier. Marcy glided forward and the water closed over her head. She surfaced when seaweed brushed her face.

Betsy was beside her. "Let's stick together, and if either of us cries for help, we won't be calling 'wolf.' "

Marcy nodded. Janice and Gloria's heads bobbed ahead of them. It wasn't quite fair; they didn't start directly from shore. But then, they weren't Indians.

Beyond the seaweed she floated for a moment. She didn't need to rest yet, but it was best not to wait till she had to.

She flipped over and swam slowly on. This wasn't going to be so hard! Already Mother and the deserted animals looked small.

"All right?" called Betsy.

She nodded.

Now Thad and Kenny were rowing toward them.

"Don't get too close or you'll clout us with an oar," warned Janice.

Marcy felt strength in her legs and lungs. Swimming seemed easy as walking. The week's hard exercise was bearing fruit! She aimed for a tree that bulged above the green clump of the island and measured her progress on the shore. She was parallel to the pasture and Sleepy Hollow now.

Under . . . and up for breath. Under . . . and up for breath.

Now the Girl Scout shore and Boy Scout shore.

Under . . . and up for breath. Cool water on her forehead, green depths stinging her eyes. On and on . . .

181

Now the scout piers. She paused to float, panting. Home was
a long way off and Mother had disappeared. Their course had
taken them closer to the Girl Scout piers, but scouts from both
sides were watching. She grinned. *They* had to swim within
ropes!

Under . . . and up for breath. Under . . . and up for
breath.

She couldn't glide as far now. She lay on her back again. A
breeze sprang up; wavelets washed her cheeks. Her feet kept
slowly sinking, so that it was almost as much effort to float as
to swim. She turned and swam wearily forward. On, on, for the
glory of the Potawatomi!

Now they were between Oyster Inlet and the bay. At the

end of each stroke she gasped and looked at the guiding tree. Her arms and legs felt heavy as anchors. She suddenly felt all in. She floated under water, suspended by the balloon of air inside her, and then surfaced for breath. She couldn't even stay under long enough to rest, any more.

She swam on, sighing her breath out in a stream of silvery bubbles that foamed the length of her. As she rose and sank she heard snatches of conversation about her.

"How you doing, Marce?" Janice called anxiously.

She nodded and swam doggedly on. No, it was too far. She was numb. She wanted to let go and sink like a rock to the bottom. "Great White Spirit," she moaned, "help me! For the Potawatomi!"

She floated again, gasping. Her lungs felt raw. She couldn't make it. She should head for the boat and hang on the side. The waves slapped over her face. She choked, struggled over, and swam on.

"You're almost there!" Kenny shouted.

The strip of shore did look closer! Trees and branches were now distinct! Fresh strength surged into her body.

"I've got my second wind!" she panted triumphantly to Betsy.

The waves died in the lee of the shore. Far below, scrubby moss clung to the orange bottom. Ahead the boat hovered near the beach with Janice and Gloria already in it. Jip, who must have run all the way from home, raced up and down the shore and wagged them welcome. She took a final stroke, let down her feet, and touched on tiptoe.

The weight of the water made her chest seem crushed, and

183

her knees were weak as seaweed. She half stumbled, half swam to shallow water and lay resting. The sun behind her eyelids oscillated whitely, and she had a small headache. But she was filled with weary contentment.

"I made it!" she murmured out loud.

Thad splashed over. "I had the inner tube ready, but you didn't need it. Now let's hurry and unload so Kenny and I can swim back."

She stood on wobbly legs and sank onto the rear seat of the boat, back to back with Janice and Gloria, her feet dragging in the water. Wet suits puddled the seats, and water trickled through the cracks to add to the bilge the turtles were sloshing in. Jip sat carefully among them, and Betsy straddled the prow, looking like the Red Queen with two inner tubes around her waist.

Kenny and Thad rowed through the channel and down the broad middle aisle of the lily pond. Marcy basked in the sun while her heart and breath slowed down. She paddled her feet languidly and watched Janice slip a tiny turtle over the gunwhale. The pink-edged shell glided away and disappeared under a lily pad.

A delicious relaxation crept over Marcy. She felt content with the world. Now if she could curl up somewhere and go to sleep . . .

On the soggy shore behind the island there were a few shacks with holes in the screens. Piers tilted at all angles. Waterlogged boats were tied alongside, and propped fishpoles dangled their lines in the clogged water.

"Cabbage, I sure wouldn't want to have a cottage in here!"

said Thad. "No beach, no place to swim — you can't even see the lake!"

"What's that?" Kenny waved a lily-draped oar. Some upright sticks stood beside a plank-and-sawhorse dock.

"Pull over," said Betsy. "Maybe it's a fish trap."

The boys scraped the boat over the lily pads. Betsy shucked her tubes and climbed out. Jip, Thad, and Kenny followed.

The older girls moved into the rowing seat. Marcy caught at the slimy lily stems with her toes. Her legs in the tepid water were ringed with scum. She looked dreamily over the pond.

The boat backed, leaving a gap between the prow and the pier.

"Hey," Betsy said, "pick us up! Nothing here worth seeing."

"Swim for it," said Janice.

"You know we can't. It's too mucky. Come on and get us."

"What'll you give us if we do?" Gloria called.

"We'll give you a kick in the pants!" Thad threatened.

Marcy looked around. "Oh, go get them."

The girls turned the boat in a half circle, so that they and Marcy faced the dock.

"Say please," said Gloria.

"Please," said Betsy.

"Pretty please," said Janice.

Betsy glowered. "Pretty please."

"Pretty please with sugar on it," said Gloria.

"I won't!" Betsy snapped. "You come get us!"

Laughing, Janice and Gloria back-watered. Kenny reached out to catch Marcy's hand. With a jerk the rowers pulled on the oars and the boat jolted away again. Kenny teetered and nearly lost his balance. "Ugh!" he cried in alarm.

Janice and Gloria tittered. They began to scull in again.

Betsy wheeled and strode off the dipping planks. "Let's walk! Who wants to ride with them, anyway?"

"But we were going to swim!" objected Thad.

"I'll row for you tomorrow. Come on, whoever's going with me!"

Kenny shrugged and followed, and Thad, after a baleful look at the rowers, did too. Jip trotted willingly.

"Now see what you've done," said Marcy.

"Oh, come back, for gosh sake!" called Janice. "Can't you kids take a little joke?"

"Talk to them, Marcy," begged Gloria. "We were just kidding."

"Come on back!" yelled Marcy. The boat clunked alongside the pier and she climbed out. The tribe disappeared into a swampy green jungle.

"Well, let them walk, the stubborn mules," said Janice. "You ride with us, Marcy."

Marcy wavered. Her legs still felt weak and she ached in the very depth of her marrow. She'd been looking forward to the long ride with the sun beating hot on her back.

"Get in," urged Gloria. "We'll beat them home."

Marcy turned. "No, I better go with them."

"All right for you. Be a dope. I don't care," said Janice.

Marcy hurried along the path. Dirty water squished up between her toes. She shoved through the bushes and cattails and caught up with the rear of the procession.

"They were just kidding," she puffed.

"Smart alecks," sniffed Betsy. "We'll walk."

"But you have to row for us tomorrow," Thad reminded.

"I said I would, didn't I?" said Betsy irritably.

They slogged along in silence. They'd never been this far behind the lily pond before. It was muggy and blistering. Black gnats stung Marcy's legs. A big fly zoomed round and round her head, trying to land in her hair. Her swimming suit was itchy, and she felt desperately tired. "Aren't we going home?" she asked.

"Not by the shore path," Thad explained. "Betsy says they'll just row alongside us and yell things. So we're going to see if we can't cut around behind the Girl Scout camp and come out in the pasture."

"We've been meaning to explore behind here, anyway," Betsy called over her shoulder. "Now is a perfect time."

"Oh," said Marcy.

They left the swampy area and followed a tangled fence up a grassy hill. At the woods the fence turned; they climbed it and cut inland. The terrain here was like that behind the bog and Boy Scout camp — long ridges and irregular hills pocked by pot-shaped valleys. Old trees strained the sunlight, and it was cool and dry.

Marcy lagged behind. She wished she'd stayed with the boat.

"Hey!" Thad's excited voice rang out ahead. "Look at this huge vine! It'll bear my weight, I bet!"

When she caught up, he was swinging out over a hollow on a long vine, part of a plant whose coils were all but choking a gnarled tree on top of the ridge. Kenny was jerking another

187

vine free, and Betsy was jumping up and down impatiently, urging Thad to give her a turn.

"Hot cabbage!" she exulted. "Here's a new test for our strength! Another Indian game!"

Marcy sat on a fallen trunk. The bark was rough on her bare legs. She absently scaled off bits of lichens and fungus, and a musty smell arose. Maybe if she rested for a minute she'd work up energy to swing.

She watched Thad whoop by. At the turn of one swing her gaze remained fixed, her eyes clouded with a film of fatigue. She gradually became aware of the image of the hollow. Something was peculiar down there. She shook her head and blinked. Things fitted into focus.

Her tiredness rolled up and snapped away. She jumped to her feet.

"Look!" she shrilled. "Look! Look! Those trees are *bent!*"

Betsy stared. Thad and Kenny stopped swinging. In the hollow where Marcy pointed five or six old, old trees bent to the ground, around the cattail patch in the center, as if washing their few strands of hair in the dried-up pool.

The tribe looked mutely at each other, then scrambled down the hill. They slowed at the bent arches and tiptoed under and around them.

"They're awfully old," breathed Kenny.

"A hundred years," said Betsy.

"More than that," whispered Thad. "Two hundred, at least."

"They haven't *fallen,*" said Kenny. "They *grew* this way."

"And no tree would grow like this *naturally.*" Excitement

188

mounted in Betsy's voice. "Maybe one, but not all these. They had to be tied down — when they were saplings —"

They stopped before the biggest one and stood in awed silence.

Kenny spoke after a bit. "To tell a direction."

"Or for a trap — or a lean-to —" added Thad.

"Two hundred years ago," repeated Betsy.

Marcy reached out and touched the shaggy bark. She drew back her hand and looked around with shining eyes. *They* seemed almost to be here; she could picture them tying down the slender branches. Their moccasins had touched this very ground!

She glanced down and gave a startled cry.

There, beside her foot, lay a perfect arrowhead.

Chapter

15

THE TRIBE was playing lacrosse on the lawn behind Kenny's garage. Marcy swung her net toward the ball and missed.

"I have a headache," she declared crossly. "I'm going home. Come on, Sugarpuss."

She strode off through the twilight. She didn't really have a headache and the lie burned on her tongue. But how could she keep her mind on a difficult game when even now Janice and Gloria were on their way to the scouts' Honors Council, and after that would hear a star talk? She fingered her arrowhead, at the center of the wampum necklace, where she had fastened it after its miraculous discovery several days before. It gave scant comfort.

Outside the doors under the porch Sugar stopped and cropped grass. Marcy stood disconsolate. Did she dare carry out the plan she'd been debating all day? If so, she must go now —

"I *will!*" she cried out loud and, shoving the goat into bed, slammed the doors and hurried to the porch. Sugarpuss blatted in vain as Marcy pulled Jerry's clothes from under her pillow and hastily pulled on her disguise. She scrawled a note for Mother and Daddy, who were out fishing, and streaked down the path, buttoning her hood under her chin as she ran.

She slowed down at the thicket. No need to get to the council too soon. The swamp was loud with frog calls, and fireflies turned the willows into winking Christmas trees. The dark wigwam looked lonely and almost strange, since the Potawatomi had deserted it lately to comb the woods of the *new* Happy Hunting Grounds for more signs and relics of Indian ancestors. Thad and Kenny had even postponed their long swim.

She squatted by the wigwam entrance. She was an Indian warrior who had been a captive. Now after many moons he had broken his bonds and come running home on soft moccasined feet. He tiptoed through the dusk, to surprise his family. A little smile played on his face. He knelt — he peeped inside . . . the wigwam was empty. His squaw and papoose were gone. The fireplace was cold; he felt it. It had been washed by many rains . . .

She squeezed out a tear and it trickled down her cheek. Her heart heavy with grief, she wandered back to the garden. The frogs stopped gunking while she went by. A large bird flapped out of the gloom.

The garden seemed abandoned, too. She could barely locate the stunty cornstalks among the lush weeds. After the rains several weeks ago she had propped the spindly shoots and re-packed the roots, but even with that care the maize had not prospered. She returned dolefully.

Her melancholy fell away as she headed into enemy territory, and a tiny balloon of excitement began to blow up in her stomach. A few stars pricked through the sky. It was a perfect night for star gazing!

Sleepy Hollow was deserted. She followed the now familiar path through the woods and archery range, behind the stockade to the long slope. Trees ended; a fire shone.

She snaked forward as close as she dared. Down the hill things were like the last time — well, not quite, for packed among the boys were Janice and Gloria, their faces pink in the firelight. The star counselor had his arm flung around the telescope, as though it were a dog that he was fond of. With a wiggle of delicious joy she settled to wait. The Milky Way glittered above her. What would it look like, magnified?

The council dragged on. Stories, and singing, and scouts marching up to receive this honor or that. Marcy looked up at the constellations. Last time she'd wondered what their Indian names were; now she knew from Thad's books that the Dipper was the Broken Back and the star at the bend was the Old Squaw with the Papoose. She burrowed deeper in the grass and rubbed her back where an ant had crawled in. The stars wavered. She drowsed, until a new voice, warm with interest, startled her awake. The star counselor! She crept farther forward.

192

He was talking simply, of the planets: their distances, how they might have been formed. The hot cinder, Mercury; cloudy Venus, Earth's twin; red Mars with its icecaps and strange markings; the asteroids swirling out there in space, some no bigger than a grand piano — the disintegrated remains, perhaps, of a planet like Earth; the nine moons of cold Jupiter; Saturn's remarkable rings; the sensational discovery of little Pluto. He spoke of other suns and solar systems — black cosmic clouds — cold dwarf stars — flaming novas — other galaxies — the space — the stretch — the infinite!

Marcy sat enthralled. She'd heard lots of it before, at school. But science class was not held on a windy hill with stars twinkling overhead. It had never seemed as awful as now, under the very planets, where the black reaches of space stretched out and on forever.

She felt overwhelmed. Her mind circled thousands of light years out into the void, perched on a star, and looked back at Earth. There was North America, just as it looked on the globe, and Wisconsin, snuggled up against the two Great Lakes, and there the spot of a tiny lake, and a grassy hill, and a strange girl on top of it who was herself, alone, swirling in space and looking up.

"So small," she whispered wonderingly.

The young man stopped abruptly and looked at his watch. "I've gone way overtime, and I meant to show you — oh, well, line up quick and have a peek at the moon. It's just coming up. Then there's a snack in the mess hall before taps. Hurry!"

Marcy's mind plunked back to earth. She leaned forward intently and watched him adjust the telescope. The scouts lined up noisily. Two of them stamped out the fire till only scattered red coals remained.

She looked at the ragged moon rising above the trees, and the balloon inside her swelled some more. The moment was almost here! There went Janice and Gloria, with Red and Jerry behind them. They peeked briefly and hurried up the hill toward the stockade.

She sidled to a spot a little way behind the end of the line, and faced the wrong way. Nobody paid any attention. The hooded sweatshirt and scout pants made her look like any other camper. She jammed her hands in Jerry's pockets and whistled nonchalantly. Ten more to go — five more — four — three — two — now it was the last scout's turn! He took a quick look and galloped off. Marcy hung back.

"Okay, Junior — you're last," said the star counselor.

Her stomach flopped completely over. She swallowed hard, then turned and tiptoed forward, almost afraid to look.

"Go ahead," said the boy.

The telescope gleamed in the light of the dying coals. She touched the metal cautiously and it sent a cold shiver racing down her spine. She closed one eye and pressed the other to the eyepiece.

Before her hung an uneven section of orange. It was the familiar moon, but, oh, how unfamiliar! The man-in-the-moon spots were plains cut with long gashes and pimpled with craters. It gave her an odd feeling of distance, at once so close and yet so far. And seen this way, the moon did not seem to give off light at all any more, but was simply hanging there — *in* the light! She had known; now she could *see* the truth!

She swallowed. "It's — it's —" Her voice was husky.

"Pretty wonderful, isn't it!" agreed the boy. "Here, I'll show you something else."

Marcy stepped aside while he adjusted the telescope. "See the Big Dipper? The star where the handle bends?"

She nodded at the sky.

"Look hard at it. See anything?"

Marcy squinted, and suddenly grinned. "Another star! Just above! That must be the papoose!" She blushed. "I mean — the Indians called that star the Old Squaw with the Papoose on Her Back, but I never noticed there *was* a papoose till just now!"

The boy looked curiously at her. "Well, the Arabs called it Alcor — means the Rider. Same idea. It shows you've got good eyes. But here's something the Indians never suspected. Take a look at the Old Squaw in the telescope!"

She peeped. Thousands of light-years away in the night two fiery globes rubbed surfaces. Nearby gleamed a fainter star.

"See?" said the counselor. "Alcor's rotating around a *double star!* Two suns! You can't see *that* with the naked eye!"

"Two suns!" marveled Marcy softly.

"Here, let me have it again." The boy squinted at the sky, swung the telescope in a wide arc, peeped, and adjusted it again. "Sort of hard to find," he apologized. He moved it slightly and took another sight. "There." He stood back. "What do you think of *that?*"

The telescope pointed nearly up. Marcy knelt and looked.

Far, far away, oh, millions of miles it felt like, hung a pale pink globe with rings surrounding it, all blurred together like a

196

spinning colored top. It seemed suspended in rapid motion. "Saturn!" she gasped. "It's Saturn! Why — it's just like its pictures!"

She looked at the boy with shining eyes. He grinned. She bobbed under to look again. There it hung on a tilt, with its great rings — two light ones, with a dark one in the middle — faint, and fuzzy, and incredibly beautiful.

"Saturn," she whispered. "*Saturn!*"

"It's pretty late," said the boy. "The rest have gone. I'll show you some more some other night."

She backed up. He knelt on one knee and started disassembling the telescope. She stood at his elbow like a sleepwalker, Saturn still dazzling in her eyes.

"Better run," he said. "You'll miss your cookies and cocoa."

She didn't move.

He swiveled and looked at her even more curiously.

The balloon in her stomach swelled a fraction larger and burst. "Thank you!" she gasped. "Thank you!" Her hood fell back and her braids swung free as she ran blindly toward the hill.

She crashed through the woods. Her ears pounded and she burned all over. She barely felt the ground beneath her feet. She stumbled through brambles and pitched over logs, climbing up and running on, beating down the flaming excitement that was at the same time consuming her and charging her with energy.

"Saturn!" she panted. "Saturn, Saturn!" She burst out of

the woods, into the light. Down the slope was the misty bog. She stopped with her feet planted wide apart, and laughed while the tears streamed down her face.

"Saturn!" she shouted out loud, and sank down in the tall grass. The world tipped slowly back into focus.

Her heartbeats in her ears slowed to dull tom-toms. She leaned back on her elbows. Somewhere, up there among the bright pinpricks, was the one she had seen.

Her elbows slipped. She lay flat with arms and legs flung out. Stirrings within her struggled to be expressed. They had to be said, before she could ever move again.

"This night I saw Saturn!" she whispered solemnly. She paused a long time, letting the words sink in, waiting for new words to rise up.

"This night I saw Saturn," she repeated. "Before, it looked like any other star. And now it does again. But I know that it has *rings* — three of them, swirling around — because I've *seen* them —"

She lapsed into silence. Her mind spiraled off and away, refusing to be bounded. Words wouldn't work. They couldn't express what she wanted to say. No words could tell of the clearness — the realness — the greatness — and yet the smallness of things. Oh, she'd thought she'd known, but she hadn't *really* known, before. There was a universe of difference now. She closed her eyes, breathing hard, then opened them to the sky again. There was no earth; it was all universe. And there was no time; it was all eternity. She was here, but she was everywhere. It didn't matter. What did matter was space . . . and Saturn . . . and God.

Slowly she rose to her knees and stretched up her arms toward the stars.

"Great White Spirit," she cried in an exultant whisper, "thank you for tonight — tonight, for letting me *see!*"

Chapter

16

SHIVERING, Marcy sat cross-legged on the stump at the top of the hill. The late-afternoon sun stretched her shadow before her, her head spilling over the hill. She found it sitting like the Cheshire cat in a tree halfway down.

It had been so scorching all day that the family had had an early supper and then had gone for another swim. And now she was cold. Her finger tips were puckered and the nails blue, and her arms were stippled with goose bumps. Underneath her the stump slowly gave off its stored-up heat. The sun penetrated her back. She wrung out a trickling braid. Like a blotter, the stump absorbed the water down thousands of tiny cracks, and turned black.

A motion on the path caught her eye. A wasp was crawling out of a hole! Her wings, like last year's jacket, didn't cover her narrow waist and fat round abdomen, which was shiny black with an orange band. Marcy had seen wasps before, circling paper nests, and more than once she'd given up her mud-pie spot when they had come in swarms to roll up mud pellets for their celled houses under the eaves, but she'd never yet seen one that lived in the ground! She sat very still.

The wasp covered her hole with a plug of earth and buzzed into the air. She zigzagged uncertainly, then dived into the grass beside the stump. Marcy sucked in her breath in surprise. Diving and rising, the wasp was attacking a smooth green caterpillar!

The fat victim rolled and unrolled rapidly, flinging himself about in violent contortions. Her heart went out to him, but she did not stop the drama. She couldn't change wasp habits by saving one worm. It was the way things were.

Now the wasp was astride the caterpillar, grasping his fat neck in her jaws. The worm struggled feebly.

Marcy dug her nails into her palms as the wasp stood high on her long legs, lifted the front end of the worm, curved her abdomen under his body, and jabbed in her stinger. The worm was instantly quiet. Marcy let out a long, quivering sigh.

The wasp remained still for a moment, then jabbed the caterpillar several times more. She squeezed him around the neck with her jaws and dragged him to her hole, lifted the lid, backed in, and pulled him down after her.

"Well!" said Marcy out loud. After a time she tiptoed to the spot. Was the show over? She crouched to peek, but startled back as the wasp came crawling out. Busily, the insect began biting away loose dirt from the hole's edges.

"Why — she's filling it!" Marcy breathed, astonished. "She didn't have time to eat that big caterpillar! She must be burying it!"

The wasp jammed down the earth with her head and scraped in more from the outside. When the filling was level with the ground, she picked up a small pebble in her mouth and pounded till the spot was firm. Several times she scraped in more earth and hammered it, till there was no sign that a hole had ever been there. And then she flew away.

Marcy flopped down and marked the spot. Would the wasp be back? There had been something final in the way she buzzed off. Why had she worked so to bury the worm, and then left? Was it food for later? But wasps didn't eat caterpillars, did they?

She wrinkled her forehead, and then laughed. Baby wasps did! Hadn't the tribe found bugs and eggs together in a wasps' nest once? This wasp had been laying an egg, and the worm would be fresh food when the egg hatched!

Marcy grabbed a twig and then hesitated. No, she wouldn't dig it up. The wasp had worked hard, and now the job was finished, and perfect. Marcy would leave the worm and egg hidden there, a secret.

A secret! Saturn spun to the surface of her mind from that shallow depth where for several days now it had been filling her with little spurts of gladness.

She glanced at the blue sky. Somewhere up there, she knew, was the splendor, spinning forever in the night! And right here in the ground — just as invisible — was another splendor. Saturn's bright disk revolved over the wasp's smooth hammered spot.

Marcy pondered. The planet and the wasp hole were the same magic feelings, really — but no, more than that — their very *togetherness* was new and awesome. One circled all the foreverness of space; the other you could hold in your hand — yet you had to feel just as much to hold the tininess as you did the bigness! You didn't understand them, all of them, the big and the little, the miracles and the secrets, but they were all there inside of you, and you knew.

All there inside of you! Saturn and the wasp hole!

Marcy's stomach churned with a strange excitement. She was just a speck beside Saturn, yet over the wasp she towered like a giant. She was huge and little in herself! She couldn't understand herself, wholly, either, but it was a self that could contain both the hugeness of Saturn and the smallness of the wasp hole — and to look at her, who would suspect that? A secret in space, and a secret in the ground, and inside of her the most secret secret of all!

She carefully picked up the tiny pebble the wasp had dropped. Nearby was a bit of tinfoil. She rolled the pebble in it and poked it deep in the corner of her pocket. It would be safe there till she could put it with her special treasures. Then she bounded down the path.

"Mother! Janice! Betsy! Thad!" She tore onto the porch.

The cottage was deserted.

She ran to the shore. Sugarpuss raised her head from grazing and gave a questioning maa.

Marcy hurried to the end of the pier and scanned the lake. "Hey — where is everybody?"

The sun was down now. A few Boy Scout crafts dotted the lake. She looked toward the thicket and her gaze traveled past it around the curve of the shore to fasten, amazed, on a strange sight. A great white mist was lying heavily on the water! Not the usual little wisps that drifted off the bog, but a cloud-from-the-sky, a cottony white wall that looked solid enough to touch!

"Where *is* everybody?" she yelled again, but this time for an entirely different reason.

There was no time to hunt for them; the mist might roll up and away before she could get to it! She jumped into the boat and undid the chain with fumbling fingers. Her oar cracked against the pier and jammed. She jerked it loose, replaced it in the rusty oarlock, and scooted over the calm water.

She glanced over her shoulder. The mist was still there, bulging amoebalike, its tail still in the bog. She skimmed past the cottages and the thicket. The white bank lay just ahead. She pulled hard, left the oars trailing, and glided. There was a last glimpse of clear air — the dusky pasture on the far shore, a clump of sheep drinking at the edge — and then she was engulfed in a cold white world.

She couldn't see the oars, or her bare feet against the push board. The mist blanketed the water and pressed damply on her face, filling her hair, her nose, her chest. She breathed deep its boggy mustiness.

She felt apart from everything. Time stood still. All movement and sound had stopped. This must be how a little spit bug

204

felt, inside his house that foamed around a grass stem. Or an angel, floating through the billowy spaces of heaven.

Or perhaps — she caught her breath and clutched the gunwales — perhaps this was the Great White Spirit himself!

She looked wide-eyed at the whiteness, and then, clasping her hands tightly, slid onto her knees in the bilgy water of the boat bottom. She pushed the thought out of her mind and let it seep back slowly, the way she sometimes allowed milk to trickle down her throat till she was forced to swallow. Cloud or fire — wasn't that how He always came?

"Great White Spirit —" she whispered.

A long moment passed.

An oarlock creaked, and something rammed the boat.

"Hey! We hit something!" exclaimed a high voice.

"Grab it!" a deeper voice answered.

Marcy scrambled back on the seat and fumbled for the oars. She didn't want to talk to people now. She gave a firm pull. One oar clunked something hard. She backed frantically with the other, but her boat swung slowly alongside another rowboat. She recognized the curved white shape. Boy Scouts! With a surge of fury she banged the fist holding her gunwale.

"Ow!" The hand snatched back, but its mate grabbed hold before she could shove away, and a pudgy face loomed close to hers. "Hey! It's one of those wild Indians! Feathers and all!"

"Let me go!" shrilled Marcy.

The face of the boy who had spit on Kenny peered out of the gloom. "It's one of them, all right! She helped tie me up! And her sneaky little brother stole some grub from our cookout! What'll we do with her?"

205

They whispered together.

Marcy felt panicky. She must jump overboard! It was getting dark; they'd never find her in the mist. She could paddle around till it lifted, then head in to the public beach. She edged toward the far gunwale.

"She's getting away!" yipped the pudgy one.

She sprang, but a hand caught the end of one pigtail. Her neck jerked back and she fell against the seat.

"Let me go!" she screamed, tugging on her braid.

The boys laughed.

"What nice long hair Pocahontas has!" Spitter tweaked it. "I've been *wanting* a nice scalp to hang from my belt."

"Say — me too!" cried Pudgy.

A chill of horror raced down Marcy's spine. She clutched her pigtails close to her head. Surely they wouldn't — they couldn't — she screamed, and jerked her head again, frantically.

The boys rolled into her boat. Spitter held her mouth while Pudgy threw her anchor into the scout craft.

"Now, look," said Spitter, "this won't hurt, but if you keep on jumping around you'll stab yourself! Got your knife, Jack? Thanks."

Marcy heard the blade click. With a squeak she stopped thrashing and lay still. One didn't fool with an open knife.

Spitter took his hand off her mouth.

"Don't you dare!" she threatened in a wobbly voice, her heart numb with terror.

Spitter laughed and twisted her arm, so that she was forced to the bottom.

Jack sat on her back and pressed her face down.

"Be careful of that knife!" she choked. "I won't move! I promise!"

"Hold it tight while I cut," Spitter instructed.

Marcy felt a braid jerked taut. She bit her lip to keep from screaming and lay rigid. This couldn't be happening! It was all a horrible nightmare! The knife began to saw back and forth and the hairs growing from the tender places in her neck smarted and pulled unbearably.

"Darn dull knife," muttered Spitter. "This's like cutting wet rope."

Marcy's tears mingled with the bilge. Her long braids, that hadn't been cut since first grade! Her shoulders shook.

A last few hairs jerked and stung, and the pressure relaxed. "There!" exclaimed Spitter triumphantly. He flapped the severed braid aloft like a captured snake. "Wait'll the guys see *this!*"

"Now this one for me!" Pudgy grabbed her other braid.

"Cut your own," said Spitter.

"Why won't you do it for me?" whined Pudgy.

"What'sa matter? You scared? Here's your knife."

There was a clunk. "Oh," said Jack. "I dropped it."

"Clumsy!" snarled Spitter.

Jack half rose and Marcy whipped around and bit his ankle as hard as she could.

"Yeow! She bit me! She bit me!" He lunged for her, but she was over the gunwale in a flash. Instead of hitting water, she tumbled into the scout boat. Her arm struck an anchor; she pitched it over the side and shoved away. She was free! Free! She sprang for the rower's seat.

"Catch her!" shouted Spitter. "Quit blubbering and listen!"

Marcy, snatching the oars, stopped. That's right — they'd hear her rowing! On all fours, like a cat, she crept to the prow. Now she could paddle with her hands, silently, away from their voices.

"I can't hear her!" said Jack. "And I'm bleeding!"

"You dope! She's got away — and in our boat!"

There was the scream of a siren from the scout shore.

"All boats in!" cried Jack. "*Now* what'll we do? We can't go in and we can't stay out!"

"Row! Row!" cried Spitter. "She's here somewhere! We have to find her!"

Marcy paddled silently, scarcely daring to breathe, while the scouts floundered and quarreled. She grinned grimly — they were rowing with the anchor down! Their voices got fainter. Now the mist was lifting; stars were floating in the water, and over the bog a fingernail moon was just setting. They might spot her now, but she had a head start! She sprang for the oars and rowed wildly for home.

At the dock she fastened the boat with a seldom-used padlock and dashed with the oars up under the porch. She hid them among the fishpoles and sank down on Sugarpuss's hay. Now — now she could think about her loss. Her head felt strangely light and lopsided. Oh, it couldn't have happened! It wasn't true! She lifted a trembling hand. Damp bristles met her touch.

She bent her head on her knees and cried with great, wracking sobs. Sugarpuss wandered up, bleating mournfully.

208

"You're crying, too," choked Marcy. She put her to bed, closed the doors, and slipped up to the porch. In the lighted living room Mother and Janice were playing double solitaire. How could they sit as if nothing had happened? She walked in and stood by the card table.

"Hello, dear." Mother didn't look up. The game went briskly on.

"Your deuce, Mother!" called Janice. "On the ace of hearts!"

Mother played it and Janice slammed on a three, four, and five.

"Oh, you," said Mother, still fingering her three.

Marcy strangled a sob.

Mother glanced up. "Why, Marcy, you're filthy! What's the matter? What in heaven's name —"

"I've been scalped," Marcy squealed, almost inaudibly.

"Scalped!" Mother and Janice cried.

She nodded dumbly and turned for them to see.

There was a flabbergasted silence. Then Janice tittered, and Mother burst into a laugh.

"It's not funny!" Marcy screamed, and tore into the bedroom, slamming the door. She flung herself on the bed and dragged a pillow over her head.

Mother and Janice burst in, trailing cards behind them.

"Darling!" Mother cried. "Of course it's not funny! But one pigtail off, and one pigtail on — like 'Diddle Diddle Dumpling' —"

"Marcy, *honey!*" Janice put a hand on her shoulder. Marcy wrenched herself away and rolled over, carrying the pillow

209

with her and screaming into it. In a gasp for breath she heard
Mother.

"But where were Thad and Betsy? I thought she was with
them —"

Marcy flung off the pillow and sat up. "I was alone in the
mist, and the Boy Scouts rammed me and cut off my — my —"

"But why just *one?*" Janice changed a snicker to a cough.

"Because I got away, that's why!"

Mother's face was troubled. "I don't know all of what you Indians have been up to, but it seems to me the scouts are going a little far —"

"We haven't done anything to them in a long time," Marcy wept.

"Would you like me to talk to the camp director?"

Janice broke in hastily. "Don't you think it's time Marcy got her hair cut, anyway? She can't be a little girl all her life! I think her hair's curly; I'll cut off the other braid and trim both sides and she'll look awfully pretty!"

"I don't want to look pretty! I want my braid back!"

"I'm afraid that's impossible," said Mother. "And it certainly can't stay this way, unless you want to start a new style. Why don't you let Janice cut it, dear?" She stroked Marcy's head and removed the broken feather.

"You'll have this braid to keep beside your bed, with your tooth and arrowhead," wheedled Janice. "And you can watch while I do it."

Marcy looked over the end of the iron bed into the wavy mirror on the washstand. Her distorted face, tear-streaked, stared back. One black braid hung down — on the other side, short ragged wisps. She gasped and her eyes filled again. She looked at her mother piteously. "I could almost sit on them," she quavered.

Mother smiled sympathetically. "They'd have to come off someday. You can keep this braid to show your children! And it isn't everybody that gets scalped and lives to tell the tale."

"Indians should *do* the scalping," said Marcy hollowly. "It's a terrible dishonor to the tribe." Her face brightened as she remembered. "But I bit one till he bled, and I got their —" She stopped. She'd better not mention the boat in front of her sister.

Janice was fussing with the cut ends. "They left enough here to work with. I'll fix you up okay." She sniffed. "Your hair smells funny, baby —"

"The boat water. They tackled me."

"No, sort of — well, moldy. Look, Mother — it *is* moldy!"

"Oh, it can't be!" Mother looked and poked and smelled. She took the remaining braid and pulled the strands apart. She felt and sniffed some more, and finally looked suspiciously at her youngest daughter.

"Marcy — did you comb your hair today?"

"No."

"Yesterday?"

"No."

"The day before yesterday?"

"I don't remember!" Marcy protested. "I always brush the top part and put in barrettes. It stays neat, in braids."

"Yes," agreed Mother, "but it stays wet, too. And then in this hot weather —" She grinned. "Darling, I don't know if this will make you feel any better, but you'd have had to have a haircut, anyway. Your braids are all mildewy!" She and Janice burst out laughing.

Marcy scowled at herself in the mirror and at the china pin trays filled with hairpins and nets. She scowled at the tattered wallpaper and at Mother and Janice laughing in the glass at her.

It was too much. She couldn't cope with all the feelings that had flooded her today: the wasp and Saturn, the mist, hatred for the Boy Scouts, fear and grief and shame at the scalping, mingled with triumph over the bite and the boat — and now, the ridiculousness of mildewed hair! A great sob burst out, and turned into a laugh, and back into a sob again.

Mother and Janice flopped down and threw their arms around her. Laughing and crying, they rolled together on the lumpy bed.

Chapter

17

"TONIGHT'S THE NIGHT!" cried Owl Eyes vengefully. She squinted up through the cattails. Behind them the rushy end of the lily pond was alive with rhythmic peeping.

"Ugh," seconded Chief Thunder Cloud.

White Feather nodded, a little more vigorously than she needed. It was four days since her scalping, but the tickle of hair bobbing around her ears was still an interesting sensation.

"Do you suppose Mother suspects?" Crafty Fox worried. "Daddy ordered us to leave the scouts alone now, you know."

"Daddy's never been scalped!" Owl Eyes blazed. "How *can* we leave them alone? We have to revenge White Feather!"

"Ugh!" Chief Thunder Cloud agreed promptly.

"Anything *we* ever did could be put right, like beds or turtles," Owl Eyes raged on, "but *hair* — long, beautiful hair that's taken years and years to grow —"

White Feather's throat tightened. Like continually picking the scab off a sore and making it bleed afresh, Owl Eyes hadn't let her sister forget her terrible loss for a minute.

She continued, full of wrath. "Daddy orders *us* to stay away. Why shouldn't Janice, too? The traitor! Trading boats with Red in the middle of the night! Why don't they give her a uniform and let her *live* there? *We* don't want her!"

"She's being *friendly,*" Crafty Fox put in witheringly. "Daddy said if we couldn't be *friendly* —"

"Ugh," interrupted Chief Thunder Cloud. "Taps."

The tribe was silent while the silver notes rose, fell, and faded across the lake. A moment later, nearer by, Girl Scout taps repeated the call.

Crafty Fox shifted. There was a crackling sound.

"Stop making that noise!" Owl Eyes was edgy. "What have you got, anyway?"

"Nothing!"

"Well, don't do that on enemy territory. You'll give us all away."

"Ugh — last light out in Sleepy Hollow," said the chief.

White Feather shivered. Soon they would push out of the sheltering reeds and paddle across the lake to carry out the most daring war plan of all! All week end they'd tried to figure something that would half equal the enormity of the scalping. If only they still had the scout boat! They could take it to the middle and load it with rocks till it sank. But unfortunately it

215

had been mysteriously traded for their own the very night of the scalping. Janice wouldn't admit to it, but who else could have unlocked the padlock? And who from the camp but Red would have been able to complete the transaction? Oh, they were guilty. The tribe had been shunning Janice ever since.

All other ideas for revenge were too trifling — like pie beds — or too terrible — such as puncturing the canoes. Still, out of a dreadful idea of Crafty Fox's, had come Owl Eyes' brainstorm.

"We've tried every way we know to get rid of them this summer," he'd sighed, "and they're still stuck tighter than bloodsuckers. I bet they'd leave in a hurry if we burned down their stockade! Then they wouldn't have any place to eat."

"Don't be silly," said Owl Eyes. "Can't we think up some really *good* idea?"

"If there was a fire, they'd ring the gong," White Feather mused.

"What gong?" asked Thunder Cloud.

"The one hanging behind where they kept Sugarpuss. There's a sign that tells how many gongs for what, like fire or a boat capsized."

Owl Eyes' eyes snapped. "I've got it! We'll give those scouts the scare of their lives! We'll get even for scalping a —"

"But how? How?" interrupted Crafty Fox.

"Can't you see? We'll ring the fire gong!"

"But you just said we *couldn't* burn down the mess hall!"

"Don't be stupid; we won't burn down anything. It'll be a false alarm! This way they'll be routed out of bed —"

"Ugh!" cried the chief. "All for nothing!"

216

"I don't see why we couldn't light just a *little* fire," said Crafty Fox. "Maybe just a little grass fire somewhere?"

"No," said Owl Eyes.

Over the week end it had been impossible to sneak out. Last night it had rained. But tonight was starry and the skinny moon hanging over the far-off thicket was trying to catch a little cloud on its horns. Daddy had gone, and his order was buried in the minds of the Potawatomi like a burr in a thick sock whose prickles pierced through only now and then.

"Ugh," said Thunder Cloud softly. "Time to go."

The tribe climbed into the canoe. Crafty Fox crackled.

"Stop that or we'll leave you behind!" Owl Eyes said sharply.

They left the rushes and struck across the lake. It was a coolish night for early August, and small waves slapped the canoe sides. White Feather buttoned Jerry's hood under her chin.

The chief guided the canoe toward the Turtle Swamp. To avoid detection, they were arriving from a new direction. They glided into the slough, brushed over lily pads, and gently clunked the mainland.

"Listen," warned Owl Eyes.

A long silence, except for night noises.

The tribe climbed out and huddled on the bank.

"Now wait at the gong till we're all there," Owl Eyes instructed. "And keep out of sight. Chief Thunder Cloud, the flashlight?"

The chief winked a tiny light.

"Okay," said Owl Eyes. "Don't forget to hold your hankies over the mallet handle. And don't drop them; we can't leave any clues!" She paused. "Anything else? No? Then on to the revenge!"

Tensely, White Feather led off. The grass sighed as the rest skulked after her. She swung wide around some tents and climbed the long hill to the mess hall. Keeping within the trees, she circled behind, watching the black form of the stockade. Ah, there was the shed; right here should be —

She yelped and pitched over something hard. A faint reverberation hummed. She lay frozen with terror as the noise died away.

"What happened?" Owl Eyes glided up.

"I fell through the gong," White Feather whispered, rubbing her shin. "The sign's somewhere on that tree."

The chief flashed his light. After a waggle or two it fastened on a white board lettered in red and black:

```
EMERGENCY GONG

ONE:   MAN  OVERBOARD
TWO:   BOAT  CAPSIZED
THREE: SWIMMER  MISSING
FOUR:  FIRE
```

He flicked the beam off again.

"I'm glad fire gets four," breathed Crafty Fox, "because we'll each get a chance to bang it."

"Line up by age," ordered Owl Eyes, "and run as soon as you've had your turn. Crafty Fox, you first; your legs are shortest."

218

Crafty Fox fingered the mallet. "I wish I could have a practice shot."

"Well, you can't. Every one counts! Now shut up and listen."

White Feather held her breath. She heard the ever-chirping crickets, the whisper of leaves — but no paleface noises.

"One for the money," the chief said softly.

"Two for the show." Owl Eyes poked White Feather in the back.

"Three to get ready," said White Feather

"And four to GO!" cried Crafty Fox, and swung the mallet.

GONG! boomed the gong. White Feather jumped at the sound but caught the mallet as the Fox dashed away.

GONG!

The handle stung her hand. Owl Eyes snatched it.

GONNNNNNG!

Owl Eyes' blow was loudest. White Feather ducked behind the gong tree while her sister thrashed past. As leader of the revenge, she'd wait a minute to be sure everyone got safely away.

GONNG!

The sound reverberated down the hill and rolled away to silence, as the chief, like a cow in a cornfield, galumphed past. Then the camp was still again. Had anything disturbed the calm night?

Suddenly lights flashed on in the mess hall. Footsteps pounded from the Ridge. Three or four flashlights bobbed like fireflies.

"Fire!" rang a terrified yelp.

"Where's the fire?" A frightened shout.

The revenge was a success! White Feather grinned and turned to run.

Ahead, underbrush crashed and there was a gleam of light. "Fire!"

She darted to the side and nearly collided with a pajamaed figure galloping along the path.

"Where's the fire?" Lights blinked closer.

She whirled. More shouts behind her! She was surrounded! Where could she go? The sign on the gong tree caught her eye; she leaped for it frantically and shinnied up, just as a flashlight beam swept the trunk.

For a minute she could do nothing but hang on while her heart thumped in her ears. Then she peeped down.

The area below was filling with bedlam — shadowy shapes, shouts, and darting lights. More scouts pounded up to the growing crowd. The shrill cries of "Fire!" began to be mingled with querulous voices demanding, *"Where's* the fire?"

She began to enjoy herself. It would have been a shame to miss this fun!

A yard light suddenly bathed the area in brightness and exposed her like a coon in a tree. She scuttled around the trunk.

"Let's have some order here! Quiet! Quiet!" rang a stern voice, and an angry man strode through the crowd. The paleface leader!

"All right!" he barked. "Has anybody seen a fire?"

There were murmurs, and then a few scattered No's.

"Where's your discipline? Have you located who turned in the alarm? Patrol leaders — why aren't you out looking for the

fire? Did you examine the mess hall? Who checked the Hollow, the Ridge?"

There was more murmuring. The scouts, no longer frightened, stood belligerent and chastened under the cold eyes of their leader and counselors.

"Well, get going! The rest of you stay here."

A dozen or so boys ran off in various directions.

White Feather gasped with a dreadful thought. The tribe must be searching for her! They'd run right into the patrol leaders, like Peter Pan's lost boys popping out of the tree into the arms of the pirates! Her mind unaccountably jumped to a nursery verse.

> Four little Indians,
> Potawatomi —
> One rang the gong and ran
> And then there were three.

She went on with the rhyming, desperately, for something to do. Three little Indians — what would rhyme? Few? New? Do?

> Three little Indians,
> What can they do?
> One stumbled through the gong
> And then there were two.

> Two little Indians,
> Both on the run.
> One captured by the scouts
> And then there was one.

> One little Indian,
> Too dumb to run [she grinned wryly].
> The palefaces found her in a tree
> And then there was — none!

The patrol leaders were pelting back now. One by one they reported no signs of fire.

She took a deep breath. So far the tribe was safe!

"All right," said the head paleface. "This is somebody's idea of a joke. I'd like whoever gave the alarm to step forward and own up like a real scout."

Absolute silence.

"Is everyone here? Counselors, check your boys."

There was a flurry of movement while the scouts arranged themselves by tents.

"All here, Mr. Maddox." It was Red reporting.

"And nobody will own up?"

The pajamaed boys, now shivering unhappily, shifted from foot to foot and looked suspiciously at one another.

"You understand this is not just a minor prank," the pale-face chief went on. "You've all been told the importance of the gong: that it must never be rung except in an emergency. And yet someone tonight gave a false alarm. Who will own up?"

Whispered denials crescendoed.

Mr. Maddox looked grim. "Very well. General swim will be cut twenty minutes every day for a week. Now — no boy should call himself a scout if he will let a whole camp suffer for his misdeed."

There was a long, sullen silence.

"If he cares to come to my tent and own up in private, very well. I promise punishment, but nothing a scout can't take manfully. Counselors, I expect you to talk gravely to each of your boys. John and Rex, you'd better patrol here till morning."

White Feather clung, dismayed. Treed, for the night!

Muttering, the boys began to disperse. Suddenly there was a shout.

"Fire!"

The camp stood electrified, staring at a gleam of flame near the boat dock. Then a dozen voices raised the cry "FIRE!" and everyone raced pell-mell down the hill. In a second the clearing was empty. White Feather skinned down her tree and galloped to the Turtle Swamp.

"Here she is!" cried Crafty Fox.

She tumbled in the canoe and with swift strokes Chief Thunder Cloud shot it out of the swamp.

Nobody spoke till they were safe on the lake. Then Owl Eyes cried angrily, "What happened to you, anyway?"

Panting, White Feather related her escapade. Before she had finished, she was feeling quite clever, and recited Mr. Maddox's speech, and her own impromptu verses.

"And then, just when I thought I'd have to sit in the tree all night, along came this fire — and everybody ran, so I did too, and you were all still waiting! I was afraid you'd go blundering into their —"

"Look who's talking about blundering!" exclaimed Crafty Fox.

"What sort of boobs do you take us for?" demanded the chief.

"You ought to thank us for rescuing you," said Owl Eyes, "while you were sitting in a tree making up poetry."

"Rescuing me?" White Feather asked stiffly.

"We didn't dare go hunt for you," said Owl Eyes, "because we saw scouts thrashing around, and then Crafty Fox said —"

" 'Let's build a fire!' " Crafty Fox supplied.

"*You* built the fire!" exclaimed White Feather.

"Who do you think built it — Santa Claus?" said the chief.

The Fox continued. "And they said, 'Why?' And I said, 'Then all the scouts will come running and give White Feather a chance to get away, if she's caught or hiding.' And they said, 'We haven't any matches.' And I said, 'I have a lot, and news-papers, too —' "

"That's why he was crackling so," Owl Eyes explained. "All that paper under his sweater."

"I brought them along just in case," Crafty Fox said smugly. "So we sneaked down by the boathouse and wadded them up in a clear space, and lit them —"

"And Crafty Fox's plan worked like a charm!" said Thunder Cloud.

White Feather frowned. "What if I'd had a broken leg?"

"Well, you didn't," said Owl Eyes.

The chief began to paddle again. White Feather squeezed out angry tears. Crafty Fox! Wind Bag was more like it! She'd been leader of the revenge, and they hadn't given her any credit at all!

The canoe rounded the point and the front of the camp hove into view. The mess hall was bright as a movie marquee, and tiny beams speckled the hillside, getting thicker, like a star cluster, around the place where the fire had been.

Crafty Fox hugged himself with glee. "They're all in a lather!"

"Looks like a carnival!" crowed the chief. "What a revenge!"

Camp lights were still on when the canoe glided to a stop at the Richardses' pier.

"Hello," said Janice. She was in the rowboat. Jip thumped his tail in welcome and made a little sound in his throat.

The tribe didn't answer.

"What have you savages been up to now?"

"Nothing," said Thad.

"I heard those gongs."

"So did we," Betsy declared. "So we paddled over to see the fire."

"How did *you* know those gongs meant fire?"

"I saw the sign on the tree the day I rescued Sugarpuss," Marcy put in hastily.

"I wouldn't trust you kids any farther than I could see you," said Janice. "I wouldn't be surprised if —"

"Go ahead — tattle to Mother like you always do," cried Betsy. "But I dare you to prove it! And even if we did do it, it's not near as bad a thing as scalping somebody!"

"I'm not going to tattle," said Janice. "You'll get what's coming to you eventually. I've been waiting for you, though, to tell you something interesting. But of course if you don't want to hear —"

"Oh, we'll hear it," said Betsy.

"But it won't be interesting, coming from *you*," added Thad.

"Red came over tonight, just before taps, to say he'd felt it was his duty to tell Mr. Maddox — he's the camp director — about Marcy's braid —"

"How did Red know? That old boat thief!" shrieked Marcy.

"I told him; I thought it was funny."

Betsy howled with rage. "What *right* do you have to interfere? Now the grownups will all be in on our private war!" She paused. "What did Mr. Maddox say?"

226

"Well, he was sorry, and got the braid from the boy, and heard about some of your other exploits, and got Thad's headdress —"

"We'll never get it back now!" Thad cried.

"Wait, I'm not through yet! Red said Mr. Maddox wasn't mad at all, but was interested to know there was a tribe of Potawatomi still living in this territory, and that the headdress showed skilled workmanship —"

"He said *that?*" Betsy's voice was pleased.

"I did the beads," said Thad.

"Children!" Mother called. "Come up; it's long after bedtime!"

"In a minute!" shouted Betsy. "Go on, Janice."

"Well, Mr. Maddox said that a lot of scout lore was learned from the Indians and patterned after them."

"I know; it talks about Indians all the time in their —" Thad stopped abruptly and looked warily around.

"And he said the scouts wanted to learn about the Potawatomi, and wondered if your tribe would come over and tell them about some of your activities — like how you made your tomahawks — at a council meeting sometime, or do some of your tribal dances, or tell some of your tribal legends. I think it would be fun. Maybe you'd let me go along. You said once I could be Old Nokomis."

The tribe sat stunned.

"And then he said that you Indians might be interested in some of the scout activities, like the rifle range, and the telescope —"

The telescope! Marcy swallowed hard.

227

"— or some contests, like swimming and archery —"

"Why didn't Red tell *us* all this?" Betsy found her voice.

"He tried to. He stopped at the wigwam first, and then here, and then Kenny's, but Kenny's granddad said you'd all pulled off in the canoe — oh, yes, I forgot — Mr. Maddox bawled out the guy who scalped you, Marce, but he didn't punish him, because being drydocked for losing his boat, and getting a black eye, was enough punishment —"

"What black eye?" asked Marcy.

"Jerry gave him one when he recognized the braid. Red says he really beat him to a pulp."

"Oh," said Marcy in a small voice.

"Well, we'll have to think it over," Betsy said brusquely. "I don't see how we can accept — we're at war. Besides, he might change his mind about wanting us — now."

"You can report to Red however you decide," said Janice. "And don't worry about *me*. *I* won't tell anybody!"

The tribe climbed out of the canoe, and, with an "Ugh," Kenny disappeared toward home. Betsy tramped ahead up the path.

"Marcy?" Thad, with Jip trailing, caught up. "What do you think?"

"I don't know," Marcy said irritably. She turned off into the trees beyond the range of the porch lights. Dread clouded her heart. Her earlier snit was forgotten in the greater danger hovering over them. Already she could sense it. She didn't know what any of them were thinking. The tribe felt split, and that was what the scouts wanted, to destroy them forever. But it mustn't happen — the tribe was what mattered!

228

And yet — the telescope —

She tore off a piece of bark and crumbled it into hard bits. The telescope, or the Potawatomi — that was the choice. She longed to go back, to look through it again — and yet she must help keep the Potawatomi together, mustn't she? Her eyes smarted and she threw the bark crumbs on the ground with a furious motion.

That was what was so awful! She didn't know how she herself felt about the terrible proposition!

Chapter

18

ALMOST A WEEK after the false alarm the tribe climbed the stile and padded Indian file across the pasture. They were walking around the lake. Behind them, like unpressed orange hair ribbons, the last of the sunset lay crumpled across the sky. A few stars flickered uncertainly and decided to remain lit. A pale half-moon brightened. Bats circled, and from the reeds two granddaddy frogs groaned in rhythm.

Jip's breath came in snuffs and his tongue nearly lapped the ground as he led the way. Kenny, next, flicked on the flashlight. The dusk instantly seemed darker. Marcy, scuffing at the rear, shivered and put on her sweater.

It was always eerie, walking around the lake at night. The

shore path that she knew by heart took on strange shadowy dangers. Landmarks loomed unfamiliar, and every sound was intensified.

They crossed the other stile into Girl Scout territory. The path here clung to the hill and rippled like the rickrack on Marcy's summer dresses — first up among the tall grass and black juniper trees, then down, where the ground squished and the tips of reeds pricked their hands.

A bugle call wafted across the lake.

Marcy frowned. Always before, walking around the lake had started out toward the wigwam and returned through the pasture, but now they had to go the opposite way, in order to sneak through enemy lands after taps — especially since they didn't know yet whether the scouts suspected them of ringing the gong.

They'd had a solemn powwow the day after Red's message, but there had been something awfully wrong. Each brave had tried to sound out the others without giving his own opinion. Nobody had wanted to make a decision. The same apprehension White Feather had felt the night before had gnawed at her stomach. They'd finally agreed to wait a week and decide then. No one had spoken of it since — and tomorrow was the week. She had to make up her own mind tonight.

Jip's toenails clattered.

"Pump house," called Kenny. The procession tramped over the box jutting out of the hill. Marcy stopped on the tar-paper roof for a moment to feel the pumps throb like a volcano under her feet, then hurried to catch up. The path leveled off on the pebbly shore.

"Girl Scout piers," announced Kenny.

"Shall we sit on one?" asked Thad. "And talk about things, like we always do?"

"We don't need a rest yet. We're just a quarter of the way," Betsy decided. "We'll sit on the Boy Scout pier, if no one's about."

They rounded the point and filed past the shadowy racks of canoes. Now came gently rolling wild lands, where huge oaks raised gnarly arms against the charcoal sky.

"Shooting star," chirped Thad.

Marcy glimpsed the end of the fiery trail. A shooting star must look glorious through the telescope! You couldn't look at one deliberately, of course, for how could you know when it was going to shoot? But an astronomer must see one once in a while, by accident. Perhaps the star counselor . . .

She forced the thought from her mind; it was too dangerous. She should think instead how many things the enemy had changed since they'd come. She glanced across at the pier gleaming in the moonlight and the boathouse like a scar at the foot of the hill. They'd ruined the Happy Hunting Grounds, of course, but they'd changed other things, too, things you wouldn't ordinarily think of, like the direction people walked around the lake. Were there still more ways — silent, secret ways — that she wasn't aware of? The sorts of things you couldn't fight?

She stood still. "They've got us all split up! We *used* to be a tribe! *Now* what are we?"

Snatching the tufts off a clump of grass, she tramped after the others. "We're blood brothers, aren't we? We all felt alike

232

the night of the first war dance, didn't we?" Her voice rose. "Then why don't we feel alike now?"

"What?" asked Betsy, looming just ahead.

"Nothing." Marcy subsided, but her thoughts went on. The tribe was like a school of fish, with the worms of the enemy dangling before their noses. She pictured for an instant the green forms, fins slightly waving, glassy eyes staring. Would they flash away with a swish of their tails and be safe? Or would they snap? She knew, guiltily, what her own worm was, and how strong the temptation!

The way sloped down into the rushes before the lily pond, and the path became springy. The dank smell of stagnant water closed in, of vegetable things rotting in oil-coated puddles, now bronzy in the moonlight. Hummocks poked up from the mucky ground.

"Water," warned Kenny.

"Water," repeated Thad.

"Careful, water," said Betsy.

Marcy took a long step over the trickle that made Almost Island a real island most of the summer. Cattails screened the moonlight. The noisy swamp quieted at their approach, and they walked in a little circle of silence, but as soon as they passed, the creatures commenced their groaning and trilling.

The path became firm and a hill loomed at their left. They were on the shore proper of the island now. They crunched along the stones till the lily pond's channel, frosted with moonlight, blocked their way. The lake on their right danced merrily with diamonds, but the pond curling behind the island was calm and mysterious.

233

The older tribesters rolled up their pants legs; the younger shucked their blue jeans. Marcy waded into the channel, shattering the moonlight. Kenny and Betsy clutched the unwilling dog and staggered across. They dumped him on the opposite strand and churned back for their shoes.

"Clam!" cried Thad. "Betsy, get my sock floating there!"

"Hurry up, Marce." Betsy passed her. "I've crossed twice already."

Sand slipped under Marcy's toes. Her legs prickled as water inched to her knees and up her thighs. Squashy leaves on the bottom indicated the deepest part. The leaves ended; the bottom sloped up to land. Dry pebbles clung to her feet. She brushed them off with her socks.

Thad wiggled his foot into his wet stocking. "How can I tell if I have any bloodsuckers?"

"You can't," said Betsy. "Let's go."

The path twisted through semiwild land and then reached civilization, the cottage row on the side of the lake opposite their own, where it went along sandy beaches, over piers, on top of stone walls and catwalks around boathouses, and sometimes on a lawn, close to the porch of a cottage. Lights threw out squares of gold. Radios blared, glasses clinked. From one pier voices laughed raucously as a motorboat buzzed the shore.

The tribe traveled in silence till they were past the settlement.

"It sure is honky-tonk around there," Thad remarked.

"Completely paleface," sniffed Betsy.

"Ugh! Here we are at-um bay! Cover-um up skin! Poison ivy!"

234

Ahead, taps hung over the Boy Scout camp like a singing mosquito, and in a moment the Girl Scouts echoed. Out from shore, oars creaked; an anchor splashed and chain rattled out. Somebody fishing. Marcy's mind jumped back to an earlier thought: worms.

The rest of the tribe had worms tempting them, too, but she wasn't quite sure what sort they were. Except Kenny's. His was obvious. Hadn't she seen him grimly practicing his archery, and lashing himself to greater speeds in the water? The tribe couldn't give him the kind of competition he wanted, but a whole camp of palefaces had offered to. . . . Would he vote for peace at the powwow tomorrow?

The path ended at a boathouse jutting into the water. They climbed a long flight of steps to another path, crossed a field, and followed the fence that marked Boy Scout property down behind the Turtle Swamp.

Ahead, the boys were arguing about the best way to walk silently.

"Heels first over stones," Thad insisted. "But toes first on grass or twigs. I can prove it!"

"You've been saying that about lots of things, but you never do!"

"I can; I'll prove it tomorrow, maybe!"

"You're both elephants," Betsy commented. "Now shut up — tents."

They crept past the swamp. At the point, the lake twinkled in fullness again.

"There's the Boy Scout pier," whispered Betsy. "We'll rest before the last lap home. Watch out for settlers!"

235

The boards spanked as they walked to the end. They stretched out on the cool deck. Marcy looked up. Earth faded away and there was only the moon-bright sky.

Well, tomorrow it wouldn't matter if they *were* caught here — if the worms were wiggly enough. Would Thad snap? His worm must be a friend. How else would he know those little bits of information about the Boy Scouts? Thad was crafty; perhaps he *could* have kept a friend secret from the tribe. Now, Betsy —

She'd seemed pleased at Mr. Maddox's praise of the war bonnet; maybe her worm was flattery. Marcy shook her head at the sky. No, not Betsy. The rest of them might snap and be pulled wriggling in, but all this week, with everything undecided, hadn't Betsy been more vehement than ever? Hadn't Betsy been the only one to keep any fun in their Indianing?

"Shooting star," grunted Kenny.

Marcy watched the streaking arc. It all came back to the stars again, how she'd vote. For peace or war? For the stars or against them? Would she snap or wouldn't she? She writhed in indecision.

"Another one!" cried Thad. "Cabbage, there's a lot tonight!"

"The Indians sat around this lake once, looking at the shooting stars." Betsy's voice was dreamy.

Marcy sat up and stared across the sparkling water. "You're selfish," she whispered to herself. "You can see the stars without a telescope." It was like Betsy'd said at the beginning of the summer — give a little bit and the tribe would be gone. It might happen so slowly they'd never notice till too late, but they'd be swallowed up, like worms now, not fish, and the tribe

236

would be part of the fish, or nothing at all. The palefaces would
have won, just as it always happened in Indian history. Thad
and Kenny might vote for peace, but Betsy saw things clearly.
She'd vote for war.

So — Marcy took a deep breath — she'd vote for war, too,
and that might make a tie, but in case of tie the tribe would
follow Betsy.

The stars swam in her eyes. It was a hard price to pay, but
sometimes you lost the stars in order to save them. After all,
what could you see from a fish's stomach? She suddenly felt
better than she had all week. The decision was made! War it
would be!

"Where is God?" asked Thad.

"Everywhere," said Betsy.

Silence.

"Shooting star," reported Kenny.

Silence.

Jip's tail thumped. Betsy jerked upright. "Somebody's coming on the dock!"

"Freeze and maybe he won't see us!" said Thad.

"In this moon?" hissed Kenny. "Let's rush him and push him in the shallow water! I'll blind him!"

The tribe clattered forward as the chief flicked on the light.

"Hey, lay off!" A familiar voice spoke.

"Relax." Betsy stopped. "It's only Jerry."

Kenny turned off the beam and Jerry creaked up to them.

"Hi," he whispered, giving Jip's ears a pull.

"What are you doing here?" Betsy demanded. "It's way past taps."

Jerry's grin flashed. "I sneaked out. There's a special show going on I want to see."

"Why aren't you in Whitewater, then?" asked Thad suspiciously.

"This is better than the Strand." Jerry swept his arm over the sky. "It's a *real* motion picture. There goes one!"

"Oh, *shooting stars*. We've been seeing lots of those," said Thad.

"That's just it. If the moon weren't so near full, we'd see lots more. They're the Perseids."

"Perseids?" Marcy took a step nearer.

"August eleven. It'll be best after midnight when the earth'll be meeting the meteors head on. Right now it's having to catch up."

"How'd you know there'd be a lot tonight?" Thad persisted. "There goes another one."

"Well" — Jerry sat down and the tribe followed — "you know there're asteroids that go around the sun just the way we do — well, once one disintegrated to just little rocks and things, and a funny thing, its orbit intersects ours, so once a year we

238

go through all those bits, and they rub on our atmosphere and flare up like matches on a matchbox."

"Was Perseid the name of the asteroid?" asked Betsy.

"No — I guess it didn't have a name. But some years there's a whole rain of stars and they all seem to come from the constellation Perseus. It happens again sometime in November, only then they're called Leonids, because they seem to come from Leo."

"There's a Perseid!" Thad cried as another arc flashed.

"How do you know all this?" Marcy asked. In spite of her decision she couldn't help feeling a glow of warmth for Jerry.

"I earned my astronomy merit badge this summer. Keith — he's the instructor — sure makes it interesting. Say, I bet he'd let you all look through his telescope some night, if I asked."

"Cabbage!" breathed Thad.

The tribe lapsed into silence, watching for Perseids. The pulse of crickets was loud from the shore.

"Say, we've been wondering what happened to you kids." Jerry changed the subject. "Mr. Maddox said maybe we'd all be getting together for a swimming meet or something. Gosh — I'd be afraid to swim against the chief!"

"Ugh," grunted Kenny modestly. "I'm no good."

Marcy quivered. Oh, how cleverly he was dangling the worm! He knew Kenny's soft spot as well as she did! *But why all this talk about Perseids?* She blanched in horror. He knew *hers,* *too!*

And how about Thad and Betsy? Did he know theirs when even she, their own sister, wasn't sure? How could she warn the tribe to be wary? What even could she warn them *of?* Oh, *he* was the one who should be called Crafty Fox! But Betsy — Betsy would see through him! Betsy was unassailable.

"Why didn't you send a message?" Jerry asked. "Even refusing. Then we could have sent you another one and had some fun dickering."

"Well," Betsy said slowly, "we heard you were being punished — on account of the gong — and we thought maybe Mr. Maddox thought — that we —"

"Oh, no, not after Janice said you were all over at Kenny's all evening."

"But she and Red both knew — ouch!" Thad subsided at a fierce pinch from Betsy.

Jerry went on smoothly. "And he realized it couldn't be one of us, because we were all by the stockade when the fire was lit by the boathouse, so he figured it was boys from town. It's all blown over now."

"Oh." Betsy's voice was strangely small.

Marcy's mind reeled. Janice and Red had protected them! Jerry knew and was hiding it, too! They all wanted peace! How could the tribe resist the pressure? Oh, they could, if they were united! They could, if only Betsy stood firm!

"How about it?" asked Jerry. "Are we going to have a truce?"

"Maybe, maybe not," said Betsy. "We're going to decide tomorrow."

Thad buttoned up his jacket. "It's sort of cool out here."

"Want to know the temperature?" Jerry studied his watch in the moonlight for a few moments. "It's seventy-one degrees out."

"How can you tell by your watch?" Thad demanded.

"By the crickets. The hotter it is, the faster they chirp. You count the number of beats in fifteen seconds and add thirty-seven. And that's what the temperature is."

"No fooling!" marveled Kenny.

Silence fell over the pier again.

Marcy lay down. Kenny was on his back, too, and Thad pillowed his head on Jip. Jerry and Betsy sat dangling their feet in the water. Marcy eased a little closer to their backs, in order to hear if Jerry spoke. Already he had twitched worms before her nose and Kenny's; would he try to tempt Betsy to want peace?

She tipped back her head and could just see the stars between their shoulders. A Perseid blazed. The breeze moved wisps of her hair and the water slapped against the dock pilings. The night was peaceful. Maybe Jerry hadn't realized what he was saying. He wasn't really so bad. Maybe he should be made an honorary Indian.

Jerry spoke softly and Marcy alerted her ears.

"I didn't *just* come down to see the Perseids."

Betsy didn't answer. Marcy stopped breathing.

"I knew the tribe was walking around the lake. Janice told me."

There was a long silence.

"I was watching for you."

Marcy felt uncomfortable. The stars glazed in her eyes.

Jerry cleared his throat. "I mean — watching for *you*."

The boards creaked slightly. Marcy tried to keep her eyes rigidly overhead, but they moved slowly, against her will, to

241

the seated figures. There were no longer any stars between their shoulders!

Her heart gave a lurch and blood pounded in her temples. Why didn't Betsy push him away?

Jerry's voice reduced to a whisper and she strained to hear. She felt guilty eavesdropping, but she couldn't stop herself.

". . . warts . . ."

She strained harder. Jerry's whisper came again.

". . . warts are gone . . . but . . . I thought? . . ." The soft question hung in the air.

Warts gone! Above, the stars swayed giddily. Marcy clutched at the pier, feeling as though she were under water, fighting toward the surface with bursting lungs. *Warts* gone!

Her mind flashed a rapid series of pictures. Betsy, knocking the wart medicine from the friendly paleface's hand; pitching it into the swamp — no, just pretending to pitch it, pitching a rock instead, and hiding the medicine somewhere; Betsy, furtively dabbing it on, day after day — and now Betsy, sitting shoulder to shoulder with the enemy, while his fingers discovered that hers were smooth and wartless!

Her hand burned as if it were the one being held. Her stomach flopped with warring feelings — a hot, pulsing excitement that she didn't quite understand, and a cold dread, which she almost did.

Like a spider, still on her back, she inched to the other side of the pier and sat up. The boards creaked, but Jerry and Betsy did not notice.

She took a deep breath. So *that* was Betsy's worm! How awful! And she had never even suspected!

242

And the tribe, what would become of the tribe? Tomorrow would be the powwow, and Betsy would vote for peace, and so would she, for it would be no fun Indianing without Betsy. What would ever be fun with Betsy again?

She stood up shakily.

"It's getting late," she choked. "Let's go home!"

Turning, she almost ran off the dock.

Chapter

19

"WE-UM KNOW what peace means," began Chief Thunder Cloud, "and we know-um what war means. Question is: do we want peace — or-um war?"

The solemn tribe, in full feathers, sat cross-legged with arms folded. Only Wag-tail grinned, his lips curled back as he panted. Sugar browsed almost out of sight beyond the willows.

White Feather rubbed her thumbs over the smooth pebbles she held in her fists — a black one for war, a white one for peace.

"We've tried all summer to drive the palefaces away and they've hung on like horseflies," Owl Eyes said. "Maybe we ought to try a little peace, and if we don't like it, declare war again next summer."

White Feather snorted. She knew why Owl Eyes wanted peace. Next summer she'd be acting just like Janice, and fat chance of any more war then!

A thought like a chilly finger poked into her middle. Hadn't her own hand tingled on the pier last night? Maybe next summer she wouldn't want war, either! She fought back the idea, but it was still visible, like a penny in ice, and she couldn't deny it. And if not next year, then the year after, or the year after that. It was something you couldn't help, and she would probably like it, and the knowledge filled her with helpless rage.

The discussion went on like a fitful fire, sputtering, nearly dying, reviving for a moment, then sinking. They rehashed the war from the very beginning and guardedly felt each other out. White Feather took little part. What was the use? They'd been hooked, all of them, and Owl Eyes worst of all.

"Well," said the chief, "if no more talk, we take-um vote. Shut-um eyes and cast-um lots."

White Feather groped wearily for the lopsided clay bowl in the center of the circle. She might as well go along with what the tribe wanted. There was a plunk, then two more. She hesitated. She wanted peace as much as the rest; yet was she the only one who realized what would happen to the tribe? Let *them* vote for peace — *she'd* be faithful to the Potawatomi till the end! She switched arms and dropped her stone over the rough rim.

"Ugh. Open-um eyes."

The bowl held three white stones and a black one. The tribe looked at one another. White Feather felt her face redden.

"Well," said Owl Eyes at last, "I guess it's peace."

245

"Ugh."

"What next?" asked Crafty Fox.

"Peace treaty?" Chief Thunder Cloud suggested.

"Sure," said Owl Eyes. She looked almost apologetically at her sister. "Just because we're going to have peace it doesn't mean they can push us around. We're still the Potawatomi! We'll dictate the peace terms, and if they don't like them, we'll go back to war! You write the treaty, White Feather; you're best at writing things. Now, we mustn't forget to put in about turtles."

"Or my headdress," said Crafty Fox.

White Feather got a paper and took down suggestions. Her spirits rose a little. After all, Owl Eyes didn't seem any different after last night. And this was sort of fun, like the last truce. They were a tribe again, figuring things out together for their own good.

After much erasing and changing, the first draft was finished.

Owl Eyes read aloud, " 'The braves of the Potawatomi Indian Tribe of Pleasant Lake, Wisconsin —' "

"Why doesn't the lake have a more Indiany-sounding name, like Lake Koshkonong has?" murmured Crafty Fox.

"Because this isn't Lake Koshkonong, you clunk," said the chief.

" '— agree to peace with the Paleface Settlement on the following terms:

" '1. No further stealing of Indian Territory by palefaces.

" '2. No scalping, massacring, or drowning of Indians, or putting them on a reservation, or stealing Indian livestock.

" '3. Hunting, fishing, and exploring rights on the lake belong to the Potawatomi forever, except for the area of the Pale-face Camp.

" 'a. The Potawatomi will allow the palefaces to fish from their dock and the shore at Sleepy Hollow.' "

"That's the only place they're allowed to fish, anyway," objected Crafty Fox.

"Shut up," said Owl Eyes amiably.

" 'b. All turtles caught must be let go within a week.

" '4. Return of scalp cut off of brave White Feather, and ceremonial headdress stolen from brave Crafty Fox.' "

"Good," said Crafty Fox. "I hardly got to wear it."

"And that's all, so far."

"Ugh. The ceremony," reminded the chief.

Owl Eyes scribbled a bit. "Okay, how's this? 'If the palefaces agree to these terms of peace, the Potawatomi invite them to a council to smoke the calumet and bury the hatchet —' "

White Feather sat up straight, blazing with an idea. "And a feast! A real Indian feast, to show them that savages eat just as well as they do — even better — and have more fun at it!"

"Maize from the garden?" The chief was dubious. "There isn't —"

"Good idea, White Feather!" Owl Eyes flashed an approving look. " '— and an Indian feast' — when?"

"Day after tomorrow?" suggested Crafty Fox. "That'll give us two days to get ready."

"Ugh," nodded Chief Thunder Cloud. "Friday. Night of full moon."

" '— and an Indian feast, night of the full moon, at the Potawatomi wigwam.' There. Anything else?"

247

"What if they don't?" asked Crafty Fox.

"Don't what?"

"Agree to these terms of peace, like you said at the start."

"Oh," said Owl Eyes. She wrote some more. " 'If the pale-faces do not agree, war will continue, more terrible than ever. BEWARE THE POTAWATOMI!' How's that?"

"Ugh! Okay!"

White Feather carefully copied the treaty and added a P.S.: "Don't send too many palefaces on account of the feast." She rolled it up, tied it with a willow thong, and addressed it to Mr. Maddox, General, Paleface Stockade.

The chief paddled erectly over to deliver it. Crafty Fox sat in the bow holding the Potawatomi flagpole. A white flag of truce fluttered just below the thunderbird.

The two left behind watched from the thicket.

"It's all right, about the peace, White Feather," Owl Eyes said without looking at her. "We'll have fun. We've done about all we can do in war, now. It was getting awfully hard, thinking up things to do."

"I know it," said White Feather. "It's just — oh, well, skip it."

"And your feast idea is wonderful. You'll have to tell us what to do. You're the squaw and I don't know a thing about feasts."

White Feather realized with a lurch that she didn't, either. But it was her last chance as an Indian! She'd show them!

"Look," said Owl Eyes. "They're almost there."

Scouts swarmed around the boat dock like bees. The yellow

craft touched, then moved away, and the bee cluster bunched up the hill toward the stockade, surrounding their queen bee, the bearer of the message to Mr. Maddox.

All afternoon the tribe waited eagerly for an answer. Suppertime came and they had to go. When they came racing back, a white envelope was before the wigwam door, weighted with a rock. Crafty Fox pounced on it, and then at the chief's thundery look, handed it respectfully over. Thunder Cloud ripped it open.

"Read it out loud!" Crafty Fox danced a jig of impatience.

"Ugh." The chief cleared his throat. " 'To the Potawatomi Indian Tribe: The Paleface Settlement fully agrees to all the terms of the Peace Treaty, and will send eight palefaces to the peace-pipe ceremony and feast on Friday next, an hour before moonrise. The palefaces hope that after peace is declared, the Potawatomi will now and then enrich the camp with their presence at festive occasions, at which times they might show the activities and handicrafts of their own tribe, or speak about Indian lore, or initiate the camp into Indian dances and ceremonies. In return, the palefaces would like to offer the facilities of the camp, and engage in games and friendly rivalries with the Indians.' Signed, 'M. Maddox, General of the Stockade.' "

"They've agreed to everything! We've won!" said Owl Eyes smugly.

"Hot cabbage!" whooped Crafty Fox. He grabbed White Feather and jumped up and down.

"Hurray!" began White Feather, and then squelched her

249

feeling of gladness. Why was she cheering? They hadn't won; she knew better. She jogged behind when the others raced home to report the news.

Mother and Janice were just finishing dishes.

"Oh, what fun!" squealed Janice. "Please, can I come too? Please?"

"Now you want to play Indian," said Thad.

"Oh, now," said Mother. "I don't see how Janice can hurt your fun. And she does know the scouts better than you do. She can be a go-between. Didn't the pioneers often use interpreters?"

"We don't need an interpreter," said Betsy.

"I've helped you some before, even though I wasn't an Indian," said Janice reproachfully.

"She'll try to boss everything," Thad said. "And she thinks Indianing is silly. She said so."

"Well, I've changed my mind, and I won't boss, honest!" Janice whirled with arms out toward Kenny. "Chief Thunder Cloud, *you'll* let me, won't you?"

"Ugh!" Kenny backed away hastily.

"Well, I guess one more won't make much difference," said Betsy.

"Oh, you darling!" Janice engulfed her in a wet dish towel. "Red told me all about it, and wanted me to come *so* much! I was dying to tell you at supper, but I knew you hadn't heard yet."

"Ugh," said Kenny morosely.

Marcy took Mother aside. "About food," she said. "I'm squaw-in-charge, and I want it to be a feast like the Indians really could have had, just from things around here. To show the scouts."

"Can you use anything from your garden?"

"Well, things didn't grow so well. But I thought, vegetables the Indians *might* have grown, like maize and onions and squash — you know — all baked together in a pit, the way the Indians did. You know how."

"I'm sure I don't know how," Mother said doubtfully. "But you could use our oven —"

Marcy frowned. "No, that won't do."

Thad sidled up. "I know how to cook in a pit."

"You? How?"

He led the way mysteriously to the bedroom, dug around in his clothing drawer, and brought forth a worn paper volume.

"Handbook for Boys," read Marcy out loud. "Boy Scouts of America — but where — how — ?" She made a grab for it.

Thad jerked it out of reach and opened it up. "It tells about cooking in a hole somewhere — here — here it is, with pictures. It's called 'imu' — is that an Indian word? 'Dig a hole and line with rocks. Build a fire in the hole and let it burn to hot coals —' "

"That's it!" cried Marcy. "But Thad — where'd you get a Boy Scout Handbook?" She clapped her hand over her mouth and her eyes widened. Thad's worm! He *did* have a friend! No wonder he knew so much about the Boy Scouts! "They gave it to you," she accused.

"No, I found it in the wigwam the night we wrecked their scavenger hunt, and it sure helped on my brave day! I've been reading it and I know enough to be a Second Class Scout, easy!

251

And those merit badges — why, I could already pass fishing — and canoeing — and maybe archery."

"You mean — you *want* to be a scout?"

"Oh, not here," said Thad hastily. "It's more fun to be an Indian. But maybe at home — well — when there aren't any Indians —"

Marcy swallowed the lump in her throat. First Betsy — now Thad. Was she the only one still trying to hold out in her heart against the Boy Scouts? "Let me see that 'imu,' " she almost whispered.

Thursday the clearing buzzed with activity.

"Look! Blackberries!" called Owl Eyes, returning from the mailbox with a heaped can. "Is the chief back yet?"

"No," said White Feather. "Here, help me hang these toma-hawks on the mulberry tree."

"The bows and quivers should go up, too, and the sling-shots," said Owl Eyes. "Say, the clearing looks neat!"

"It ought to!" Old Nokomis said. She was patching a hole in the wigwam. "White Feather's had me practically *combing* the grass!"

"Which peace pipe should we make?" Crafty Fox held up a page of diagrams from one of Daddy's Indianing books.

"Um. That one's prettiest," Owl Eyes pointed.

Crafty Fox flipped the pages. "I wish I had time to bead some knee bands. Oh, and here's how to make moccasins!"

"There's lots we could do if we had more time," said Owl Eyes. "A proper drum — some rattles — and our old bows and arrows are a disgrace! But we'll fix all those things later. We'll

252

have to do things *really* right, if we're going to go telling the Boy Scouts!"

"I'm glad Mother was a dancer," said White Feather. "She says she'll teach us a harder Indian dance, and help with the costumes."

"And Daddy keeps bringing books," said Crafty Fox. "I liked that last one, on Indian legends."

"I know an Indian song," called Janice.

Crafty Fox grimaced. "Well, don't sing it. Your voice wobbles."

"Here comes Thunder Cloud," said Owl Eyes as the canoe sliced in to shore. The tribe hastened to unload the bulging sacks of groceries the chief had bought in town with his granddad.

White Feather checked down the list. "Maize, squash, eggs —"

"They can be wild duck eggs," said Crafty Fox. "Or turtle eggs —"

"— onions, potatoes, nuts, fish —"

"Not that we couldn't have caught them," the chief defended, "but we don't have time to sit around fishing."

"— flour, milk, butter, apples, a honey comb — and tobacco."

"Old Plug Chewing Tobacco!" The Fox gleefully sniffed the twist. "Let's mix it with other stuff, so it's like Indian tobacco!"

"Ugh. We fix-um," promised the chief. "And look. Old yellow curtains from Granny. Crafty Fox, you and me make-um *real* breechclouts!"

"Good," said Owl Eyes. "But make the pipe, first. Janice, you clear the shore of any dead fish. And we have to dig the imu pit — and get stones to line it — and gather wood —"

"Ugh! To work!" ordered the chief.

That night it took Marcy a long time to get to sleep. A meal for thirteen people! She'd never before made a whole meal for the six in her family — just parts, like mashed potatoes or chocolate pudding. And boys ate so much. If the food were raw — or burned — then what would the palefaces think of the Potawatomi?

She felt under her pillow for the directions Mother had helped her figure out, and fell asleep murmuring the memorized schedule.

Friday was clear and hot. All morning the tribe and the half-breed Nokomis labored, and after lunch, lined up for the big push. White Feather, squaw-in-charge, consulted her much-thumbed paper.

"Chief Thunder Cloud, keep the fire going *hot* in the imu pit — and the rest of you go get big leaves —"

"What for?" asked Nokomis.

"To wrap the food in, for baking."

"That's dumb! Why don't you use aluminum foil?"

"Because we don't want to."

"There's a roll at the cottage. It won't burn, either, or —"

Tears sprang to White Feather's eyes and she turned around. "Nokomis," said Owl Eyes coldly.

"All right, all right," said Nokomis. "Can't I open my mouth to make a suggestion around here?"

"No," said Crafty Fox. "Come on, let's go." The tribe charged off.

White Feather wiped her eyes and examined the plump ears of maize. They already had their leaf wrappers and needed only to be wetted down. The fish, still chilly from their night in the cottage icebox, were gutted and scaled, but had their heads and tails. She'd leave them on; it would add to the effect. She carried the potatoes to the lake and scrubbed them. Sugar-puss wandered up and nibbled at the fish-soaked newspaper, bobbing her head and trailing a long strip, like a beard.

Owl Eyes raced up with an armload of leaves. "Now what?"

"Well, wash them, and wrap these potatoes — and Nokomis can cut the squash in big chunks — and Crafty Fox can wash the fish —"

"Say!" said Crafty Fox. "This is like the first Thanksgiving, except the Indians are giving it for the palefaces!"

Heap by heap the food was chopped, salted, wrapped thickly in leaves, and wetted down.

"Ugh!" shouted the chief. "Fire pit hot-um 'nuff! Bring-um grub!"

The feast makers carried down dishpanfuls and armloads.

"Ugh! Thunder Cloud hot-um 'nuff, too!"

"Are you sure the stones are really ready?" White Feather looked doubtfully into the coals.

Thunder Cloud spat on a rock and the spit, with a report like gunfire, sprang into steam.

"Okay, okay! It's after two-thirty, isn't it? The food shouldn't overcook — just three to four hours."

The chief squinted at the sun. "Just-um time!"

"Now go fast, so the pit won't cool off!" White Feather instructed. "First save some coals to heap on top; then spread the rest out even."

The boys seized the shovels.

"Careful!" Nokomis warned. "We're all barefoot!"

"Now lay the corn in a row, and the rest on top."

Food flew in a jumble as the tribe pitched eagerly. The coals hissed and turned black.

"Now the rest of the coals," cried White Feather, "and a thin layer of sand, and this gunny sack, and then a *whole lot* of sand!" She suddenly felt all atremble, and squatted down while the boys obeyed her orders. Her face was flushed.

There was still lots to do before tonight. But the important part — the squaw part — was in the ground! Nothing to do now but wait, and hope that it would cook to perfection!

Chapter

20

CRAFTY FOX hung out from two willows and scanned the sun-dappled water. "What if they don't come?"

"They'll come," said Owl Eyes, "or Jerry would have told us."

"Jerry." White Feather smacked the nut she was cracking so hard that it squashed to powder. If it weren't for *him,* there wouldn't be any peace, and her insides wouldn't feel like jumping beans. She sniffed. Well, this was what he'd been after from the start.

"I don't see them yet," Crafty Fox worried.

"It's not time yet," said Owl Eyes. "Is your bread okay, White Feather?"

"Why shouldn't it be?" White Feather snapped.

"What's eating *you?*" asked Crafty Fox.

"Wait till *you're* in charge of a feast for thirteen people," said Owl Eyes, "and see how *you* feel."

"It was her idea," said Thunder Cloud.

"It's not just *that,*" White Feather muttered. She stamped to the edge of the thicket, where the bread twists, coiled on sticks like snakes, leaned toward the fire. She turned them, then squatted and stirred the embers.

Funny, on this same spot, ages ago, had been the frenzied dance that began the war. That night their souls had leaped aloft with the spiraling sparks; tonight, hers felt sullen and smoldering, like the slow flames that now spread like a miser's hand over the red-gold coals.

A scream came from Crafty Fox. "They're starting! Three canoes!"

In spite of herself, White Feather felt a thrill of excitement. She sprinted for the wigwam for her arrowhead-and-wampum necklace, adjusted her feather, and ran to line up with the

others on the beach. She took her place and folded her arms, glancing sideways at the tribe.

The chief and Crafty Fox wore real breechclouts and looked very grim and Indiany with their painted chests and tan bodies. The chief's headdress and Owl Eyes' new bonnet waved proudly. White Feather had a stab of misery, thinking of her braids. They were what had always made her look the part, before. Well, she had her arrowhead, anyway!

Wag-tail came and stood alongside. Only Sugarpuss spoiled the effect by poking her head from the thicket.

"Where's Janice? I mean, Nokomis?" asked Crafty Fox.

"If she can't get here on time it's her own lookout," said Owl Eyes.

The canoes approached rapidly.

"There're *nine* scouts!" Owl Eyes whispered in alarm. "We won't have enough food!"

"Ugh," the chief snickered. "Look-um close in first canoe."

"Janice!" Crafty Fox yelped. "Wearing some sort of sack!"

The canoes skimmed up and scraped the beach. The guests hopped out.

Chief Thunder Cloud raised his arm. "How. Welcome."

"How, Big Chief Thunder Cloud!" Jerry returned the salute. "Big Chief, may I present Red, Howie, Pete, Goober, Rory, Spider, and Brinkerhoff. Palefaces from our stockade."

The scouts grinned and bobbed their heads.

White Feather scanned the faces. Most were vaguely familiar. She did not see her scalpers, though, or the scavenger-hunt scouts, except for Jerry.

The chief bowed gravely and pointed to the tribe. "Owl

Eyes. White Feather. Crafty Fox. Wag-tail. Sugarpuss." He paused at Janice, standing midway between the groups. Her Indian dress, brown and fringed at hem and sleeves, came to her knees. Red and yellow crayon designs decorated it. She blushed self-consciously.

"Ugh," said the chief finally. "We call-um Old Nokomis. What *you* call-um?"

"Minnehaha!" blurted Rory, the smallest scout. Everyone laughed, and the awkwardness of meeting was over.

At the edge of the clearing the scouts stopped and ogled.

"Wow!" cried Howie. "Look at the arsenal!"

White Feather smiled, pleased. The clearing *was* impressive. All the weapons hung on the mulberry tree. The neat fireplace had the chief's new council seat at the head of it, a log with a board back rest painted with Indian designs. The chief had also decorated his paddles, and crisscrossed them over the wigwam entrance. The drums sat on either side, and above, the flag was freshly washed.

Brinkerhoff — or maybe it was Goober — knelt and poked his head in. "So this is the tepee I've heard so much about!"

"It's a wigwam," said Crafty Fox. "Don't you know the difference?"

"What's for supper? Goat sandwiches?" Spider lunged at Sugarpuss. She skinned away with a blat and a twitch of her tail.

"Hey! Careful of my goat!" Rory knelt, and Sugar nibbled a tuft of his hair. "I was chief goat keeper," he explained to White Feather. "Her and me are old friends." He rubbed the goat's nubs of horns. White Feather felt a friendly surge.

"How do you like my dress?" Janice asked Owl Eyes.

White Feather jumped. Her bread! She raced for the fire and snatched the twists back. Thank goodness! Only one was really burned, though the rest were well browned. She stood surveying the coals.

"Great White Spirit," she whispered, "make the food just right — not burned, not raw —"

Her prayer was cut short by the mob tearing from the thicket. Chief Thunder Cloud seized a shovel and beat the fire. "Open up-um pit!" Scouts stamped on the flying embers.

"Stop it!" White Feather cried, wrestling for the shovel.

"Let White Feather direct it." At Owl Eyes' command everyone fell back.

White Feather took the shovel and carefully scraped away the coals. A singed, fishy steam vapored up. The imu pit was open!

With the fire tongs she lifted a charred lump and laid it in the dishpan. The crowd murmured. She watched anxiously as the chief took a twig and pushed aside the layers of leaves. It was a potato. He punctured the skin and with a cloud of steam it split open like snowy popcorn.

"Ah!" sighed the hungry mob.

He speared a bit, blew, and tasted. "Ugh! Good!"

Relief engulfed White Feather, and with a heart almost singing she lifted the bundles into the pan. Only the top layer was charred. "Eggs. . . . I think squash — fish —" Like the hum of insects she heard the sweet noises of anticipation. Her ears glowed hot.

Chief Thunder Cloud bore the feast back to the clearing,

261

with everyone pressing, like cats around a farmer carrying milk pails from the barn.

"Use a catalpa leaf for a plate," ordered Owl Eyes, "and you'll have to eat with your fingers, and there's only one apiece of everything, so don't take more than your share."

"Just a minute!" Pete darted toward the shore. Two others sprang to follow. He returned with a huge watermelon, and Goober and Brinkerhoff with a case of pop piled high with marshmallows, cookies, and candy.

"Firewater!" breathed Crafty Fox. "But where's my headdress?"

Jerry stood. "Accept, O Chief, our poor paleface gifts."

The chief bowed his thanks. Then he spread his hands and a hush fell. "Great White Spirit," he intoned, "gaze on-um Peace Feast. May there be-um many more, with-um big harvests and plenty game. Ugh."

He sat, and the hungry feasters fell to. White Feather unwrapped and served, her stomach still churning with anxiety. She was glad she was busy, so no one would wonder why she wasn't eating.

"Say, this is good!" Spider munched an ear of corn, harmonica fashion. "I'm glad we're not at camp! They're having Spanish rice."

"Did all of you do the cooking?" Jerry asked Owl Eyes.

"We helped, but White Feather's our squaw-in-charge," Owl Eyes replied. "She planned it all. It was even her idea."

White Feather colored at Jerry's quick, admiring grin. In confusion she crammed in her first bite.

"White Feather?" said Rory. "Hey — we want the cook! I mean — we want the squaw!"

The scouts took up the chant. "We want the squaw! WE WANT THE SQUAW!" White Feather choked on her bite. The chant changed to:

> "Get a wiggle on, get a wiggle on,
> Don't sit there with a giggle on,
> Get a wiggle on, get a wiggle on,
> And make us a speech!
> SPEECH! SPEECH!"

White Feather looked beseechingly at her fellow Indians. "Get up, you dope!" said Janice sharply.

She stood. Everyone clapped madly. "I don't know what to make a speech about," she said.

"She don't need to talk, she can cook!" yipped Rory.

"Sit — down!" a foghorn voice bellowed. Someone pulled her shirttail and she tumbled down, laughing and embarrassed. But everyone else was laughing, and then they were all paying attention to the feast again and not to her. Her heart still pounded wildly, and she felt very gay and giddy. She realized she had not even noticed what her bite had been, or whether it had tasted good!

Nearby, Wag-tail waited for bites to be thrown his way. Sugarpuss traveled nimbly about, snatching leaves and potato peels.

"Hey!" Pete yelled. "More Injuns!"

"Don't shoot!" cried a familiar voice. "We're from a friendly tribe!"

White Feather whirled. The scouts scrambled to their feet. Daddy and Mother, draped in bright blankets, were standing at the edge of the clearing! Daddy had a feather poked in his hair, and Mother had looped several strings of beads around her neck.

"Oh, Mother! Daddy!" cried Owl Eyes. "Do come and eat!"

"We're not going to stay but a minute," Mother said. "My chief just arrived from working at the salt licks, and we're going out for antelope steaks. But we couldn't resist coming to see how you were getting on. My, doesn't your camp look splendid! Chief Thunder Cloud, where did you learn to decorate paddles so nicely?"

"Ugh," said the chief modestly.

"At least *taste*," ordered Crafty Fox, and the visiting Indians sat down. They were plied with samples.

"Things are awfully good," approved Mother. "Everything has a flavor a civilized oven couldn't possibly match!"

"Oops — nearly ate a fish head!" said Daddy. "Or are we supposed to?"

"Thank you for letting us barge in." Mother stood and the scouts jumped up again. "Good-by, Mrs. Richards. Good-by, Mr. Richards."

"Just call me Sitting Bull," grinned Daddy.

Mother gave White Feather a squeeze. "Your feast is a wonderful success," she said softly. "You'll make some brave a fine squaw someday." Then she and Daddy pulled their blankets around them and disappeared through the trees.

White Feather's eyes stung. She wanted to crawl into the

264

wigwam and weep, she felt so queer. "I'm happy!" she whispered and, sitting down, tore into the remainder of her meal with ferocious hunger.

The Indian feast finished with apples, berries, honey, and nuts, and then came the paleface food. Red cut the melon with a long scout knife. Even Sugarpuss received a slice, and nibbled it with pink-fringed lips and a dribbling chin.

The scouts insisted on cleaning up afterwards. While they buried the garbage in the imu pit, the Indians readied the clearing and lit the ceremonial fire. The chief sat solemnly on the council seat and the tribe squatted on either side. The scouts returned and silently sat in a large half circle across the fire from the Indians.

The full moon, like a great orange, was just rising and flooding the lake with orange juice when Chief Thunder Cloud stood erect. The thicket was still, except for the gunk of a frog in the swamp.

He raised his arms. White Feather remembered the earlier ceremony when they had chanted "Blood, blood, blood!" For an instant her resentment against the scouts flared like a match, but died as quickly. She couldn't keep it burning, and, strangely, she didn't care.

"Great White Spirit, Protector of the Potawatomi, you-um lead us through two moons of war. You give-um strength to bows and sureness to arrows. You bring-um us to victory. We-um ready now for peace."

White Feather watched the scouts. Every face was serious. She felt proud of Thunder Cloud. He was doing well.

265

"Give-um strength to peace treaty. Let neither side break-um vows. Be-um guiding spirit now of palefaces, as well as Potawatomi. Ugh."

The chief sat. The circle shifted, slapped at mosquitoes, and was still. Owl Eyes stood up, holding a paper.

"My headdress," Crafty Fox reminded in a loud hiss.

She nodded. "Listen, braves and settlers, to the peace treaty." She slowly read the document.

At the fourth clause Crafty Fox burst out, "But they *haven't* returned it!"

"A moment, O Indians!" Jerry dodged into the dark and returned with a cardboard box. The chief folded back the flaps.

"There it is!" Crafty Fox grabbed the bonnet, examined every feather, and finally, satisfied, put it on his head.

Chief Thunder Cloud peeked in the box again. "Ugh. Scalp." White Feather received her braid without a change in expression.

Once more the chief reached in the box and brought forth a blackened arrow. He looked puzzled.

"From the very first raid," explained Jerry. "It landed in the fire."

The tribe exchanged glances. So that was why the message had been ignored!

"You Indians have some stuff to return, too," Nokomis reminded.

The chief frowned at her as Crafty Fox brought a bundle from the wigwam.

"Ugh. Paleface garments saved brave White Feather. We

266

thank-um. And here-um paleface handbook, paleface scalps."

"Thank you, O Chief," said Jerry.

Owl Eyes finished the reading and then each side signed.

"Ugh. Crafty Fox, place-um Indian scroll in wigwam; fetch-um shovel and tomahawk."

Crafty Fox plucked down the shabbiest weapon on the tree. The chief turned over a little dirt near the swamp, and then the scouts gave a hand until a narrow trench had been dug. Red unfastened a rusty scout ax from his belt. The chief knelt and laid both hatchets in the hole, their handles crisscross. He crumbled a handful of dirt over them.

"May-um wrath of thunderbird descend on who-um disturbs these buried hatchets!" He paused. "Peace."

"Peace," chanted the tribe.

"No more war," he said.

The scouts joined in this time. "No more war."

"No more scalps."

"No more scalps."

"No more blood."

"No more blood."

"Peace," said the chief.

"Peace," echoed the group.

Thunder Cloud and Jerry filled the trench and tramped it down. Then everyone settled around the fire again.

"Ugh. Bring-um calumet."

Crafty Fox vanished and returned with the peace pipe. The stem was a smooth twig and the bowl colored clay. Bark thongs ending in tufts of feathers hung down, and a string of gaudy beads festooned the stem. A scout whistled in amaze-

267

ment. The chief and Crafty Fox beamed at the appreciation of their handiwork.

The chief pinched a tangle of Indian tobacco from a bulging leather pouch. He tamped it in the bowl and Crafty Fox set a coal from the fire atop it with a forked twig. Thunder Cloud sucked in, blowing smoke out in little puffs. The tobacco glowed red, faded, glowed again. He lifted the pipe aloft and said the ceremonial words.

"Great White Spirit — him who smoke-um calumet and then break-um treaty, may he tread on-um coals hot as this forever and ever."

"Forever and ever," echoed the tribe.

"Him who smoke-um calumet and then break-um treaty, may he feel arrows pierce-um heart forever and ever."

"Forever and ever." The scouts picked up the response.

"Him who smokes this calumet and then break-um treaty, may he never come to Happy Hunting Grounds but wander with empty belly through dry lands with-um no game, no fish, forever and ever."

"Forever and ever."

The chief took another puff and handed the pipe to White Feather. She took it gingerly. What if she choked?

All eyes were on her. She touched her lips to the hollow stem and sucked. Hot smoke coated her tongue. Almost gagging, she blew the smoke out and gulped in fresh air. Tears flooded her eyes — but she'd done it, without even coughing! She triumphantly passed the pipe to Owl Eyes.

Owl Eyes made the tobacco glow red and coughed just a tiny cough as she handed the calumet to Jerry. He took a long puff and passed it on. It made the rounds of the scouts, who managed without mishap, except for Spider, who got a choking spell and had to crawl away and take a swig of firewater. Red smoked, and then Janice. There was no sound in the thicket except quiet breathings, disguised coughs, and swamp noises.

Nokomis passed the calumet to Crafty Fox. White Feather watched anxiously. What if he botched things at the very end? But he'd smoked before — didn't he manufacture his own brand of cigarettes, Pine Brothers, from pine needles wrapped in toilet paper?

Crafty Fox fondled the pipe so long and lovingly that Janice nudged him to hurry. He withered her, took several little puffs, and handed the pipe to the chief. Thunder Cloud gently thumped out the glowing plug of tobacco. He stood.

"Ugh. Peace now strong as Indian tobacco. Peace between-um Potawatomi and palefaces strong-um as dried willow bark. Peace spread-um over lake like wings of Potawatomi thunderbird. Ugh. Peace ceremony ended. Go in-um moccasins of peace."

A pang pierced White Feather. "It's over," she whispered. But the ceremony had impressed the scouts. She was proud to be a Potawatomi.

The scouts murmured. They seemed reluctant to move.

"Well," said Goober, "this has been a lot of fun."

"Maybe we can get together again," said Brinkerhoff. "Mr. Maddox said he'd ask you to come over and visit camp."

Owl Eyes grinned wickedly. "It won't be the first time!"

"And you know what?" said Red. "Mr. Maddox is awfully

interested in your Indianing — he wants an Indian division of camp next year; maybe we'll rename the Ridge 'Indian Ridge' — we wouldn't be the Potawatomi, of course —"

"Can I tell the rest?" asked Janice eagerly. "He says he knows a *real Indian* that might come and live in a tepee — his name is Joe Bazooka — and teach Indian lore and make totems and stuff —"

"And it's you kids that gave him the idea," finished Red.

"Cabbage!" yipped Crafty Fox. "A real Indian!"

"We could have some more ceremonies yet this year," said Owl Eyes, glancing at Jerry. "We could maybe make a few honorary Potawatomi."

Jerry's ears turned red. "Hey, Chief," he said hastily, "what sort of tobacco did you put in that calumet? It sure packed a wallop!"

Thunder Cloud handed the pouch around. "Well, shredded chewing tobacco, and willow leaves, and pine needles, and corn silk —"

"It makes me sick just to hear about it!" groaned Spider.

"How did you make the pipe?" asked Howie.

"The stem was hardest," said Crafty Fox. "One of my books said to use an ash stem and poke out the pith with a knitting needle, only we used an old bicycle-tire spoke — after we finally found an ash tree."

"And we made six clay bowls to be sure we'd have a good one," added the chief.

"Gosh — is that a *real* arrowhead?" exclaimed Pete.

White Feather let the scouts examine her necklace while she told them about the discovery at Bent Trees Hollow.

"That was the day I was s'posed to swim back across the lake," Crafty Fox said to Rory. "I'm going to do it yet! Maybe Mr. Maddox would let you try, too."

Rory's eyes lit up. "Gee! Do you think he would? I don't think I could swim the long way yet, but I bet I could make it from our dock to the Girl Scout piers! Why don't we swim it that way this year, and next summer try the long way?"

"Okay," agreed Crafty Fox. "We can make it, easy!"

The scouts asked about the wigwam, the council seat, the tomahawks. Finally the talk lagged. A breeze sent ripples slapping the shore and the willows soughed. A scout began to hum and others joined in with words — "There's a long, long trail a-winding . . ." The Indians sang, too.

They sang on and on — at first dreamy, poignant songs that made a little catch in Marcy's throat, and then gradually more rollicking ones, till finally they were all stamping and roaring out the words.

Then the singing stopped as abruptly as it had started, and everyone just looked into the embers.

"I have an idea," said Red. "It's early yet — what say we paddle across the lake? We can hide the canoes in the reeds, and Howie knows where there's a haunted house. It ought to be plenty spooky tonight with this full moon."

"It's spooky *any* time!" Howie declared.

"Let's go!" The group jumped up with one accord.

"Wait for me!" Marcy cried. "I have to put Sugar to bed!"

"Run! We won't start without you," ordered Jerry.

Marcy spurred the goat to a gallop. At the cottage she shoved her underneath, slammed the doors, and raced back.

271

The moon silhouetted three floating canoes. A scout sat in the stern of the fourth, still beached, and another stood on shore.

"Hop in — you're riding with us, Pete and Brinkerhoff. And Jip."

She settled beside the dog on the slatted bottom and sat catching her breath. Pete shoved off. The moon made the figures plain in the other boats. Janice, Red, and Howie in one; in another, Betsy paddled bow and Jerry stern, with Goober in the middle; and in Kenny's canoe, Thad and Kenny paddled with Rory and Spider on the bottom. The tribe was sprinkled in all the canoes, a part of the yellow fleet, sailing with it and not against it!

Jip licked her knee. She patted him and watched the black whirlpools the paddles made as they drip-dipped in and out of the silvery water. Strange — to be riding in a scout canoe with boys she'd never met till tonight! Her paddlers chatted about things at camp, but she didn't listen. She dragged a hand in the lake and looked at the sky.

As her body calmed, the question she'd been feeling all evening formed into words. "Why do I feel so good inside?" she whispered. "When I thought I was going to feel so bad?"

It wasn't the telescope; she'd known for several days now that she'd be looking through it again. And it wasn't forgetting Jerry and Betsy. She hadn't forgotten. They'd sat together all evening, but hadn't acted silly at all. Even Janice had acted okay.

It was partly because the feast had been such a success. A thrill ran through her, and she basked for a moment in her

272

glory — "We want the squaw!" and what Mother said! She'd never had a real chance before to do any squawing, she'd been so busy being a brave. But squaws were important. What would they have done without one tonight? Yes, she liked being a squaw. . . .

She skimmed her hand along the surface, and the tops of her thoughts foamed behind as bubbles of light, and there was something deeper, blacker, underneath.

What was it? It had something to do with the war . . . she'd thought they'd lost, but had they really? For the Indians had dictated the peace, and given the feast, and now in the paleface camp they were going to do things, not like scouts any more, but like Indians! Although in history it happened differently, this was proof that it needn't happen that way all the time. The tribe had conquered the scouts by making them Indians!

But there was more to it than even that. At first they'd wanted to drive the palefaces away to have the lake just as it always had been. The war was over now, and they were still Indians, but the lake *was* different. She had been afraid — but what if the lake had never changed at all? It would still be a lump of ice. Maybe a glacier would go over again sometime, but it would melt eventually, and then the lake would be there, or another lake like it. You couldn't stop things from changing.

Things changed, but even then they were the same. Like Jerry said once about their bodies, how the cells were being replaced all the time, so that you were practically a new person every seven years. Yet she was the same Marcy Richards that had been there when she was little, even if every speck of her was different! What was it that was the same? Not her body, be-

273

cause that would someday die. It was something you couldn't touch or measure. You could only feel the "me-ness," and know that it was true.

Under the canoe, water gurgled. The boys were silent. She gazed at the silvery lake, surrounded with an uneven black fringe of trees and hills, and then looked up.

The stars — they changed, too. Sometimes the Little Dipper could hold water and sometimes it couldn't. Even Polaris, millions of years from now, wouldn't be the North Star; Vega would be! The telescope man said so.

She felt she understood, and it was making her feel all right about everything, and it was a secret, like Saturn and the wasp, that you couldn't talk about and expect anyone else to understand. Things were different, but they were still the same. Maybe she'd outgrow Indianing in a few years — but maybe not. She could still be an Indian when she wanted. Even Mommy and Daddy had been Indians tonight. Things didn't stop. They had to go along to have any meaning.

She sat up suddenly and shouted, "Walla walla woo hoo!"

"Walla walla woo hoo!" three voices rang back across the water. The tribe was still the tribe!

"Walla walla woo hoo!" the scouts echoed. No, it was more! A tribe with friendly allies!

"What did you do that for?" Brinkerhoff rested on his paddle.

"I just wanted to prove something," Marcy said contentedly. She smiled and hummed softly her favorite song.

> From the Land of the Sky Blue Water
> They brought a captive maid . . .

She touched her feather fondly. She was the captive maid, and these were her captors, paddling her swiftly away from the Land of the Sky Blue Water, but her heart was not afraid. Weren't the wings of the thunderbird spread out over the lake, protecting them all — the deep, midnight blue, the feathery black?

But, no — her gaze traveled up the moon path — tonight everything was silvery. The wings were not thunder heavy. They were light and sequined with stars. They had been there when the Indians looked up two hundred years ago. They were there now, spreading over the Potawatomi and the palefaces. They would be there when she was old, and young Potawatomi were riding the lake: the changeless wings of the Great White Spirit.

And below, she was moving across a sea of peace in a world of silver. The sparkling bubbles rushing from her fingers were the her of a moment ago, and what she would be in a minute were diamonds coming to meet her, and she was all contained in one sea of silver, lapping at every tiny inlet around the dark shore, the same and yet dancing, dancing, every second different. And underneath was the black, still water — the understanding and the deep content.